HELIUM

HELIUM

Jaspreet Singh

B L O O M S B U R Y
LONDON • NEW DELHI • NEW YORK • SYDNEY

First published in Great Britain 2013

Copyright © 2013 by Jaspreet Singh

Bloomsbury Publishing Plc
50 Bedford Square
London
WC1B 3DP

www.bloomsbury.com

Bloomsbury Publishing, London, New Delhi, New York and Sydney
A CIP catalogue record for this book is available from the British Library

ISBN 978 1 4088 2916 5 (hardback)
ISBN 978 1 4088 3821 1 (trade paperback)

10 9 8 7 6 5 4 3 2 1

Typeset by Hewer Text UK Ltd, Edinburgh
Printed in Great Britain by CPI Group (UK) Ltd CR0 4YY

For P. K. Page
1916–2010

ਉਡੇ ਉਡਿ ਆਵੈ ਸੈ ਕੋਸਾ ਤਿਸੁ ਪਾਛੈ ਬਚਰੇ ਛਰਿਆ ॥
ਤਿਨ ਕਵਨੁ ਖਲਾਵੈ ਕਵਨੁ ਚੁਗਾਵੈ ਮਨ ਮਹਿ ਸਿਮਰਨੁ ਕਰਿਆ ॥੩॥

— ਰਾਗੁ ਗੁਜਰੀ ਮਹਲਾ ੫ ॥

How I wished during those sleepless hours that I
belonged to a different nation, or, better still, to none
at all.

— W. G. Sebald, *Vertigo*

1.

Bubbles

Now as I assemble my notes I recall the beginning of my sabbatical year, and my uneasy decision to spend some time in Delhi with Father, who was recovering from a serious surgery. It is still hard for me to picture his body on a bed, although I see clearly his face, and faintly unstable hands. Certain things, firmly connected to a body, can never be erased, especially hands. Papa sent an email without much sarcasm or hidden meaning: 'worst is over'. As usual his words cut right through me.

I didn't fly directly. My secretary booked a necessary stopover in Europe, where I attended a previously planned event on rheology. That is when, following a partially understood mechanism, a complexity of uneven forces, the volcano Eyjafjallajökull erupted in Iceland. The unexpected event occurred on the very first day of the Brussels conference. The TV channels showed surreal never-ending clouds of volcanic ash. Eyjafjallajökull, we were told, woke up after a long slumber and released gritty plumes as high as ten kilometres containing particles as small as sixty microns in diameter, spreading southward. These (rock and glass) particles generated fears of aircraft engine failure and grounded almost the whole of Europe.

Stranded, with every passing hour I felt as if through no fault of mine I had slipped into an uncertain in-between

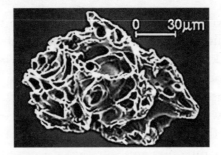

world. What made the flight cancellations particularly eerie was that they came into effect barely a few hours after a student presented an insightful, paradigm-shifting paper on the rheology of lava flows.

Stuck in Europe, I recall now how I gave up all hope of departure. But a week later the ash cleared, and the moment the flight finally took off, the skies displayed a beautiful hue of lavender, and as I drifted in and out of sleep Eyjafjallajökull merged with Vesuvius, and with Hokusai's many views of Mount Fuji, another volcanic calamity, and together the ensemble merged with 'roots' of an old shadowy memory of my father driving me for the first time to the engineering college, the IIT.

Nine hours later we landed at the Indira Gandhi International Airport. The touchdown generated a near spontaneous applause from almost all the passengers aboard. No one was waiting to receive me. Because of the uncertainty I had not bothered to inform Father about the exact time of my arrival. Otherwise he would have sent the black BMW (as an overture to establish a truce between us). Nevertheless, I felt a strange sense of freedom arriving in the city of my birth as a mere outsider after a gap of nearly twenty-five years. It was dark; as usual the air of Delhi was heavy with nefarious gases. I took a taxi. Surprisingly the driver didn't overcharge.

4

The taxi zipped through the highway to the heart of South Delhi. 'You are my first customer of the day, and it is bad luck,' he told me, 'to overcharge.' The driver, an elderly man with a two-day stubble, spoke in a candid no-nonsense manner, although the unnecessary laughter that followed puzzled me. 'Is it OK to overcharge the second or the third customer?' I said. He poked his short neck in my direction and stared as if I were a shadow of a figure from some imponderable era. 'Sa'ab-ji, no one overcharges these days. The thirty extra rupees are merely the convenience fees.'

So much time has passed by since that cab ride. I am gathering these notes five years after my volcano inter-rupted flight. It is important to clarify a few things about myself. Thirty years ago, after completing my undergrad-uate degree at the prestigious Indian Institute of Technology, Delhi, I proceeded with grad work in rheol-ogy at Cornell. Why Cornell? Because it was the only school that offered me a full fellowship. Ironically I teach at the same university now as a full professor. Once or twice during the Bush years I strongly felt like leaving my new life – carefully assembled in Ithaca – and starting all over again in a more enlightened European country, but my body responded strangely at the mere thought of it. Cornell, Ithaca, New York 14850–2488, for want of a better word, is 'home'.

Father was deep asleep by the time the cabbie dropped me at the gates. Our old sentry carried my luggage to the room allocated to me. For some reason I had no recall of that room, and the harder I tried to remember, the more I felt blocked. Twenty-five years of absence is enough to diminish and erase certain memories. So much time gets needlessly lost, or twists silently, circulating as minor

5

eddies and vortices. Truth is that during the last twenty-five years I had met Father not even once. I was still repelled by the very idea of having to confront him in the morning. But how could I forget that the room I found myself in was actually my mother's bedroom?

The sixteen-metre by eight-metre room had nothing in common with its traces in my flickering memory. Even the smell was different. Certain irrevocable things, it was clear, had taken place during my absence. Almost half of the room was now filled with hunting trophies. Stags on the walls. For a while my eyes rested on the chiru, the endangered Tibetan antelope. Its shy upward gaze brought to mind the nimble baby pronghorn I had spotted not so long ago in the mountains in the US. Right across the newly varnished door I noticed a paralysed moth resting on the skin of a blackbuck. The hangul above the window had huge antlers, and Little Red Riding Hood was walking away from me, about to vanish again in the dense forest of its antlers. Such was the state of my mind when I arrived in Delhi.

Thirsty, I poured myself a glass of ice-cold water and sat in the living room staring at framed photos of my children, who to this day have not visited India.

Mother's black-and-white portrait, high up on the wall, surveyed me as I surveyed my children. The blown-up photo had lost the original aspect ratio; as a result her high cheekbones and big youthful eyes appeared crooked. A moth had attached itself to the bottom right of the brown frame. This is not how I remembered my mother's face. Sitting in the velvet armchair, I heard an echo of her voice. Softly she enquired about the well-being of my children, whom she never met. We held hands, and then she was gone. I missed her more now that I was in Delhi.

She died before my kids were born. I could not come for the cremation. (I didn't come.) For several days in Ithaca in the US, after I heard the news, I would experience her walk in my rooms, and hear her body rustle and crack bit by bit like a mechanical object. The only time I wept.

But how could I forget her bedroom? Mother moved to this part of the house when I was still in high school. She found some solitude in the separate room, I remember. She used to call the room 'my jahaz' – my ship. Strange, I was convinced then that all her problems were really my fault. Often she would stare for hours on end at her shawl or voluminous sari. Unlike me she was less conflicted about Father. She avoided head-on collisions by using his words, and her own protracted silences.

Before I describe him fully in flesh and bone, let me articulate one faint but significant detail, because sometimes the lost moments do return in a new form. Something within me, ever since my grad-student days, has always been curious about 'change' and the 'mechanisms of change'. Or rather: the mechanisms of forgetting. How past becomes past. My work, to put it simply, deals with the memory of objects and materials. Most things in this world of ours change. Every substance transforms. I have come to this awareness not as a historian, but as a scientific observer. Although I never fail to admire the distilled beauty of the sentence: *Everything flows*. Rheology, my specialisation, is the science of deformation and flow. Even so-called 'solids' flow: stained glass in old churches is thicker at the bottom.

My work focuses on the flow of 'complex materials', the ones with 'memory'. Water, for instance, doesn't have memory, but blood remembers its past. Volcanic lava flows and clays, too, carry within them some deep traces of unresolved past.

7

In the morning I met Father. It was his first week back home from the hospital. The surgery had basically eliminated any chances for heated arguments or the usual hostility between us. For years I had dreaded the very idea of a reunion. And now I was standing no more than fifty centimetres away. We shook hands; his were sweaty. Father looked more fragile than I had imagined him during the flight. The only thing constant, immutable and unchanged was the small mole on his left cheek. His hair had thinned. It was clear he had dyed the strands black before losing faith in the project completely. Father's sparkly eyes blinked like window shutters as he explained a few procedural details of the surgery, and quite unexpectedly, he asked the nurse to leave the room. Then in an extremely concerned voice, he enquired about things in Ithaca. 'Everything is going as expected, in fact, better than expected,' I lied. *Worst is over*. Carefully I avoided any talk about my estranged wife, or my failed/failing marriage. I did mention my sabbatical though, and my plan to edit an anthology on the deformation of biomaterials. I don't think he understood.

Right after breakfast I took a taxi from our house on Amrita Sher-Gil Marg to the IIT campus. Because of dense smog I was unable to notice any major alterations in the engineering campus. Or a large number of puddles and stray dogs. To my surprise the office keys were ready; all I had to do was sign a special form. However, the room looked a bit run-down, different from its picture, the one the Chair had sent me via email. I must explain. IIT gave me a tiny office for six months to facilitate my sabbatical. The office, a favour, like all favours, came with a price. The first thing they demanded nefariously on the day of my arrival was to help conduct a PhD exam.

I was still dizzy, mildly feverish and foaming with jet lag.

However, the student did an outstanding haze of a presentation. When I was his age, work as good as his was often described as 'fucking good'. What I relished about the talk were the old-fashioned no-nonsense slides – helpful because I had not read the thesis. Hurriedly I flipped through the document and found he had even cited a paper of mine that had appeared fourteen years ago in *Physical Review A*. My colleagues asked the candidate questions about the assumptions of the model he developed and the data he generated. One of the key applications of his work was to help clean up soils in heavily industrialised areas, and damaged soils in areas like Bhopal.

But these notes are not about tragic industrial disasters or Dow or Union Carbide. I am assembling material connected to an unspeakable event that took place barely a month before Bhopal. How those three or four days in the past ruptured my relationship with Father. Ruptured is the wrong word. With years a lot of dust has settled on our so-called relationship, but the passing of time has made little difference, or rather neither of us has changed or relaxed the way we expected each other to. He knows I know he is not innocent. Nevertheless he considers himself justified. My absence, now that I think about it, has been an immense loss; my long voluntary absence kept me from participating in the colossal transformation my country has gone through, making me a stranger to the city where I grew up. The gap of years has not even helped determine the 'why' of my troubled relationship with Father. Troubled, once again, is the wrong word. The word I would like to use doesn't exist. But, to move ahead, it is essential to venture near the interstitial spaces of language. I must unravel the primary mechanism(s) of the problem. Gather evidence. How else would I figure out the mechanism of my own grand failure . . . ?

There was a professor of mine who used to emphasise the difference between 'dependent' and 'independent' variables. If the population of human babies, for instance, starts falling (in a city like Bhopal) and the population of black dogs starts rising simultaneously, it would be wrong to jump to the flawed conclusion: the dogs are responsible for killing the babies. It would be erroneous to rely on simplistic cause-and-effect correlations, because we are really dealing with two independent variables here.

During the PhD oral examination, for some unknown reason, my mind drifted to my own student days, and I could not help thinking, amid a jumble of stray thoughts, about the most harrowing event I ever witnessed. The event that made me stare directly into the dark face of history.

On the morning of 1 November 1984, my professor, who taught us introductory courses in engineering, was killed brutally during the pogrom that followed Indira Gandhi's assassination. I was nineteen years old then, a boy about to become a man.

The professor was over six feet tall, in his early forties, and taught us Feynman's Lectures and a class on failure analysis, and he had also screened 8mm films of collapsing structures. I recall now his lecture on Karmen Vortices, and the collapse of Tacoma Narrows Bridge, and phase diagrams of a major industrial accident.

I first encountered him not in a classroom, but in the student residence. In 1981 my mother had accompanied me to the residence with two items of luggage (a black aluminium trunk and a roll of bedding) and she had ventured beyond the visitors' lounge for she wanted to personally test the quality of the canteen, and there

Professor Singh, the boys' hostel warden, spotted her. Instead of getting mad, he walked up close (yellow tie fluttering in the wind) and asked if he could be of assistance. He reassured her and joked *if your boy doesn't like the 'spartan' food here he could always eat at my place*. The warden's accent and choice of words conveyed three or four crucial years spent abroad. British, American, Indian English, strands no longer distinct, fuzzy, like a superposition of sine and cosine waves. Even his majestic turban looked Westernised.

I recall he pronounced 'ethane' like '*eh* thane' and skipped an 'i' in alumin(i)um. But it was really hard to pigeonhole him. Sometimes he would arrive without notes in the lecture hall, a bit unprepared (or so it seemed) in blue rubber hawai chappals, as if woken up in the middle of a research paper, and he would try a few partial differential equations spontaneously with a coloured chalk on the board, and then use his left hand to rub out those beautiful micro-symbols and try again and was not afraid of making mistakes. He rarely opened the thick textbook on the desk.

Nelly and my place. A few months after joining IIT, the day I topped the class, he extended an invitation. A real invite in a soft-spoken voice. *If you are free this evening you are most welcome to dine at Nelly and my place.*

Nelly and my place. The molecules of air around me vibrate still, gathering evidence. *Come to our place.* I still hear an echo of that ghostly voice, but am unable to foresee what fate is riveted to that cheerful face. Professor Singh's actual area of specialisation was helium. The second element in the periodic table – 'He' – the so-called noble gas. Colourless, odourless, tasteless and monoatomic. The invisible 'He' atoms don't interact much with each other (or with others), preferring 'isolation' or 'solitude'. The gas doesn't 'burn', no combustion reaction in the presence of oxygen. Slowly it keeps escaping our earth's gravitational field. To this day I am able to quote his lectures. *If we are not careful on Planet Earth, in thirty or forty years not many atoms of this ludicrously light element will be left behind. All our primordial helium has already vanished.*

Liquid helium, the coldest fluid, boils at extreme low temperatures, around minus 269 degrees Celsius. In the lab the professor, wearing a white lab coat over a tweed, would demonstrate a purple glow under very high voltages, purple like a jacaranda flower. Helium gas is also capable of altering the human voice radically, although this demo never took place in his presence.

That day Professor Singh invited me to dine at *Nelly and my place*. I got delayed by a full hour, apologised. I could not reveal the real reason for delay. Accompanied by a bunch of classmates I had gone to Chanakya to watch my first adult film. The 'obscene' images involved two or three fully exposed breasts, nipples longer than mulberries, enough to give me a huge hard-on. Simultaneous pleasure and pain of a kind I had not experienced before. Plus, the campus gift shop was closed to mark an optional religious holiday, and I felt embarrassed arriving empty-handed. Hesitantly, I rang the bell. The bookshelves and other objects in the house suggested this family was steeped in deep knowledge about the world. By now I have forgotten many details, but this I remember. Twelve or thirteen shelves in the living room. Books spilling all over. More, a flash distillation. *Encyclopaedia Britannica*. The Nobel laureates series. European, American fiction and poetry. Not a single science and engineering text (only one on 'Bose–Einstein Condensates' borrowed from the library, a monograph on the Dutch scientist, Onnes, and the first editions of Feynman Lectures.) This is Nelly's territory, said Professor Singh.

Nelly was perhaps the most beautiful woman I had ever encountered, a serene Sikh beauty, and the most refined. She would call him 'Mn' with a sense of ease that Indian wives of that generation didn't normally possess. (Mn or 'em en' stood for Mohan and was the best chemical tease.)

She greeted me with a sardonic smile. In fact, both Nelly and Professor Singh had the same sardonic smile.

She had studied literature at a state college in Punjab, and was much younger, only eight or nine years older than me; they had married after he returned from the US. When I arrived at the house she was playing a musical instrument, a rabab. Her two children, a boy and a girl, were asleep in the bedroom. In our class she was known as Mrs Singh; everybody fancied the 'khubsurat sardarni'. Until that evening I had only seen the enigmatic Nelly from a distance; I will never forget the bread pakoras she fried, not with dhaniya-tamarind but with what she called cranberry chutney. That was the first time I tasted cranberries. There was a layer of spicy potatoes in the pakoras. She served channa-kulcha as well and cashew burfi and chiki as dessert. The professor seemed more relaxed that night; he unfolded his beard, and loosened his navy-blue turban. Two or three strands of grey in his robust beard. Nelly had on Ella Fitzgerald songs and now and then she would step out of the house, and this seemed to annoy him but he didn't express his annoyance properly.

After dinner Professor Singh did something unusual. He washed the dishes.

Nelly retired to her room without wishing us goodnight, and I ended up discussing 'dimensionless numbers' all night long with my teacher. By the time I departed, both

13

of us sensed a new layer of relationship sprouting, the layer commonly known as friendship.

These days the *Times* often runs profiles of highly qualified immigrants returning to India. Better jobs, better quality of life. Good life in Bangalore or the Los Angeles-style Millennium City, Gurgaon. To me these returns are not even half as interesting as Professor Singh's decision to return when it was really hard to return.

'Why did you?' I had asked him that day.

'Perhaps you know the answer. When I hear the national anthem, an electric current goes through me.'

Often I would go to his office. The walls had developed cracks and the electrical wiring was visible. The left side was covered with awards and commendations and important citations. On the right wall hung a huge black-and-white photo of the so-called great leader, Indira Gandhi. Even then I found her hideous because she had imposed the dictatorial Emergency only six or seven years ago. One day, her bleached hair appeared yellow to me.

I stopped going to classes for a while (in the final year) because I was sick with jaundice. Everything around me turned yellow (including my shit and urine). While convalescing I felt as if coming into contact with everything for the first time. Objects strange and familiar through surge and flutter of marigold yellow. I almost fell down ... Stumbling through a meta-stable state of diminishing nausea I walked into the college to collect the handouts I had missed. Professor Singh finished his lectures at eleven on Tuesdays and Thursdays and I showed him my new face then. I remember, too, the faint odour of chemicals in his office. In the cupboard there were four or five dark brown

14

bottles, and liquefaction apparatus no longer in use. One Tuesday morning I was still in the office when a weighty parcel arrived. He unwrapped, in my presence, a yellowish book. The thing had arrived all the way from the New World.

'Do you know where Ithaca is?' he checked in a husky voice. Up until that day the place Ithaca was merely a Greek myth; I was completely unaware of the names of American university towns. Somewhat hypnotised by his accent my gaze fell on Professor Singh's tennis shoes. For some mysterious reason he always kept them in the office under his desk. The package was mailed by his friend (a room-mate during the grad-student days) at Cornell. He asked if I were interested in reading the 'the periodic table' by a man 'who belonged to some other world'.

The author, a complete unknown to me, had organised 'seemingly harmless' memories around twenty-one chemical elements. Neither a hardback, nor a proper paperback:

Zinc	29
Iron	37
Potassium	50
Nickel	61
Lead	79
Mercury	96
Phosphorus	109
Gold	127
Cerium	139
Chromium	147
Sulfur	160
Titanium	165
Arsenic	169
Nitrogen	175
Tin	184

the uncorrected proofs. Curious, I borrowed the wondrous 'book' of 'memory and alchemy' a week later. The friend had inscribed the title page and inserted a copy of his typed review, the one he had submitted to the *Times*. I have no idea why I still remember the expected launch date, 19 November 1984. First English edition. The reviewer/friend, overly generous, claimed it was an admirable and 'true' translation. Little did I know then that the author would commit suicide three years later on 11 April, 1987.

Chaucer, Tennyson, Manto. Chekhov, Mishima, Maugham. These are the bookmakers I had read so far, men who belonged on my father's bookshelf. I had even read Joyce's 'Hell-Fire Sermon' in *A Portrait of the Artist as a Young Man*. But I had not encountered anything remotely close to Primo Levi's alchemy, a voice so restrained and gently ironic and devastating. There were parts I couldn't comprehend fully, but this didn't stop me from getting entangled with the twenty-one irradiating elements. It is hard for me now to convey the sheer delight and pain I experienced being exposed to that old-fashioned way of doing chemistry, involving not just the highly privileged sense of sight, but also smell, touch and taste. A few days later, Professor Singh distributed handouts during his lecture. The stapled material included the first two pages from the Italian author: 'There are so-called gases in the air we breathe. They bear curious Greek names which mean "the New," "the Hidden," "the Inactive," and "the Alien." Indeed so inert, so satisfied with their condition that they do not participate in any chemical reaction, do not combine with any other element, and for precisely this reason have gone undetected for centuries.' Levi connects the world of molecules to the world of humans, to the world of his own family members, explained Professor Singh. *The little that I know about my ancestors presents many similarities to these gases* ... Uncanny as the whole affair appears in retrospect, it was during his advanced elective on cryogenics that I had learned that almost a hundred years ago in 1882, while analysing the lava of Mount Vesuvius, a previously known 'extraterrestrial' element was detected for

16

the first time on Planet Earth. Before this discovery it was largely believed that helium existed only in the sun.

Professor Singh would spend long flickering hours inside and outside the classroom discussing material not directly on the syllabus. Blinking rapidly he would expand those mere footnotes and old-fashioned Kodak slide projector shows (for some reason I am unable to forget the grainy photographs of Giorgio Sommer) . . . Vesuvius, he told us, is best known for its eruption in AD 79. In a single night those ancient, bustling Roman cities of Pompeii and Hercula-neum were buried under a seventeen-foot-thick layer of dust and pumice pebbles as a result of a catastrophic pyro-clastic flow. Toxic gases and extreme high temperatures perished all plant and animal life on the slopes and made the river change its course. Within hours the mountain looked stark naked and its shape changed as if all that weight and volume was really a small lump of Silly Putty in the hands of a titanic god (or – should we say? – a demon).

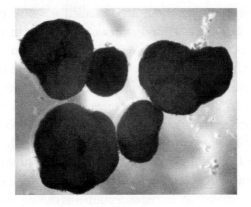

When my turn came to ask the IIT doctoral candidate a question I thought of asking something from *The Periodic*

Table. He had not heard of the book. So I posed a question on cadmium, chromium and arsenic. Something connected to the shiny beads of mercury floating on soil samples in central India, and the student figured out the answer, and then I posed a problem even more directly connected to his area, a question about mountains of toxic waste still piled up in Bhopal. How deep into the soil and water have the toxic chemicals penetrated? Especially organo-chlorines. The student paused and I checked my watch. Then he chalked an equation on the board, and I learned something new. The answer was incorrect, but his approach was solid (as they say), and this assured me that the kid knew his stuff, and it also pained me that this bright boy would leave the country and neither clean the soils nor design reaction vessels, some other asshole would do that and industrial disasters would continue to happen. That was pretty much the end of the exam. Afterwards the candidate was asked to step out of the room for a few minutes. We discussed whether he deserved the Dean's honours list, and the door was opened. Congratulations, Doctor! The committee members took him to the faculty club for lunch. The student invited all of us to a grand party that evening. I declined. I excused myself and walked aimlessly through the campus, and then for a long time stared at my favourite purple-blossomed jacarandas. How voluptuous they looked now that I was back . . . a purple carpet of flowers under the trees, and seed pods, which looked like vaginas. A feeling came over me that if only I had stayed behind in India my life would have followed a different turn.

For hours I rode the new Metro aimlessly. I had missed the major phases of its construction – the Metro operated now as if it was the most natural thing in the city's circulation. Rajiv Chowk (new name for Connaught Place), Jantar Mantar and the Old Delhi railway station. Yamuna

River, across Yamuna. Remote areas like Noida shrank in time, only ten minutes away. The city had changed in so many ways, and in so many ways for the better.

How excited I was in the beginning of '84. My parents lived not far from the recently constructed Olympic-sized Nehru Stadium. We had just won the cricket World Cup, and two Indians were being trained by Russians to go to space on Soyuz or Salyut. I recall my father had bought a colour TV to watch the historic moment. So what does India look like from up there? Prime Minister Indira Gandhi had asked. Sare jahan se achha, echoed the astronaut's voice. Best in the world.

Just as I was walking around imbibing the sheer energy of the city my cellphone rang. 'Sorry, sir, I don't want to give the impression I am hounding you.' The IIT grad student's voice, not very clear, superimposed by sounds of howling children. Who gave you my number? 'The Chairman, sir,' he explained. 'Please come. You are invited to a gathering at my place. Eightish.'

'Not possible, not tonight, I am occupied.'

Despite my better judgement I succumbed to his persistence, and decided to surprise him. Cancelling the dinner appointment with Father was easy; I then took a taxi to Jor Bagh. Because it was dark the elite neighbourhood resembled a Western city, no trace of slums, although even here the posh brick walls smelled of male piss. The houses in Jor Bagh were big, however, and majestic, and competed with the ones designed originally by Lutyens during the times of the British.

The student's house had real cops posted outside, alert and jumpy, loaded with carbines. Ten or fifteen Mercedes and BMWs and Bentleys chaotically parked by the gate. I asked the driver to wait and presented myself to the guards, who frisked me and then ejected me in through a metal detector.

Inside I was unable to locate the student or my colleagues. The veranda was densely packed with intermingling people. Not a single familiar face. I made it to the large high-ceilinged room on the ground floor, a dining table in the middle, no chairs, hundreds of bottles of Sula wine, the wine which had made me throw up only a day ago. A woman in a red jacket was looking at the miniatures on the wall. Nude Radha and Krishna. Like most women at the party she was in a skirt and black leather boots. She had the most voluptuous calves.

Liveried men served kebabs and drinks, and the kitchen was occupied by a maid in a sari. She told me to check upstairs. Chote sahib sometimes goes to the kotha, she said in Hindi. The stairs were steep and up there I found a terraced garden with a pergola, and the suffocating smell of raat ki raani. Something started blinking and shuffling not far from me – an orphan cellphone. I picked it up and placed it on an empty chair, and walked slowly towards the small room at the other end of the terrace; the room, a slab of concrete and glass as if done by Corbusier himself. Dim light, the door ajar. Bookshelves. Russian writers. Music CDs. I walked in. The student I was looking for was there. He was not alone. He was in a position normally described as missionary, the woman's legs and feet wrapped around him. His skin, darker than hers. His neck turned and our eyes locked for a brief second; after that my gaze drifted to the Russian authors, then I stepped out.

'Thayroh,' he said in Hindi, then switched to English. 'Please don't leave, wait for me, sir.'

There I surveyed the city at night and its awkward, uncomfortable sounds and smells. Those two minutes have stayed with me, the man's butt and the woman's thigh. The way the woman's mouth had widened, the way the boy-man didn't seem to care about my intrusion. Slowly I moved down the stairs to the Sula room; the voluptuous woman was no longer there, but there were loud waves of chattering. Floating around, I entered a small dimly lit room with a solitary yellow armchair. Without a third thought that is where I took refuge.

Often old memories flicker within me on encountering the deeds of the young or the very young. Nothing shocks me any more. Why would someone with his background go for a grad degree at IIT? Mere idealism? His father had enough money and power to send him abroad to Oxford, Cambridge, Harvard. I felt as if I were staring at my younger self in a mirror. I, too, didn't want to go abroad. However, my decision was not as bold as his. I did move to Cornell. Whereas he sits the Joint Entrance Exam, All India Rank: 48. Finishes his undergrad degree, and immediately enrols in the grad programme. But what I saw on the roof terrace was more than a question of enrolment. As if I were looking at myself. Some significant but lost slice of time and space. When I was a young student, I, too, started seeing a woman a few years older than me. The affair started as pure lust, rightly or wrongly, and soon mutated into something special. Something more real. They always do. (But I shall divulge such matters a bit later.)

That afternoon, right after he had discussed Pompeii and Herculaneum, Professor Singh sent me out of the class. Perhaps I had disrupted the lecture, although I remember this vaguely. As I was leaving he turned to me, smiled sardonically: Kal bhi nahin aana! Later I stood outside his office next to the bare semal tree with

21

blood-red blossoms, then walked in with uncalculated slowness. I didn't say sorry, and he demanded no apology. As usual, without permission, nervous as hell, I occupied the threadbare chair. He was typing a research paper, inserting a couple of sketches of two stable helium isotopes, ^{3}He and ^{4}He, using that old-fashioned 'photocopy' and 'cut and paste' technique. 'So what are your plans?' he asked. 'India or the US?' Those days I was open to working in my own country after graduation. In fact I was also open to sitting the GRE exams. 'Are you a man with a plan?' he asked. I told him I had kept both options open. 'Then you have no plan.' He gave me a piercing look. 'Go abroad, but come back.' It was rare to see him less open to discussion. His mind was already made up. 'It is too bureaucratic, and too hierarchical, and too feudal here. People have insecurities,' he explained bluntly. 'A few years of exile will do you good. You are young and ambitious. You will see the world. You will be better accepted by the powerful – here – after that onion-skin higher degree from the US.' He didn't reveal his own details and decisions. I found out later. Most of the staff members in his own department accepted him only after a famous American professor, a Nobel Laureate, praised Professor Singh's work during a keynote lecture at the academy of sciences.

The next day the IIT colleague told me he knew nothing about Professor Singh's family, but he took me through a long corridor to the Chair's office, who said that Nelly (according to the grapevine) had moved to the hill station of Shimla. A 'friend' had come to the office to collect Mohan's papers 'but we,' said the chair, 'didn't have the key ready, and even if it had been ready we would not have passed the boxes on to someone who claimed to be a mere friend'. The papers were still in

22

storage until last year in the cryo lab. Early this summer during the annual clean-up, partly due to an oversight and partly due to a stupid clerical mistake, they got shredded.

Don't expect me to remember everything. A lot has simply faded away. Also, I am not implying that other teachers were crap and he was the lone phosphorescent giant. Perhaps premature death transforms a teacher in the eyes of the student. Even if the person was unpopular, immensely disliked, he becomes a myth, even mediocre students transform him into a benign myth. Small details, small movements made in the classroom, acquire more weight. Words said and unsaid more significance.

I figured out only in the final year that thirty or forty minutes before the lecture Professor Singh would lock himself in the office and pace up and down and contemplate, in other words prepare his so-called spontaneity. (This was a pedagogical device and when I started teaching at Cornell I basically emulated the same technique and it delivered wonders and made me somewhat popular with the students.)

I shall never forget my last visit to his office. The 19th of October, a faultless day like any other. The laburnum quivered in the sun, I recall, so bright it hurt my eyes. I placed the borrowed item on his heavily cluttered desk; sheets and memos spilling over, glacial mountains and ice fields of exam papers and clogged lava flows of lab reports. Still weak, recovering from jaundice, I was in a way rediscovering the world; everything around me felt new and alien. Even the smells I took for granted in the past, and the dewy brilliance of objects. Without wasting words he checked if I had the energy to walk back to the hostel. I nodded. But he insisted on driving me in his white Fiat, which he drove slowly for my sake. On the way we talked about Maxwell's demons, he was also curious about my recently formed opinions and thoughts on Levi. I was unable to express myself properly. I said something about Levi's dark sense of humour. How he made use of snake droppings once to manufacture lipstick! Then we discussed briefly the chapter that left a huge impression on me. How the author had dealt with hunger. What really happened inside the 'concentration' camp. Up until that day the words 'dilute' and 'concentrated' were simply connected to the density of molecules in solutions (and not human beings). The writing had disturbed me, pushed me out of my comfort level. Those pages were set in a world I did not know.

Soon afterwards our class was divided into two groups for factory visits. The first, led by Professor Acharya, travelled to the Mathura Refinery and the ONGC offshore oil rig in Bombay. This was a five-day affair. All the plain and good-looking girls in our class signed up for this trip. If I had not been sick I, too, would have done the exotic trip, and if I had been fortunate enough I would have held that particular good-looking girl's hand. But 1984 was not a fortunate year. Special, not fortunate. Professor Acharya was a complete asshole, a postgraduate of Imperial College, London. I am glad I did not accompany him. His sick jokes repelled me, and so did his New Age fixation on Krishnamurti and other so-called gurus. The chairman accepted my request to join the second, relatively small, group instead. This one was led by Professor Singh, the two-day visit to factories up north. We left on 30 October.

Because I was unwell my father drove me to the station that day. He insisted on shaking hands with my teacher, and Nelly was there on the platform too. Although it was late autumn, her light cotton sari exuded the feel of summer.

24

Her cleavage visible, if one paid attention. The train was to depart at seven in the morning. 'Is your father an IPS?' Professor Singh took me aside. I remember his soft voice. 'He appears to be a terribly important man.' Father's uniform made it obvious that he was an elite Indian Police Service officer; however, civilians found it difficult to decode the meaning of the stars and ribbons and medals and other signs. While we were still floating on the platform, when my professor and my good father shook hands I felt strangely proud (and I didn't bother about 'what other students would say'). One of my hidden subconscious hopes got realised that day, a perfectly ordinary day like any other. Precisely at that moment I became aware of my 'double bond'. Blood and friendship – now that I think about it. 'Please take care of my son,' my father requested Professor Singh. 'He has just recovered from jaundice.'

The train was still at platform number one, the neon sign SECOND CLASS RETIRING ROOM flickered randomly. Where I stood I noticed tracks of birds permanently embedded in cement. Two silverish-hued pigeons were fluttering about completely oblivious to the human mass. The platform was definitely not a good site for a group shot because we were surrounded by a high concentration of men, waiting chaotically, elbowing women, ogling. Nelly volunteered to take the photo. We flocked together, all boys. Time was on our side then, most smiles filled with optimism, or rather entitlement. As I said before there were no female students in our group. On my laptop I have a scanned copy of that overexposed photo. Behind us the flickering neon sign. Professor Singh in the middle. One hand visible. His tie, black and narrow and angled, so unlike the symmetry of his turban. Nelly included Father in the photo, even though she could have kicked him out of the frame.

We urged her to join us in the second shot, but she looked baffled, and insisted on occupying the space behind the camera.

Several years later I wrote about the photo and the handshake and my stoic-faced father. I wrote about Nelly. No other images haunt me more. But for some reason memory fails me here, I have little recall of the onward train journey.

On 30 October we visited the pharmaceutical plant in Kasauli. (In colonial times the building served as a TB sanatorium.) On 31 October we visited the Mohan Meakin Brewery in the Solan Hills. (In colonial times it was called the Dyer–Meakin Brewery. Dyer was the father of General Dyer who ordered the Amritsar Massacre in 1919.) I still remember the enzymes, the smell of fermentation reactors and the hum of giant crushers, centrifuges and heat exchangers. Stage 3 washing with excess CO_2 to remove harmful gases from the liquid, the Bengali quality-control officer (a 'teetotaller' and a Brahmin) who tasted the 'thing' after it 'matured'. Because I was exactly six feet tall, Professor Singh made me stand next to the inebriated fermentation reactors and commanded the camera-wallah to take a shot. No one asked why. For we understood the implicit reasoning. The dimensions of my body (height in this case) a most convenient way to estimate the dimensions of the reaction vessel! 'Back home you will list the design variables and calculate the safety factors. How safe are the "safety factors"?' Alcohol was pumped like water from a muddy brown river to the bottling zone of the plant. In my ears I still carry an echo of the strange music the pasteurised glass bottles produced on the conveyor belt. Fifty thousand bottles a day.

During our return journey Professor Singh told us about the writer Kipling, who supported General Dyer even after the massacre of innocent Indians. Kipling contributed twelve pounds to the mass murderer's retirement fund, and called him 'brave'. Professor Singh also spoke about Gandhi with some admiration. 'But,' he said, 'Mahatma Gandhi was plain wrong about certain things. I cannot get used to the idea that he opposed the railways! Where would we be without the railways? There– ' I heard a scream. Someone discovered two rats in the bogie. Perhaps it was the sheer insane energy of youth that made me pick them up. Something was definitely strange about the rats, they had not yet started decomposing. Two rust-coloured bodies, freshly dead, hooked to my fingers, dangled in front of everyone. *Abe pagal ho gaya hai kya?* teased the chorus of voices. Another whisper: *Professor ki pagri main dal de, saleh!* Put them inside the professor's turban, saleh! The rats spun and wobbled when I dropped them out of the moving window. For a brief second I felt I was in my school biology lab about to begin dissections. Odour of formaldehyde. Smell of an anatomy experiment. I don't recall now my exact state of mind when after a brief pause the professor regaled us with stories about his great-grandfather. When just fifteen, great-grandfather, a self-taught chemist, joined the Maharajah's court. One day musicians came to the court claiming their music possessed the power to light up all the lamps in the palace. Demonstrate it, ordered the Maharajah. Lots of sitars were strummed and resonant ragas and raginis sung, but the lamps refused to ignite. The Maharajah, more embarrassed than the celebrity musicians, turned to the fifteen-year-old, who knew exactly what to do. In his spare time the kid, the boy, had taught himself the sciences. He dissolved white phosphorus in carbon disulphide and refilled the lamps with this magical 'oil'. The enchanted musicians kept playing their ragas and the royal audience kept swooning (and murmuring). Soon carbon disulphide evaporated in the lamps and the phosphorus caught fire. In a flash the wicks lit up high with a strange glow to dazzle everyone. There was a loud cheer in the court. And a stunned silence in the train. I don't know when exactly one of us (pretending to be drunk) came up with the bright idea to transform 'bad odours' into fragrance. (The toilet in our bogie lacked a door, and there was an ensemble of houseflies on human vomit. Someone said a new bride had been throwing up.) Professor Singh very playfully massaged the student's idea and they discussed the experimental procedure . . . He had a smile. To this day I cannot forget his sardonic smile. As engineers you are expected to be 'ingenious', he said seriously. In our country we end up becoming 'one-dimensional' and 'obedient'. We must learn to pose the right questions, and question what is considered right. Soon some of you might get involved with the three most important questions. What are they? The origin of the universe. The origin of life. The origin of mind.

Several times I have tried to recall the train journey. Every attempt a failure. Every attempt a mere fucking iteration (if I am still allowed to use that word). I recall most of us disappointed (and terribly thirsty) because the managers at the brewery had refused to gift us bottles of Mohan Meakin. 'Company policy.' This detail is perhaps the most insignificant from that journey.

The catering-wallah passed by and we ordered twenty-one lunches, eight veg and thirteen non-veg, dal and chawal and dahi and oily parathas with achar. Non-veg thalis had fish curry or mutton with gravy. I ordered fish and this detail for some reason is stuck. The fish is stuck inside me. Some chutiya mentioned surrogate mothers and then a bad joke, 'Do female mannequins have pubic hair?' and Professor Singh stared at our silliness and there was a stunned silence. Then someone suggested antakshari and we sang old film songs and Michael Jackson and Prince, and even David Bowie, until someone turned on the radio, first All India Radio, and immediately afterwards the short-wave BBC Radio, which confirmed that Mrs Gandhi had been assassinated by her own bodyguards.

Good, the bitch is dead, a class fellow said, and Professor Singh stood up and raised his voice. 'You should not talk like this. So many bullets have been emptied into the poor woman, no one deserves to die like that. To disagree with someone doesn't mean you assassinate them.'

The slow-moving train got more and more delayed, and perhaps it was one of the most difficult nights for the entire country. The delay was a tense six-hours.

Early in the morning we saw people defecating by the railways tracks, Subzi Mandi passed by, and then New Delhi station. Even before it came to a complete halt we saw traces of violence on the platform, but there were cops stationed there, and because the cops were armed with guns and lathis we thought the situation was under control. We spontaneously formed a circle around Professor Singh (for he was the only Sikh in our group) and stepped out of the bogie. I wish my father had been there to receive us, then there would have been no need to worry, but in those days cellphones didn't exist. Suddenly an angry mob, armed with the most elementary weapons (metal rods and rubber tyres), crossed the railway line and climbed up the platform. '*Khoon ka badla khoon say. Give us that traitor sardar.*' We started to run. 'Blood for blood.'

29

What broke the circle was a Vespa scooter on the platform. Sudden screeching of brakes, tyre marks, rubber smell. A photojournalist in a yellow windcheater started snapping pictures of the mob, which had fished out our professor. 'Stop taking pictures,' said one of the thugs, 'otherwise we kill you.'

The thug points at Professor Singh. 'This traitor Sikh is going to take pictures. Those who want to save him, we kill you.' He kicks the 'sister-fucker' journalist in the balls, snatches the camera, destroys the roll. I remain paralysed on my spot. He snatches our professor's suitcase. 'Sardar-ji, our mother is dead and you are not crying? Cry, behnchod. Gadar kay londay, beat your chest.' He unzips the suitcase, rummages through the contents, old and new, pulls out something that looks like a souvenir for Nelly, and a Pahari doll (most likely for his daughter) and a Himachali achkan (most likely for his son). 'Nice wristwatch.' Then the thug gestures for other lumpens to go ahead; the lumpens spray gasoline from the journalist's scooter on our teacher, slip a rubber tyre around his neck. 'Let me go. What have I done?' I can hear Professor Singh shout. The tyre constrains his arms. 'Sardar, you sister-fucker, you killed our mother. Gadar, now we kill you.'

'Stop it,' I say, 'you can't do this, he is our teacher.' 'Khoon ka badla khoon say . . . saala sardar ki aulad . . . gadar ki aulad.' Although it is early morning, his breath stinks of rum. Half of my class fellows disappear, others repeat the same thing over and over: 'This is madness.' I urge the cops to help, I tell them that I happen to be the son of a senior police officer, the most senior. At this point the chief lumpen laughs and spits in Professor Singh's face, douses the tyre with more hydrocarbons and strikes a match. A senior Congress leader, his Nehru – Gandhi khadi clothes fluttering in the wind, is standing close to the station master's office on the platform, guiding the mob like the conductor of a big orchestra. *Khatam kar do sab sardaron ko. Khatam kar do saanp kay bacchon ko. Finish them, children of snakes. Destroy them all*. He is not very tall and wears black glasses. I will never forget that Congresswallah's black glasses. I feel like confronting him, but stand on my spot, paralysed. 'This is the way to teach the Sikhs a lesson,' says a bystander. I take a deep breath. The black glasses are gone. The photojournalist is still trembling; they spare his Vespa, and we keep hearing the screams. I still hear those screams. I can't hear enough. We couldn't do a thing. I could do nothing. The only thing I was able to save was a shoe and that too was lost in the commotion that followed.

It was sickening, you had to see the horror to believe the horror and it was so unreal I almost didn't believe my own sense organs. But the fire and the smoke were so absolutely real, different from the way they are done in the movies. During the combustion I could not use my knowledge of chemistry and physics to extinguish the flames. How fast they engulfed his entire body. I could do

31

nothing. I was a mere onlooker. In the end all that remained along with the ashes were a few bones and a steel bracelet. Black like a griddle.

If Primo Levi had witnessed the moment he would have written the chapter called Sulphur differently. Sulphur is used to vulcanise rubber that is used in tyres.

Primo Levi survived the German Nazis and Italian Fascists because he helped them prepare Buna rubber during the war. In India my compatriots slipped rubber around Professor Singh's neck and set him on fire.

My father had sent an official jeep to pick me up at the station and drop me at the IIT campus. Two of my classmates accompanied me.

As the jeep passed Tolstoy Marg I saw dozens of Sikh bodies on fire. Smell of burning wool and rubber tyres and human flesh. I saw taxis being smashed. And the black cloud of smoke touched the sky. This was our Eiffel Tower. This was our carnival. Our periodic table of hate.

We passed by the church. The Bishop was standing by the giant black-painted cast-iron gates, preventing the mob from entering the church. Thousands of children, women and men had taken refuge inside.

It was a Thursday. The jeep driver was in tears, he had seen horrible things. The skinny man trembled, on the verge of a nervous breakdown. Gurdwaras on fire, Guru Granth on fire. He said he didn't want to come, but it was Sahib's order and his duty. Those days my parents lived in a mansion on Amrita Sher-Gil Marg (the road named after the 'mother of modern Indian art'), and I lived in the hostel on the IIT campus.

After this there are lapses in my memory. And moisture in my eyes. There was too much going on. Too many exams. What conversations I had with my father and classmates I

have little recall. Were they equally shocked? Soon after-wards toxic methylisocyanide gas leaked from the Union Carbide plant in Bhopal. Back at the campus I stood in front of Nelly's house and noticed that almost a quarter of it was badly damaged. Charred is the right word. There was a yellow padlock on the chestnut-coloured front door. The brick wall behind the house, between the campus and the village, was broken. According to rumours, she had survived the attacks.

Classes resumed and someone else replaced Professor Singh, and what made his death more unbearable was an empty chair; it was not his chair, but the chair of another Sikh boy in our class. He, too, had disappeared. When I had joined IIT there were two Sikh students in my class. Only one of them managed to survive and he was heavily traumatised; now he was the only one left and he seemed to have been transformed into silence itself.

Soon afterwards, maybe a couple of weeks later, we were all asked to assemble outside the hostels and form a line, and the new warden ordered the Sikh boys to form a separate line. At first I thought this was for their own safety, they were being sent elsewhere, this is the time before YouTube and Facebook and fearless bloggers, we didn't know what was really going on, media was state-controlled, people turned on short-wave BBC to find out what really happened or what was happening in the country. But soon we found out. A Dalit woman had been molested on the IIT campus and she had complained to the authorities. A Sikh boy had molested her – she knew this because he had entered her tent in a turban. The student in our class was also in the line-up (along with nine or ten others). It is to that woman's credit she didn't point a finger at those who were innocent, but whenever she stood in front of a turbaned and bearded face my heart leaped out of my body. Not one of them was guilty; we all knew who had done it. A Hindu boy had tied a turban on and had entered the Dalit construction workers' tent, but no one had the guts to report him.

After the incident the Sikh boy in our class came to me and urged me to accompany him to the market, and he told me to take him to the barber's shop and the first barber refused to cut his hair, and the second one confirmed with him several times if he was sure. 'Of course I am sure', he said. And I remember that day clearly when his hair was being cut. He had shut his eyes tight, and the crackling of the transistor radio could be heard in the barber's shop and Prime Minister Rajiv Gandhi's voice: *when a big tree falls the Earth shakes*. I say this in hindsight; when I heard the crackling radio I was too young to

34

process the lack of shock, and the force field of hate, in the new PM's words. My classmate's hair had piled up in the barber's shop. We paid. He was slightly shorter than me, and it was windy, the city still smelled of burning rubber and I asked him how does it feel. He stopped on the pavement. And then God knows what got into him, he lifted his hand and slapped me. And I was so shocked I didn't know what to do. By the time I processed this it was too late to slap him back and I simply laughed.

2.

Drops

'Dystopia' is a word I learned in 1983 while preparing for my GRE exams to apply for higher studies in the US. A compound made up of two ancient Greek words. *Dys* = ill, bad, wretched. *Topos* = place, land. A government that harms its own citizens. A state in which life is sometimes extremely wretched as a form of deprivation or oppression or genocidal pogroms. In the land where Orwell was born, 1984 was never imaginary. In India it was real, 1984 is burned fully into my retina; it recurs every day, every month, every year with its own chilling periodicity.

My memories are scalded memories. Remains of a fire. Dense black smoke flows through my veins. Delhi is a singed postcard. Smell of fungus, actinomycetes, just before rain. We waited. But it didn't rain the first week of November. That is why human ash still coats my lungs. I have given up trying to comprehend the madness that overtook the city. I summon images, try to plot them with words and numbers on a 3D graph, but words don't live up to their reputation, each one a failure. All I can do is listen to the pain of others. Perhaps it is more than my own.

Twenty-five years after the Event, on a night like this, I took the train to Shimla to see my professor's wife. Something keeps me from calling her a widow. As the narrow carriage picked up speed, I thought about the remaining days of my sabbatical, and the possibility of closure. But the past refused to become past. Outside, a thin forest of chir pines and oaks with serrated leaves, although I could not see a thing. Only a faint reflection of spiral tracks and my own face in tinted glass. There exist only two ways to deal with time, and I, several years ago, chose the wrong way. More than once I thought of standing by the open, rattling door, but I was afraid of myself.

Shimla or 'Simla' was colder than I had expected. A porter moved my luggage along the rough cobbled path to the hotel on the upper mall. I had a booking for six nights at the Peterhof (a fossil left behind by the Empire). The hotel clerk had warned me of an upcoming Hindu Party convention, a 'brainstorming' session, a so-called chintan baithak. But the event hadn't seemed to matter when I made the reservation.

The city was still waiting for the first snowfall of the season. For some unknown reason it didn't snow during January and February, I was told. Global warming was too easy an assumption or conclusion. The distant mountains, visible from the balcony, still carried the weight of snow of previous years. The Himalayas were higher there. Chiselled peaks (with names like Bangles of the Moon) flushed with strands of orange or flamingo light. My room had a musty, resinous smell and the navy-blue carpet carried white stains along the non-functional fireplace. After that long and exhausting journey I felt like taking a proper shower. But, as expected, there was no soap in the bathroom, so I stepped out to purchase a cake of soap.

Nelly, if she followed the same profession, works at a library, the IIT Chair had told me, scratching his shock of white hair. Library or the archives. She was trained as an archivist. On a departmental sheet he had scribbled her phone number. 'So much time has passed by, I am sure the number has changed.'

After a shower I shaved, then called the number. The answering machine clicked in and I was greeted by a voice choked by years of cigarette smoke, at the same time musical; the voice, darting out of the receiver, almost stabbed me. Not her, it was the voice of a man, a mediocre Indian Leonard Cohen. I left a detailed message for Nelly, and an inchoate apology regarding my failure to get in touch earlier.

Failure is the right word.

Shimla or Simla – a city six thousand feet high – was not a bad place to recover, an altermodern sanatorium, but my head pulsed like an overinflated tyre, and I was foolishly eager to locate Nelly. The best bet was to wait. I don't recall how I spent an entire day in that L-shaped hotel room, but no one returned my calls. Next day, again, I spent the first half in the room, but after lunch, feeling energised, walked a hundred metres to the edge of the hotel. Past the black cast-iron gates at a slightly lower elevation I noticed the directions to an aviary. Smallish and poorly maintained, I could tell from the outside, but something compelled me to go ahead, and so disregarding my better sense I bought a ticket and spent two or three hours inside amid a confusing ensemble of Himalayan birds.

During the IIT days Nelly would tell me now and then fragments from her past. Listening to her I would try to imagine the shape of my alternative life if a biological accident made me take birth in a Sikh family. She would tell me what it felt like washing her father's turbans. She did not romanticise the turbans the way I do. She would tell me about her kind but intimidating father, who trained as an agricultural scientist. Almost all his research focused on rice. The old man was never able to resolve the contradictions between science and religion. He knew half of the holy Granth by heart, and would recite hyper-melodious verses from the holy book and Nanak's poetry on the oddest of occasions. Waking up at four in the morning and in the solitude of his room the rice scientist would hold reasonably loud dialogues between God and Darwin. These sessions lasted a little over an hour. God would win in the end, but Darwin would make sure the dialogues started again the next day. She rarely mentioned her mother. By all standards she had a happy childhood. Nelly, I recall, never learned to swim, and until the age of eight, she was afraid of snakes and water. Her father taught her cycling; often she would ride her red Hero to school (salwar puffed up) with friends. She loved foreign films, the first one she told me was *To Sir, With Love*. In her college years, Nelly suffered a minor bout of depression. The depression did not last long and getting married to Mohan eliminated the melancholic moods completely. At least that is what she told me. Together they travelled to different parts of the country on trains pulled by steam engines, especially the hill stations. Darjeeling, Dalhousie, Ooty. When I got to know them better my persistence paid off. I found out, if not the cause, the details of that depression. One day she also confided in me a difficult episode from her teen years. She was good friends with their neighbour's daughter then. Several times Nelly watched a noisy spectacle through the bedroom window – the girl's mother holding a cane. After the beatings I always felt sad, said Nelly. Sad that my friend's mother was like that, and more sad because a part of me derived pleasure watching the beatings. Then there was a heavy mist in her eyes.

Despite a few odd recollections it occurred to me that I knew Nelly less and less. The gaps in my understanding remained despite reading at Cornell library several 'Sikh' biographies; in Shimla, looking for her, I felt the gaps more than ever, a tightening sensation as I observed the birds. I had even failed to ask, for instance, how Nelly and Mohan met. I never managed to ask the most essential questions. In my younger days I would dismiss such questions as 'auntie talk' (and in my twenties I would dismiss them as Oprah Winfrey). Of all the birds in the aviary, the ones that most caught my attention were a pair of monal pheasants. The female dull, the male flamboyant in metallic blue-red-green plumage, digging deep into the soil with his bill. Bejewelled, tessellated with heavily protruding eyes, trying to locate worms. As if he had never known fear. Observing the male I felt a mild twitching sensation in my left hand.

Over the next few days I tried another way to locate her.

Every morning I would drink two or three glasses of bottled water, put on my blue jeans and black Zara jacket, and step out for long walks. I did seven bifurcating walks, whirling around the seven hills of Shimla. The hills or mountains strangely defined, definitely not volcanic; the geometry misleading. Jakho, Mount Pleasant, Potters Hill, Bantony, Prospect, Summer Hill . . . Portions of the ageing hills still covered with trees. Nature had perished on those slopes a while ago; what remained now were simply the traces of the past. Chir pines. Chestnuts. Himalayan oaks with serrated leaves . . . Others crooked, dwarf, twisted, young . . . Himachal University library. No Nelly Kaur there. Another Tudor building on the ridge, the city library. The Cliff End Estate. The state archives. Structures more than a century old, fallen into disrepair. Railway Board Building, a cast-iron cage. In a decaying Catholic cathedral I saw the Virgin of Guadalupe. Snowdon, Medical College, Lakkar Bazaar. Three Kali temples. I even did the slums, and today more than three-quarters of the city is a hideous slum, perhaps the highest in the world, with crying children and incessantly clogged drains. Men in Himachali topis and women in incongruous white running shoes and brash, ill-mannered tourists despoiling the place. Walking around I encountered several concrete and bronze statues, shadows shortening and lengthening; the most impressive one was that of Ambedkar, the leader of the Dalits, a copy of the Indian Constitution in his hand. His bronze hand and bespectacled head glowed with utopian hopes. The Dalits, inspired by Ambedkar, were challenging old Brahmanical ways of being in the new India, not just economically and politically, but also symbolically, rightfully taking back what was denied to them for so many centuries. *I cannot give you heaven, but I can give you a voice.* One evening my feet started hurting and I sat at the base of the bronze statue, and thought of the grade-nine poem, 'Ozymandias'. Ambedkar doesn't belong to the Ozymandias category, a voice corrected the current of my thoughts. He stood for justice, dignity; an end to humiliation. An end to violence, an end to the poisonous Manusmriti, which says: All women are impure. Which says: Molten lead ought to be poured in the ears of an 'untouchable' who aspires to higher education. Ambedkar, who did his grad work at Columbia University, New York, is even more important to this country than Gandhi, who merely patronised the so-called pariahs. There: I contemplated the rest of my so-called sabbatical. My colleague's pithy statements: 'So much work, so little time. So much time, so little work.' In Shimla: I was wandering without a good probability of success, squandering precious days over something unconnected to my research interests and rising-star career status. Locating Nelly had become my new obsession. Why now? Why after so many years? As if I were a freak, accidentally summoned by the demons. I called the IIT Chair. Surprisingly he didn't scream or yell, but he wanted me to co-supervise a grad student. 'At the very least introduce the Nobel Laureate Douglas Osheroff. Only you can do that.' He flattered me . . . I wanted the Chair to help me locate Nelly. You are wasting your time, he excoriated. The cell-phone connection kept failing; then a crackling disturbance set in and it cut off. The wind grew strong. My eyes watered because of alien particles stirred by its sheer force. I shut my eyes, and my ears alone couldn't tell if the sound belonged to the rising and falling of the wind or to a body of water as vast as the Arabian Sea. For once I didn't think in terms of pressure pockets, temperature gradients, boundary layers, dimensionless numbers or aeroelasticity. Vayu, the god of wind; I brought to mind his mythical powers, and even the sturdiest of conifers, in that sparse and austere forest, I feared were going to separate one by one from the root system and fall. She sheared past the agitated branches of a tree, leaning forward, running. Dressed in red and green rags, the woman with wild black hair and wild ravenous eyes, I noticed as the figure approached closer. Not shy at all she sat precariously close, splitting a blade of grass, or staring at her calloused hands, then staring vacantly at the unsteady, swirling mountains as unreal as fog or mist. From a small bag she dug out a red-coloured fruit and let it go. Together we watched the fruit rolling down the slope until it vanished completely. She smiled and twitched, then again, and then her longish, soiled fingers tapped and caressed my shoulder. My jacket was fluttering now. I have the key to happiness, she snapped, and burst out laughing. 'Do you want to know the secret?' The cop posted in the square appeared with a stick and shooed her away as if she were an animal. 'Why are you so unhappy?' The woman, mad like the wind, chanted from a distance. 'I will go to the moon, and tell them about you. I will go there and tell the goddess about you. Nine, eight, seven . . . Moon.'

Then she laughed. 'Nine, eight, seven. Teen, doh, ik.'

The cop addressed me as 'sa'ab' and advised me and my hallucination to try the old Viceregal Lodge on top of Observatory Hill. He made a stiff but awkward movement in the wind and made a strange remark, which has stayed with me all these years. 'Now books live where the Lat Sahib used to live.' Further probing led me to more information. I had read about the lodge but didn't know that the Scottish baronial castle had actually become the Centre for Advanced Studies . . . In his own limited way he explained that the dark chapter of colonialism was over. I felt like giving the man a small tip, but restrained myself. The cop's face resembled an isosceles triangle sketched by a naive and mischievous child, something about that Euclidian nose and forehead and his black leather belt transported me to the time when I would accompany my father to remote towns and cities for police inspections (during his deputation posting). When we stepped out for long walks, uniformed men (posted throughout the city) would salute me. How delusional my childhood years were because I walked a little ahead of my father! The cop told me that the institute had a huge library of its own. Naturally I assumed I had almost found Nelly. And the archives? I checked. What is that? I didn't press further and followed the steep path, which looped up to the green posts. As I climbed up I felt a cool and green dampness in the air.

Over a hundred years ago when the British built the castle they thought the Empire would last forever. The sun would refuse to set, and the wheels of history would always move forward (for them). Those at the very top planned a giant 'non-perishable' machine assembled out of mere sandstone and limestone. The aspirations of the imperial architects matched the grand aspirations of the Empire, and its absurd rationale for plundering the colonies, the so-called white man's burden. Lord Dufferin himself oversaw the construction of the flamboyant structure, which began in 1884. His wife, the Vicereine, wrote long letters to family and friends in England about the interiors done in the most English of chintzes, reassuring the readers all along that finally there was a building in

Shimla worthy of their high rank, and in no danger of slipping over a mountain.

I have a confession.

When I rounded the road to the library and first saw the building I felt sorry for the British; momentarily it dispelled some of the sadness I carry around. Once inside the building, I bought a ticket to the guided tour (led by a sprightly man in his twenties). Most tourists parked themselves and listened quietly as if this was the most significant moment in their lives. Unable to stand still, the engineer within me made quick calculations related to materials, volumes and surfaces. Pacing up and down and tenuously attached to the obedient tourists, I marvelled at the massive electrification problems. Structural challenges. Calculations about the entire throbbing mechanism. How many faceless, voiceless men ran the grand imperishable machine? The main collection of the library is housed in what used to be the Viceroy's ballroom, with its tall windows and Gothic arches. Some very powerful and wealthy sahibs and memsahibs danced there. In the Empire's dining room there are shelves on history, archaeology and emotions. In the leaky pantry: law, technology and religion. Downstairs in the vaulted room: Indian languages and translation. The archives are in the gleaming cabinet room where the Viceroy determined the fate of millions of subjects. Research fellows from India and abroad inhabit the colonial building now. The tour was exceptionally well researched, but over in twenty short minutes. On the noticeboard by the entrance I saw announcements for upcoming conferences on Memory, Forgetting, History, Truth and Reconciliation.

It was closing time. I lingered around the pebbled path by the entrance. The pebbles, sharp and striated, did not belong there. Neither did the castle with its many architectural associations. Glancing sideways, I noticed some movement. A woman looking much older than her age stepped out of the main entrance, the so-called porte cochère, and walked to the solitary bench under the tulip tree planted by Lord Curzon. Most of her colleagues seemed to be in the mood to compete with the speed of light as they disappeared towards houses and bazaars down the hill. She was the only one on the bench, visible from where I stood. Salt-and-pepper hair. Monkeys around her; not too close. Those creatures didn't look different from Kipling's monkeys, the ones he sketched for his kids during time spent in undulating Vermont.

She was wearing a loose salwar kameez, black boots, a chunni round her neck. I walked on the crunchy pebbled path very close to the bench. It was clear this person had never dyed her hair. She noticed me, her mouth half open. I had no idea how to begin, so I stammered, 'By any chance are you?'

The face was still beautiful. But it had started to ruin. The mole below the lower lip drew unnecessary attention. Distorting symmetry. Some faces are difficult to describe using models and metaphors. One looks for traces of the old self, but all one sees is loss, and what remains feels like an unsettling fiction or a perfectly settled disguise. Let me just say that she, the woman in front of me, had the aura and grandeur of an ageing beauty.

Imagine a piercingly attractive actress who (for the sake of her role) makes an attempt to look old. Using a special wax and make-up she allows extreme undulations to appear on her forehead. Also a scar on the right cheek, and another hint of one on the brow. Such was the face I saw.

'Yes, I am Nelly Singh, I mean Kaur,' and then she looked at me for a long time.

'Raj?'

She stood up, almost hugged me, but some mysterious force made her change her mind.

We shook hands.

'Your hands are very cold.'

She asked me about things that had happened in my life, and I told her briefly about my years in Ithaca, my thesis topic, etc.

'Are you married? Children?'

The shock and excitement of having actually located her was only now penetrating my body, and I could hardly say a meaningful word. I even forgot to ask about her children. There was a book in her hand, a dusty red cuboid of light.

'How did you recognise me?'

'I knew you would come.'

'You knew?'

'Got your phone message.'

'But you didn't call me back, Mrs Singh.'

'Where are you staying?'

'The Peterhof. I mentioned the hotel when I left the message.'

'Sorry.'

She smiled. With some difficulty I scanned her face again. The oval. Big, beautiful eyes. Her nose striated, as if the make-up artist had stretched a rubber band and run it repeatedly on the young woman's skin just below the bridge.

'Mrs Singh?'

'Yes?'

'May I invite you . . .'

'Go on.'

'May I invite you to dinner this evening?'

50

'OK.'

'Thank you.'

'But I don't have a lot of time.'

Her chunni fluttered in the wind.

'In that case, shall we eat at the restaurant at the Peter-hof?'

'OK. I know what to order. But we must do it right away.'

For several years now she had worked at the institute, six years as a chief archivist.

'You have come during so much chaos.'

Nelly didn't spell out the exact reason. It was an early retirement. Her lips quivered as she spoke. She had had the 'good fortune' to assist innumerable distinguished scholars, visiting research fellows from abroad. Dr Uberoi of Australia. Dr Aung San of Burma. 'You know, Dr Raj Kumar –' she used my complete name – 'a few speeches will be made and then the director will praise me, my contribution to the collection, and ask me to say something before handing me the gift box. Standard procedure.'

The streets to the Peterhof were dirty with political posters stuck by the Hindu Party, as they were about to have their annual brainstorming session in the city, and they had chosen that fossil of a hotel as the main site. Nelly told me something I didn't know. The Peterhof was the High Court before it became a hotel. That is where the trial of the zealot (Nathu Ram Godse) took place, the man who assassinated Mahatma Gandhi. The assassin belonged to the same Hindu Party.

'And you?' Nelly asked me. 'Why did you choose the Peterhof?'

'Well, my reason is entirely personal. My parents spent

51

their honeymoon in Shimla. They stayed at the same hotel.'

I didn't tell her about the difficulties my parents had throughout their marriage, or my own troubled relationship with my father, or his surgery.

'So you were conceived in one of those rooms!'

Technically this is not correct, said Nelly. The original Peterhof mysteriously caught fire in the early eighties. She then described the fire in detail, but I was unable to concentrate. Her words assembled a strange burning image in my mind and momentarily I was overcome by a feeling of panic.

Once I had yearned to be alone with her, and now everything had changed. She had a fearless but delicate face then, the way Punjabi women are, a regal posture. She was responsive to small changes, very small alterations, in a different season. Now, in my mind, the gap between the remembered Nelly and the real Nelly acquired a complexity I had not foreseen. She was still beautiful, but crumblingly so. My memories themselves, I realised, had become viscous, viscoelastic, or elastoviscoplastic, terms I usually reserve to characterise materials and the way they flow.

So far, very carefully, we had avoided talking about Professor Singh, and she had not mentioned a single word about my changed appearance. She was not the only one. I, too, had changed. The cops had blocked the short cut to the hotel, the path which looped up the steep hill via the aviary. We followed the longer path. With the sun almost down, I felt the air become cooler. Nelly said, 'You have come at a time when Shimla is untidy, chaotic, completely taken over by the politicos. It is not always like that. There are times when research fellows take over the streets and of course while there are some who treat the institute as a playground, certain fellows get serious work done.'

We were unable to walk past the aviary, but the sounds the birds made swelled and shrank around us as if a chorus in a play. Some birds merely imitated others; and others, while fluttering about, emitted notes of incomprehension as if they had completely lost their sense of reality.

On the train to Shimla a strange image had flashed in my mind. A little girl more or less like Red Riding Hood was playing with a predator of a bird. The wolf was disguised as the peregrine falcon. Is that you, Grandmother? Are you really hungry, Grandmother? Now and then the little girl stared at a painting by Amrita Sher-Gil. But the wolf stared at the girl with murderous rage. To protect herself, the girl entered the painting . . . Little Red Riding Hood walked slowly and safely into the labyrinths of raven-coloured hair, confessing strange theories about her 'wicked' grandmother.

Something trembled at the edge of my hallucination. *Three Women*, the painting, never fails to stir me. Three women, three 'saviours', enduring what comes from outside the frame, and the bigger pain woven or braided within. Big bird-like eyes averting the surveyors' gaze, vividly coloured dresses, perfect locks of black hair. The longer one stares at those delicate faces, this one thought precipitates: those three must be out of their minds. Moving backwards or forwards or sideways offers little help. Whenever I encounter reproductions of the painting in art magazines and even in newsprint I get the feeling that perhaps I, too, must be out of my mind.

Nelly, it seemed, had not had a proper conversation for a while now. Her deep penetrating silence during our stroll spoke louder than a reptating bead of words. I was looking forward to difficult questions over dinner. In a different season, it is safe to say, she had been loquacious and had a tendency to 'cultivate'. She questioned my all-male reading list. She would often disturb my equilibrium, make it meta-stable. She is the one who persuaded me to read 'The Quilt' by Ismat Chughtai. To this day I have not been able to forget the story and its marvellous discontinuities. Perhaps start our conversation in the restaurant with 'The Quilt?' Or start with something safe. Little did I know the new developments. During my absence the Peterhof had become abnormal – almost a citadel. The man at the reception desk said that he had been looking for me. 'Where were you, sa'ab?' He was very apologetic. 'Sorry, sa'ab, we had to move your things out of the room, we made a mistake when we took the booking, sa'ab.' Momentarily I lost my temper. I rarely lose my balance. Then I scanned the place more objectively. The statue of Buddha on the lawns looked as puzzled, disappointed and harassed as me. The Hindu Party had literally taken over; saffron flags were all around and men in sinister khaki shorts were doing sinister drills on the lawns, and it was so screechingly loud it hurt my ears. Within a few hours the so-called retreat had become pure movement and action and order. Suddenly the men lifted their arms in unison and delivered a fascist salute.

Nelly suggested we try Hotel Cecil. I settled the account and we rolled the suitcase towards the building. The roof had a distinctly green copper patina. She offered to carry the smaller laptop bag, but it was heavy and I slung it around my shoulder. In the lobby of the Cecil a pianist was playing the *Doctor Zhivago* theme song and there was a sentimental mood in the air. There, too, no space was available because the Hindu Party had booked all the rooms.

On that long, more familiar Mall Road we walked towards other hotels, and soon passed by a building completely ravaged by time. My sudden breathlessness did not go unnoticed. On Nelly's suggestion we sat on a bench. Lots of horny honeymooning couples around us. Some, I thought, simply happy to have escaped the clutches of 'family'. I noticed an ensemble of monkeys. Nelly helped me distinguish two types of Shimla monkeys. Langurs and lal-walay. Langurs stay away from humans. Lal-walay are more playful, and sometimes attack for a vested reason, for they are completely dependent on the residents of Shimla for food. It is an uneasy coexistence. The brains of these macaque bandars were studied in Western universities not so long ago, said Nelly, and without delving into details slipped into a prolonged silence. Not entirely unexpected, she stared at the moss on grey rocks and barks of deodars, and then gazed into empty space. One of Nelly's earrings was missing, and very politely I decided to remark on asymmetry. She touched her ears in disbelief. The solitary earring gleamed with impatience. Perhaps it was not important, she said. 'Twenty-five years,' she said. Those two words lingered. 'You have come back after twenty-five.' I stayed silent. She took it as an invisible blow and started looking for the lost object and (because she was the luckiest woman on Earth) a few minutes later found it under the bench next to my luggage.

In her hand there was an ancient-looking book, which looked more conspicuous than my luggage; she placed it between us while putting on her earring. A red binding. Mildly damaged leather spine. Kipling. 'What I love are his stories for children,' said Nelly. 'My father was never able to read this man without getting agitated. He took it out on a sheet of paper. Once he drew Kipling as a monkey.

Darwin's theory was correct after all, he said. On that sheet of paper Kipling got a pinky-blue face, and Kipling ate the sun thinking it was an orange! And I don't think the intention was to make me laugh.'

Kipling, a hirsute monkey, an irascible old man, a bandar with a short temper. *Kim* is the only book of his I really like.

'Stay at my place,' she suggested. 'It is small and I am busy with the retirement function, but you are most welcome to spend a few days. As long as you are not pesky.'

'Pesky' – I had not heard the word for a while.

Her generous offer was hard to refuse. She stood up. The air was crisp and clear and cold. I walked a little behind her, deodars on one side and humans on the other, and monkeys swung on the canopy of branches above us. During the walk

a fleeting sense of relief overwhelmed me, but I was careful not to ask a wrong question or stray anywhere near that violent strand of memory. Once or twice she stopped in mid-sentence as if processing something, processing a thought, a pain that could not be articulated.

She lived on the slopes of Prospect Hill. A one-bedroom unit in an old run-down house. Approximately one hundred steps higher than the legendary 'starry cottage' and its fossilised red-brick chimney. No servants, not even an anonymous maid. She led me in. Bare walls. Two small windows, but not very bright. I tried to recognise objects. Her clothes were drying on the dining chairs. For some strange reason I had expected the place to be filled with smoke, but it seemed no one had lit a cigarette in those rooms for nearly two decades.

I sat on the yellow sofa and closed my eyes for a long time. There I heard the squeaking of brakes; a clogged mountain road whose existence I didn't know yet. When I woke up I noticed she had lit up two (half melted) candles. The clothes were no longer on the chairs.

'Triangulars, as usual?'

She remembered my weakness for caraway-seed parathas (shaped liked triangles) with anda bhurji and pickle. More than the ajwain, I savoured the smell of her freshly made parathas and ate more than necessary. She made tea using dried milk powder, her usual way, with a hint of medicinal banaksha, dried violet pansies. Nelly's new kitchen had Spanish tiles, patterns that reminded me of aperiodic quasicrystals, lacking translational symmetry. Something was not quite right, and obviously this didn't come as a shock. She kept quiet while cooking, and sat as far apart as possible and did not eat. She drank tea, but all I heard was mild slurping. Strange resonance. Between us a triple wall of silence. Dull unangry silence. How does one unlive what has been lived? The only thing that came out of her emerged with enormous effort, as if she was working against will. 'Twenty-five years.' Later she showed me the way to the bathroom and asked me to sleep in the bedroom.

'And where will you?'

'On the sofa.'

'No, please.'

She insisted. 'In the morning you will get disturbed. I wake up early. And I will need the living room then.'

'The sofa is all right,' I said.

She took a deep breath. 'I knew you would say that.'

Her voice came from some other world. She shut the bedroom door, and opened it again.

'If you need anything else, don't hesitate. Sorry there is no TV.'

I couldn't say a word.

As long as you are not pesky.

Unable to fall asleep I stood by the window. Nelly's institute perched on top of the Observatory Hill exhibiting a few traces of its old glory and many dots of dim light. The building looked comical – almost a folly. Inside the living room most of the objects were new, like her black boots by the entrance, or second-hand, like the slightly singed Persian carpet (and the sofa with fatigued springs), reacting with each other, but the object that seemed to carry truth, the one that drew me most towards it, was Mohan's silver-framed photo. The photo had outlasted him. On the back: *Self, London, 1975.* (This is the same year Indira Gandhi imposed Emergency.) Professor Singh in a long black winter coat with big buttons, on the steps of St Paul's and looking unusually melancholic, trying to forget perhaps his unfortunate country, or trying to remember every single detail. There were a couple of blank sheets of paper on the side table. I had a strong urge to transmute the yellow photo into a narrative. I confess I am not a real writer. But at that moment I felt if I don't find precise words corresponding to his life I would turn to stone.

One evening he found himself standing in front of a cathedral, which could only have been St Paul's. So many times he had been to London but he never got a chance to step inside the shrine, which was destroyed partially during the war . . . the damage long repaired, it carried no memory of the relatively recent German bombs or the Catholic structure before the Great Fire, the one that stood three or four centuries ago, no memory of the painting in the old cloister oddly titled the *Dance of Death*. He stood for a long time in front of the small memorial to thousands of Sikh soldiers, who had died for the British. Stepping out of the cathedral his thoughts turned briefly to the road to Amritsar, to a very different structure, the cathedral of his childhood, the Golden Temple. This is the shrine of a place where his grandparents and parents took refuge whenever struck by catastrophic events. For some mysterious reason on the steps of St Paul's the young engineering professor also brought to mind a book he had read during his college days: *The Temple of Golden Pavilion*. But it was the real shrine (and not fiction) that provided him with comfort and extremes of happiness, and despite being a man of science he often thought about the road to Amritsar.

I have only once been to the Golden Temple. Father had to go to Punjab on official duty, an interstate crime investigation, and I accompanied him and Mother. I was around eight then. We were not Sikhs, but the gurdwara was open to all humans. 'Humans'? Even at that age they were a mystery to me. And 'Sikhs'? Honestly I knew nothing about

59

the Sikhs then, and I didn't care. Once an uncle of mine said, Today at the bus stop I saw three human beings and a Sikh. And we all laughed without recognising his racism. Other than Bhagat Singh in a trilby and Indira Gandhi's shoe-licking president, I had little idea then about the Sikh community's out-of-proportion contribution to the freedom struggle and the armed forces. In school the textbooks taught me next to nothing about Sikh history, or about Maharajah Ranjit Singh and his grand multicultural Empire. The Sikhs are a proud people, only 2 per cent of the country's population, but for some strange reason don't consider themselves a minority. Most walk like kings. And have the rare ability to laugh at themselves. My uncle must have envied them. But I don't think my family had anti-Sikh

hatred ingrained in the psyche . . . At the Golden Temple I
don't recall now if we ate the 'spartan' but delicious langar
or not. It is all coming back to me now, fresh with all its
smells. Dal and chapatti served on plates made of fig leaves
(stitched to each other with toothpicks). Something left a
deep impression on me. I have not been able to forget the
visual representations of that titanic scholar and warrior,
Baba Deep Singh, the 75-year-old, who fought the invading Afghans in the eighteenth century. Perhaps I started
paying attention to the Sikh saints and warriors after I got
to know Nelly. Deep Singh's seven-foot-long double-edged
sword gleamed with confidence, and his severed head on
the palm of his own hand. Another odd memory of
Amritsar: I refused to drink the holy amrit. Mother, my

somewhat devotional mother, was very keen that I drink water from the sacred pool. That water is not so pure, I cried. That water is full of dissolved salts and acids, it doesn't make the sacred sacred. When we returned home I got sick, and my mother correlated my refusal to drink amrit with the onset of my sickness.

When in school, before I joined the engineering college, there were two Sikh boys in my class but I didn't get to know them properly. Throughout my schooldays for some mysterious reason there were always two Sikh boys in my

class. Once I sat next to one of them, and heard his views on the 'Punjab Problem'. But another close friend of mine pulled me aside. *Abe tu uski baat kyon sunta hai? – wo to Sikh hai*. 'Why listen to him? – he is after all a Sikh.'

On 6 June, thousands of families were gathered at the Golden Temple to commemorate the day of martyrdom of the fifth Guru – it was a bit like Christmas Day (or Good Friday rather) for Sikhs – when Mrs G ordered an unprecedented army action, Operation Blue Star, apparently to flush out the militants and the extremist preacher, her own creation (someone on her payroll for several years). Old newspaper cuttings in the archives are filled with this information. The shock-and-awe army action was deeply flawed and was not the only solution. Seven battle tanks rolled in . . . The Akal Takht was completely destroyed. The holiest shrine was riddled with hundreds of bullets. The treasury looted. Rare manuscripts and historical artefacts seized. The library set on fire. Mrs G's, it is said, army killed more innocent civilians than the Butcher of Amritsar, General Dyer. According to human rights reports between two thousand to eight thousand innocent civilians were killed. There is also a mention of a firing squad taking care of captive men after tying their hands with turbans. Thousands in Punjab were tortured, humiliated, thousands disappeared . . . Even if one agrees with the rationale behind the attack (the archive says), one finds the 'secrecy', the 'timing' and the 'method of attack' unacceptable.

How did I respond then? I remember that comfortable June day with clarity. That cool and pleasant summer month. No heat, no dust at all . . . We had gone to the hill station of Mussoorie; my parents played Chinese checkers all day long on the cool, green lawns of the Police Guest House, the officers' mess, and for some reason even I had no idea that something was being held from me, and believed every word that woman uttered on state-controlled TV. And she was not alone. The print media, too, was heavily biased and softly communal.

Why did the PM fail to grasp the enormity of her action? Or the anguish and scars it would cause within the Sikh community?

Operation Blue Star was the biggest disgrace in the recent history of our country.

But why?

Mrs G bought into her own 'great leader' myth: *Indira is India and India is Indira.* Myths can be dangerous. That one ruined her and thousands of others.

Nelly had arranged the books more or less the same way they were in the IIT house. Four bookshelves, not twelve or thirteen, but the arrangement was more or less identical on a smaller scale. Each title neatly bound by transparent plastic to keep away particles of dust. I was literally on my knees moving from one end to the other, and pulled out a book by Conrad, and another one by Flaubert, Volume II of

Sentimental Education (Volume I was missing). Published in 1869, Volume II, older than the building I was in. Strange smells emanated from the dog-eared pages. Old railway time-tables. The *Encyclopaedia Britannica*. Another with a red-and-black damaged spine: *The King of Infinite Space*, a biography of Don Coxeter (the man who saved geometry). Why in the world was Nelly interested in that famous geometer? Why was she reading about the mathematics of shape and space? And then. On the brown shelf I found an object with a familiar smell; it had touched my hands, also his hands in 1984.

Levi's cover photo stared out at me.

Trimmed white beard. Huge plastic-framed glasses. Schoken Books, New York. First edition. Translated by Raymond Rosenthal. I stood for a long time in disbelief, leaning against the shelf, now on my right leg, now on my left, not realising the time it was. Reacquainting myself with that peculiar style, smelling the pages, half controlling my unexpected laughter, recalling that day when the package arrived in his office, remembering that day when he drove me slowly to my hostel in his white Fiat. Those days half of my class was going through the 'asshole reading phase' (a phrase I learned in the US) reading Ayn Rand. Professor Singh introduced me to Levi while most in the hostel were under the spell of Rand (masquerading as a philosopher). I read the chapter on cerium, pages 139 to 143. How the author and his handsome friend dealt with hunger, about fascism and death factories in Europe. How they refused the concentration camp universe . . . 'Cerium' kept them alive. They 'stole' cerium rods from a storage jar in the lab and, taking a huge risk, filed them at night. Small diameter rods ignite cigarette lighters. The two friends bartered meals for fire. *Alberto kept me alive*. But. *Alberto did not return*. Four or five lines underlined in pencil; a note in the margins in dense, baroque handwriting. While reading I shut the book now and then and studied the author's beard and enigmatic, melancholic face hiding certain things. *Humans capable of such cruelty to other humans*. Depression. Suicidal thoughts. I could not help but think about the controversy surrounding his death. 11 April 1987. Was it suicide? My mind wove strange patterns and correlations. Primo Levi, born in Italy in 1919: three months after the first Amritsar Massacre in India. *The Periodic Table* appeared in English for the first time in November 1984. Random coincidences. Signifying nothing, and yet it didn't feel merely random, as if the coincidence carried a ring of inevitability. That first night on Prospect Hill at her small place I kept hearing Nelly's voice 'the light is dim, move under the lamp', but no, Nelly was in the other room, fast asleep. As I was replacing the book on the shelf two tiny photographs fell out of the pages. Like perennial migrants, the photos were impatient and keen to reveal the twists and turns of their odyssey.

Carefully I wiped away dust and scanned the images in the fragile light of the candles. The first one was the photo of thick 'fog' or 'white smoke' in our old lab. On the faintly visible bench there are traces of a completely shattered flower, a yellow rose. The professor's two children are part of the photo; I suspect he must have done a special cryogenic demo just for them. The father must have demonstrated his famous 'Coldest Experiments' in a slightly different fashion to his children ... The photo for some strange reason reminded me of Chardin's *Boy Blowing Bubbles*, but I don't think Professor Singh was thinking of Chardin when he took the photo. He must have warned the kids not to touch. Strange irony: one's fingers 'burn' when one touches the coldest fluid. A prickly feeling hard to describe: an unfamiliar kind of pain goes through one's arm. Most likely he plucked that rose from the

66

garden outside his house on the way to the laboratory, perhaps he described it in literary terms as 'Goethe's rose'. I am exaggerating. One doesn't talk to children that way. Perhaps he simply dipped the flower in liquid nitrogen. Magic. With forceps he plucked the brittle object out of the dewar flask; in the sink the frozen rose shattered like glass. In the photo the kids look reasonably amused, dark intelligent eyes. He must have entertained them further with 'helium snow'. His lab for a few minutes would have become the coldest place in Delhi, indeed one of the coldest on our earth. The second photo is also a time-ravaged black-and-white. Beyond doubt it is a demo of the lambda point, the strange transformation, the so-called 'phase transition'. Beautiful, hyper-beautiful helium-4. What made him think the kids would comprehend the very essence of his work? Sudden, extreme changes in properties, extreme confusion. An ordinary fluid becomes a superfluid. I remember. He loved explaining phase transitions with that smile of his, calling them an 'identity crisis'.

Close to absolute zero, minus 271 degrees Celsius, liquid helium undergoes the crisis that collapses all definitions.

Normal becomes anomalous then, and anomalous becomes normal. Particles cease to be particles, they become small waves, no, one giant wave, as if a startled flock of birds (or eels swimming together). Think of the flock as a giant orchestra, flying. Each airborne instrument, each bird playing the same startled tune. Everything is identical everywhere. Who am I?

Helium has a very high heat capacity, and at very low temperatures it has an absurdly high heat conductivity. It stops boiling turbulently, defies gravity. It just 'knows' how to overcome obstacles. It becomes a fluid like no other, a superfluid. No friction, no viscosity, no resistance to its flow. Strange metamorphosis.

Professor Singh must have used his own coffee cup and his deadpan voice. *Let us do a thought experiment. Arjun, Indira, imagine this cup is half filled, not with water or milk, but with helium. Spontaneously . . . Look here. Look here. On its own the liquid rises, on its own it rolls over, on its own it crawls down the outer walls of the cup. And a lot of 'He' collects at the bottom, and you can see it, first as a little drop, and then as a big one getting bigger, dangling in response to gravity.* Imagine Ganga landing from the heavens on Shiva's head. Imagine a river flowing over a high bridge. He must have derived enormous fun explaining the micro-details to his children, using strange analogies and metaphors.

That night at Mrs Singh's place I curled over with real and phantom memories of death, of tiny superfluid drops on the sofa. I forgot to extinguish the slowly melting candles before drifting to a different world, and for some unknown reason thought about 'Lihaf' or 'The Quilt', Nelly's favourite short story. A child, sleeping on a separate bed, in her aunt's bedroom, witnesses something she doesn't comprehend. On certain dark nights her aunt and her maid make love. To the child this seems like a fabulous transformation of a quilt into an elephant . . . Once in a while I heard the mad, twitching woman's voice wafting from somewhere outside, wave after disturbed wave. *I will go to the moon and tell them about you.* Her wild laughter. In my dizzy state I finished what she started. *On a Chandrayan, the moon machine, I will go and land on lava fields and frighten the gods . . . and I will tell them about you. One . . . two . . . three.*

Next morning, I am embarrassed to spell it out, I woke up with an erection. Strong light was pouring in through the window. I stretched myself.

Something happens to one's dreams when one is in the mountains. The high altitude, the changed magnetic field, all these factors influence the complex way blood flows in the brain. In my dark dream I made love to a friend of mine; the disturbing bit was that we hit each other and then fucked each other by 180-foot-high statues of Shiva and Kali and Hanuman, raw concrete, bronze and volcanic debris glowing in the harsh light of the sun. Afterwards we lifted heavy mountains on the tips of our fingers, and re-enacted Hanuman's Lanka-burning feat. *Jai Maruti*. I woke up not just with an erection, but also with a lump in my throat because in real life there was no love or lust between the two of us, and I could not make sense of the unsettling parts of the dream. My mouth filled with ash and sand, completely dry. She lived on a different continent and was happily involved with, and powerfully attracted to, someone else. Nelly was absent in the apartment; a note was waiting for me on the dining table. Yellow, legal paper. She had covered my breakfast with heavy-duty insulators and it was still hot. Anda bhurji, dahi and T-parathas. I shaved, took a mugga bath (which flooded her bathroom) and, unable to locate a fresh towel, dried myself with an old black T-shirt; after changing my clothes I dared to spend a few moments in the bedroom. Everything so clean and tidy. The kind of order I had seen before at an ex-girlfriend's place, who suffered from obsessive–compulsive disorder. Twice a day she would clean all the objects in her apartment, even books, which she would polish with a fine velvet cloth opticians use to clean prescription glasses. In Nelly's room – a familiar smell I have not been able to forget. On the windowsill, next to her comb, a tiny bottle. Trapped within walls of glass the oil was partially frozen. (Nelly used to massage Professor

70

Singh's hair with coconut oil. In winter whenever I visited their house, I would find a little glass bottle of coconut oil on the veranda, undergoing melting in the sun.) Linen on the bed as white as snow. As if she did not live alone, and was expecting someone any moment. A quilt, with rhomboid patterns, on one side. I sat on the bed for a brief minute and took a deep breath. Her smell. Still good. But like everything else, it, too, had aged. On the wall a Goya and a large framed photo of the indispensable Punjabi poet Amrita Pritam. *Aj akhan Waris Shah nu / tikon kabran vichon bol / te aj kitabe ishq da / koi agla varka phol.* The poem still invoked the Partition and its two million dead. That most elegiac line, the line that carries more sorrow than it can hold. On the side table an antique mint-coloured lamp and an extra pair of reading glasses, and an illustrated large-format Kipling.

Once I was sexually attracted to Nelly, when I was very young and she was young, and now all that feeling had evaporated, and that was not the force field which had brought me to Shimla. The reason she offered me her sofa, and the reason I agreed, was because there was no possibility of a relationship between us.

Time had ruined her, just like it was ruining me . . . And that is the only truth. Even the beauty of helium ceases one day. But let me not slip into something abstract. I must resist the urge to explain humans in terms of atoms, molecules, bosons and fermions. Flesh and blood and bones and warmth require a different type of telling. Let me travel back in time and describe a few things clearly. Busy with exams I was unable to leave the IIT boys' hostel and join Nelly for badminton for almost a month. But I kept hearing the sound of the white-feathered shuttlecock. The sound still exists and resonates in my ears. The shuttlecock drifts back and forth for no good reason. She was absent the day I returned. From the canteen I phoned. No response. So I walked to my professor's residence. The door ajar. I rang the bell, and when no one showed up, I knocked four or five times. She came. Barefoot, running, finger on lips. Shh! She was putting the children to bed.

I waited in the living room. In the adjacent room she read them 'Five Blind Men and an Elephant'. It is a spear. No, a snake. A tree. A fan. No, it is a rope. 'The Five Blind Men of Hindustan and an Elephant' – the children knew the story well, but they loved listening to every single word repeated over and over.

Finally she stopped, and the house was so quiet one could have heard a pin drop. Then I heard Arjun and Indira breathe. After fifteen minutes or so she stepped out, and told me Professor Singh was away in Punjab for a couple of days. Shall I make you tea?

I don't recall all the fuzzy details. How exactly we came to hold hands. For a long time we held each other. The eye is less a window to the soul, more a window to the body. She was beautiful, and that very moment no longer my professor's wife. But soon her body broke free and walked away. The angle at which she stood illuminated her wrist-watch, and I ran after her and sniffed her long hair. We hugged then, and she smiled and critiqued my way of hugging, and demonstrated the proper heart-to-heart hug.

We moved to the roof terrace. Where the night was dark, and proper. Up there the stars low, and bougainvillea lusty. Our secret remained within us, accumulating more and more nights, and days, and I don't know when pure, awkward lust transformed into something more real. We quarrelled, then made up. Quarrelled. Patched up again. I learned exaggerated patience. Towards her. But became more and more irritable. Towards others. Sometimes we had sex for two or four or six hours. When I witnessed that IIT grad student in a compromising position, many years later on his Jor Bagh roof terrace, I felt as if I had walked into the familiar labyrinths of a mirror. Time was replicating my story. Our narrative. Once Professor Singh returned a day early from Punjab and found Nelly and me together. The way he interrogated us by not saying anything. His prolonged silence. Did he suspect? I am not sure. One can never be. It was a fact like any other, a truth like any other. But all based on how I felt.

Like I am never sure about my childhood memories. When I was around eight, my father bought a Japanese cassette recorder. He taught me how to become a minor detective. I recorded the sounds and micro-sounds of our house, every single room. Even then I had a feeling that truth was hidden in other rooms. Because I heard mysterious sounds wafting from my parents' bedroom, I was curious about those night sounds as well. So I left the cassette recorder in their room one night after dinner, concealed and turned on. The recording lasted for thirty minutes before the tape ran out. Next day I heard the tape. My mother is not in favour of torture. My good father says some torture is part of his job in the police force. We are not a developed country yet, he says. When we become a developed country we will stop these methods. You think I don't feel bad? he asks her. My mother sounds like a closet human rights expert on the tape. My father, so naive, assumes that the West doesn't torture.

In Nelly's apartment in Shimla my mind flowed with unwanted thoughts. Slowly my gaze moved towards the floor, and I noticed a white substance. Spilled milk. Despite spending five or six minutes trying to comprehend the spill, I met with no success. Close to the refrigerator in the kitchen there was a long puddle, and it seemed to have formed on its own, without an apparent source. My whole body quivered at the sight of that substance. Nelly had woken up before me. Why did she leave the spill unattended? The thing had a peculiar shape, a strange fractal geometry, and I switched on the brightest light and scrutinised it. The source seemed to be at the top of the refrigerator; a drop fell down, then another after a long wait. I found an identical puddle of milk at the very top of the refrigerator, but nothing falling from the ceiling. I ran towards the window – it was wide open. No wire mesh. Outside a cluster of dilapidated colonial erections, buildings becoming ruins, and big red-flowering trees, and slender pines and slightly shaking oaks; the air reeked of resin, and then I noticed an introspective monkey, as if Lord Hanuman himself, and close by a cluster of monkeys, one grasping on to a milk carton, and it was then I understood the spill ... Nelly had left tea in a pot, shielded by a heavily padded tea cosy. I drank my tea black, and for a long time stood by the window, and then I closed it.

The note had been written in no hurry; it said the expected. *Namaste.* Almost involuntarily I touched those small, baroque words. Something immutable: the handwriting had not changed. I would have been happier if she had used the Sikh greeting. She left me the keys as well.

Feel free to visit my institute, my crumbling splendour.

Shimla was a bustling slope of a city at that hour despite the chill. Flocks of hill mynahs delightful as I walked down the hill and then up again. Something startled the cloud of birds as they flew low right above me, thinning and thickening the air. For a brief second the flock shimmered, then

74

soared away. I turned and caught them vanishing, rising steeply like an ensemble of tiny black data points. I turned and they shifted again into the shape of a graph of cosmic proportions. On the narrow trail I encountered a woman knitting a sweater as red as the rhododendrons. Slowly I looped around the Himachal University campus. Gliding through students made me feel young again, and old, both at once. The birds returned, another neat kink in the graph, and were gone. By the time I arrived at the institute most of the male staff members were out on the lawns basking in the sun.

Inside the library the carpet was soft and blue. But it was very cold.

Even before I entered I noticed big eyes behind the shelves staring at me, and an old uncomfortable feeling ran through my spine. Years ago Father had used a newspaper

to kill mosquitoes; the eyes behind the shelves belonged to the same photo embedded in my memory. The paper was some censored rag during Mrs Gandhi's dictatorial Emergency. From high up the same eyes stared at me now.

A few stones that made up the crumbling wall were visible. Ahead of me a glass partition. He stood as a mythical figure, the khaki-clad man behind the partition glued to a slab of a heater (the only heater in the library), grooming his intimidating moustache and simultaneously scratching his ear. I simplified our exchange (which had the potential to become Kafkaesque), 'Madam-ji's permission', and showed him the yellow sheet of paper (which carried her signature). He frisked me and pushed me in. There was no heating – the original fireplace was plugged with potted plants. The research fellows and scholars and other readers were wrapped in two or three layers, sweaters, shawls or jackets and woollen caps and gloves with dangling ghostly fingers. It was the coldest library in the world, and I was walking through the space where the British Empire had danced only sixty or seventy years ago, and the eyes of the censorship woman on the wall (Mrs Gandhi) kept staring at me; the British Empire danced when nine million Indians died of a famine, the famine occurred because of cruel taxation policy, taxes were raised to fund the Afghan wars, and the Viceroy and the Vicereine danced here and had fancy-dress parties and ate here, the dining table was able to seat 150 guests, each one got their own personal liveried waiter, and the menus competed with the menus of Queen Victoria, they did not want to be left behind, those who plundered the wealth of India, they, too, ate bull's head and wild boar, because it was on the Queen's menu in England. But now it was a library, and now most of the portraits on the walls and the power and the Raj belonged to the Nehru–Gandhi dynasty that took over from the British, but the building was so huge there was space for others, full-bearded Tagore hung on the walls and Ambedkar, too, deep and pensive, also a portrait of the first female president of India (in a spacesuit), and ex-President Sarvepalli Radhakrishnan, the philosopher, who had come up with the idea to transform the Scottish baronial castle into a castle of higher learning. This was architecture of a grand crime, and the philosopher-president had come up with a grand scheme to civilise the architecture. I moved between two front shelves; now the eyes on the wall acquired a face, and I pulled out a book and turned and there she was, Nelly, by an unusually tall window in the reading room, far from me, the faded maple-orange curtain as high as the window. The corridor of the Empire had become a reading room; stacks filled with magazines and journals, current issues on display. From where I was I saw Nelly bent over a book, taking notes, it was a corner table, a half table, on her left a pile of books, on her right a pile of papers. I felt like slowly walking up to her, but decided not to disturb.

I fluttered about the aisles, overwhelmed by dusty tomes. Some of them with damaged bandaged spines, others never touched before. Randomly I exhumed a disintegrating bone of a volume and browsed. A veil of dust particles spread around me. I didn't see Nelly leave the reading room. The creaking corner table where she was working only a while ago was empty now. Slowly I walked to her space and sat in the chair. A strong rectangular light poured in through the tall window, and I don't remember when exactly I turned to observe the spot by the shelves from where I had observed her earlier. The glare almost ruined my eyes. The face of Mrs Gandhi was visible as half a face now. I flipped open the book (*Anthropology of Violence*) Nelly was perusing moments ago, but found it difficult to concentrate. Even the doorknob looked ghostly.

'Sa'ab, if during your consultations you find a dusty shelf let me know. I will clean it. I will wipe dust that has gathered on the books.' He came to me, the man in khaki, with a strange request, which in hindsight was not so strange. 'This is a huge library,' he smiled and nodded, 'and no matter how hard I try there is always a slim layer that settles down.' I asked him Nelly's coordinates, the best way to locate her. The man walked me down the stairs to the basement where very few rays of natural light penetrated. We went through a gargantuan double door, beyond which stretched a narrow corridor lit by dim translucent globes all the way to her office. She was not in. But khaki cardboard boxes were there, bulging files and other orderly chaos. Her Burmese desk, a desktop, a swivel chair, a handcart, a jug of water (half full), a tiny white towel, and the hum of fluorescent lights. Feeling disappointed, my guide designed a little tour of the basement for my benefit, which included what used to be the wine cellar, the dumb waiter and the boiler room. The room was now a storehouse for rats, fungus and wrinkled old Victorian furniture thrown together in haphazard piles, rusted metal frames and two disintegrating cribs. White paint peeling off fragile wood. Viceroy's children?

The cribs made no sense at all, and my guide had no idea. 'Let me now show you the fire-extinguishing system, it is old but smart and relies on the melting of wax.' The man whisked me round the corner. But I lost all curiosity and ran up the stairs, away from the dark, dripping foundations of the Empire, and spent another hour in the reading room browsing through current periodicals.

Later I had coffee at Barista. In the local paper (in Hindi) there was a brief article on Nelly Kaur's retirement. What struck me the most was that no mention was made of what her life was before she moved to Shimla. How she survived Delhi. What happened to her children. Especially the children. No details of her 'monumental project'.

The article ended abruptly. *Whosoever replaces N. Kaur?*

Other papers carried nothing on Nelly. The Hindu Party convention received front-page attention. Shameless dishonesty and filthy power struggles within the party. Photos of men in khaki shorts giving the fascist salute. The *Express* or the *Tribune* (one of those papers) also ran a long tribute to Nadine Gordimer: *No violence is more frightening than the violence of revenge.* The paper also carried a piece on a thorium mine, and a huge headline: SUICIDE OF A DALIT MEDICAL STUDENT. Reading the article, for a fleeting second I thought about the 'crystallising image' that made me start taking notes. New Delhi railway station. On 30 October 1984, we left two figures behind. What happened? Did my father speak to her? Did he offer Nelly a ride home?

She was busy handing over, she had warned me. I will not be able to play a good host the next few days. That day all I did was walk and linger in cafes, and take more notes. All of a sudden I felt accumulation and transformation. My brief interaction with Nelly so far cast a new spell; I had new ideas to deal with my old demons.

There was proper heating in Barista and I don't know when exactly my shivering stopped. Two Armani-clad youths sitting a table away gave me a dirty look. They were nibbling at reddish-blue sandwiches, and it seemed the duo had popped down from Neptune. I scribbled on a sheet of paper. The flow of words drowned the inane cell-phone conversations, businesslike transactions and a faint murmur of love-smitten teenagers, necking.

For so many in '84 death began with rubber tyres . . . Sikhs were mere objects (of hatred) bonded to rubber tyres, offered to the gods . . . Agni, the god of fire, has two heads, three legs and seven tongues . . . My compatriots (under normal circumstances) don't burn fellow citizens. Under 'normal' circumstances some do transform the strange joke of an unease they feel towards Sikhs into Time (Sardar, tehre barah baj gayeh; your time's come, sardar-ji) . . . Who am I? What is common between me and other 'Hindus'? All I know is that I have not been able to study properly the microstructure of

rubber. I fail again and again when it comes to estimating the speed with which fire engulfs a cylinder over six feet tall ... But I correctly assume that an average human body weighs sixty-five kilos ... Twenty thousand cylinders means 1.3 million kilograms. 1.3 million kilograms of human mass. In the cafe my otherwise numb fingers started moving. Memories, I felt, have an elastoplastic quality of their own.

Why think of one genocide in terms of another? Why use a prism? It is impossible to compare and quantify suffering, I know. Why then? Because one story is better known and the other one completely unknown, completely distorted or filled with ominous silences. (What breaks me is the silence of distinguished public intellectuals, liberal-secular writers and established academicians.) Because this is exactly the process I follow in my own discipline, I use analogies to move from the 'known' to the 'unknown'. At first all I see are the similarities. Differences or uniqueness emerge later. Where would we be if Rutherford had not imagined the structure of an atom as a tiny solar system. Later, Bohr destroyed the solar-system model with his 'quantum', but where would Bohr be without Ruther-ford's insight? *But why am I so shocked if thousands were murdered in Delhi? Why am I shocked if the 'majority' is unable to comprehend the enormity of its actions and the pain of the 'minority'? Why does this pattern repeat itself over and over in the world? Why does the dominant group continue to represent itself as a 'victim'? Bigger genocides have happened before. Armenian. Rwandan. Native American. Genocides will happen? Regarding this I am not sure. One can never be ... Animals are much better, they don't conduct genocides.* When my fingers became numb again I called Nelly half hoping we would dine together. Bluntly she declined. She, of course, was preparing her retirement speech. I ate alone at Restaurant Splash. My table next to the only window with a commanding view of the deodar hills of Shimla and the valley below. The red-tiled boarding school melted into the deodars, which melted into the skating rink.

While eating alone I started missing my children. My wife has not allowed me to see them since we broke up. You don't know how to edit the world for children, she has a constant complaint. You scare them.

I have two girls. If I had stayed behind in India I would have dealt with the burden of the past differently. A pattern established at Cornell even before I became a professor, none of my relationships would last more than six months, maximum a year, and they all ended badly because whoever I was involved with wanted a child and I didn't. I never felt ready for children, and women would simply walk out of my life. The so-called East–West cultural clash was not my narrative. My narrative was different, and that is when (on the strong recommendation of a colleague) I saw an analyst. I, who always mocked analysis, ended up doing that and found the hour-long sessions helpful. One day during analysis I realised I had not had sex for almost a year. I think we can easily avoid being sexual beings, but that problem is more complex than our neuroses about it. Later that night after a bit of hesitation I called an escort. Before her I had never been with a paid woman.

She was from the Middle East (she told me that). When I had called, I told the male voice at the agency only the size. 36D. There are many things I remember about the escort to this day, but more than anything else her limited English, and thick ankles, her tight skirt, and oiled curly hair. The TV was on all the time when we did the act, and afterwards she started weeping. I didn't pay you to cry, I said.

'Next it is the turn of my country.'

'What do you mean?'

'War,' she explained as if I understood nothing.

'Can we do this every weekend?' I made an offer.

'No,' she said, 'I cannot do this more than once with anyone.' Then she picked up her handbag, used the bathroom and left.

Next day I stepped out for breakfast with my engineering colleague; we picked the place randomly. In fact he was the one who suggested the restaurant. Somewhere we had never been before. The waitress who served us coffee looked vaguely familiar, and it didn't take me long to figure out that she was the exact same person with whom I had slept the previous night. A corn on her right toe. Before me flashed a naked body I had not even tried to remember, also the sharp smell of sweat which had cut through my nostrils a few hours ago. I had no idea if she had recognised me. But the way her eyes avoided us when she poured warm coffee into my cup assured me that she, too, had figured me out. My colleague was sitting there, talking tensors, vectors and carbon fibres, and had no clue what was stirring in my body. She must have been in her early twenties. When I returned home I was unable to concentrate. I had breakfast at the same restaurant for the next three or four days, even the weekend, but she didn't return.

Days later I launched a search, and after a few weeks succeeded in locating her, and persuaded Asma or Azra (her made-up name) to sleep with me one last time. And then it became an obsession. I found out where she lived, the man she lived with, and the day I encountered the man for the first time I felt a strong urge to kill him. I wanted her all to myself, the woman with a corn on her right toe. I returned to my department. Something had transformed. I felt like eliminating whoever I saw, fellow professors, my secretary, and realised I needed serious help. Without help I would have become one of those rare engineering professors who run along the corridor shooting innocent people. In the end the person who saved me was my colleague. He introduced me to Clara, he persuaded me to have children, and we had two cute daughters. I thought they would not allow me to do research, but I did some of my best work after the girls were born, and I also, on the suggestion of my colleague (who turned out to understand me better than the analyst), started scribbling.

Urvashi and Ursula, my daughters, I'd give up anything to see them again.

Urvashi, our firstborn. The day she arrived, the moment I held her close and felt her heart beat, I thanked Clara silently, and decided to give up my Indian passport and become an American citizen. But just before I kissed her tiny hands and head, I had a strong urge to name her Indira – after Professor Singh's daughter. In the end I didn't.

Urvashi looks a lot like her mother. Due to a complex biological reason (or mere chance) even her skin colour resembles her mother's. One day I accompanied my wife to the day care to collect the child, and the woman over there produced a boy as brown as me. He had curly black hair, and a strange sadness in his sparkling eyes. The woman knows Clara well; every evening she pulled out the right kid (pale like her mother), but my presence short-circuited all her mental associations. I don't know how to respond to such errors of judgement committed by polite and friendly bleeding-heart liberals. Some still support racial profiling at airports. Some of them, although they deny it now, supported the Iraq War. Guests Clara invites now and then to celebrate India or Indianness. At the last Diwali

84

party one of our so-called friends revealed his abnormally large ignorance about the 'Third World'. Mahatma Gandhi was assassinated by the Sikhs, he said while eating a besan laddoo and a cashew burfi. The Mahatma was shot dead in 1948 by a Hindu zealot, I corrected Dick. Indira Gandhi was assassinated by her Sikh bodyguards, but Mahatma Gandhi was assassinated by a zealot. My response annoyed him. He left early.

When I returned 'home' Nelly was ironing her clothes. Salwar, kameez, chunni. Clothes for retirement.

'There is lots of food in the fridge.'

She kept ironing and I sat on the sofa pretending to read the paper. But my thoughts were still stuck in Cornell, the grey stone buildings, the bell tower, sleepy, misty valleys and long finger-shaped lakes, and Cayuga and Bebe and the gorges. How many times I have walked down into so many of them. How many times I have sat behind a waterfall, under a rock ledge, watching water thunder down in front of me, how many conversations in the lab simply began with the suspension bridge and the achingly small Thurston Avenue bridge and the 'jumpers', definitely not my colleague, whose marriage broke down the very same day I married Clara. That unsuicidal day, 11 May, as I found out later, is also the birthday of the genius of a physicist Richard Feynman, who himself taught at Cornell from 1945 till 1950 before moving to Caltech, where he did work on 'anomalous' helium. Before switching over to superfluid, supercooled liquid helium investigations Feynman was involved with the Manhattan Project. The dropping of the bombs over Hiroshima and then Nagasaki induced in him a depression he hadn't known before, as if something deep inside was irradiated by a conical beam of darkness. Perhaps the depression was really due to the

85

sickness and death of his wife. One can never be sure. Yet Feynman's memoirs have the kind of lightness absent in Levi's *Periodic Table*. When I go through my own darkest moments I read Feynman. That day he was sitting in the Cornell cafeteria, whiling away the time, and suddenly for some unknown reason a guy threw a plate in the air (he writes). The plate wobbled, going higher and higher. Feynman curiously observed the wobbling motion, also the motion of the red medallion of Cornell painted on the plate. The medallion went around its axis faster than wobbling. Nothing else to do, his hand sketched the motion of the rotating plate, and he soon figured out that at a certain angle, the medallion rotates twice as fast as the wobble rate – that neat enigmatic ratio 'two to one'. Feynman worked out equations for wobbles. 'Everything' flowed out of work that started as pure 'fun'. How the electron orbits move in relativity. Then the Dirac equation. Finally, quantum electrodynamics. The entire Nobel Prize, he writes, sprang out of that random plate in the cafeteria, during his unhappy days at Cornell.

'Are you sure you have eaten?' she asked again.

I turned my gaze in her direction. Nelly appeared stressed and exhausted. The hem of the kameez she was ironing twitched in her hand.

'Yes, I ate at a restaurant. After my meal I ate a paan as well.'

Our 'conversation' (I take the liberty to use that word) drifted to Hindi. I used 'aap' and she responded with the same respectful form of address, which made me uncomfortable. I had expected 'tu'. 'Aap' paradoxically enlarged the distance between us, the area of silence. Once or twice (not without delight) I detected an authentic Punjabi word wobbling out of her otherwise reasonably

86

well-modulated Hindi. For instance 'drakhat', the word for a 'tree'. And the phrase 'nutth-bhajh' which meant 'running around'. Steam kept rising from the ironing board. "What are you thinking?' she asked. Feynman, I said. Professor Singh once told me a very personal episode from the physicist's life. Although Feynman moved out of Cornell he would return once in a while to teach a course. Professor Singh worked as Feynman's teaching assistant for two terms. I didn't tell Nelly my growing regret. Why didn't I ask him more stuff when he was alive? She was hearing me, not listening, her thoughts elsewhere. I felt she needed space. Goodnight. One thing was certain. I was not going to have a good night. Wait, I will just clear this space, she said. I waited also for an invitation to the retirement event. Her hesitation to do so was not connected to tiredness. So why was she avoiding any talk about the event? She extended no informal invitation, not even a fleeting mention. I murmured the high-energy Sikh greeting – 'Victory to truth' – Sat Sri Akal. She merely smiled. Perhaps I was expecting a lot from her before re-establishing trust. I opened my Swissair bag. Mud marks inside. No way. Such lightness . . . The absence was easy to detect. I unzipped all the different parts of the bag, but that slim object with finite weight and volume was no longer there. My worst fear had materialised. My 17-inch Mac had gone missing.

My notes in the laptop, and special software and so many other documents not yet backed up. 'You're looking at me so seriously.' Nelly turned off the iron. The thing hissed and whistled one last time and died. No, I had not left the windows open. She suspected the men at the Peterhof. It was 9.07 p.m. Did I suspect anyone? For a brief second I thought it was Nelly. But I hated myself for doing so. She offered to accompany me to the hotel. I declined and literally ran all the way. Took me twenty breathless minutes to loop up the hill. What was I thinking? Visible and invisible fences. There was a huge security cordon, the circle of heavily armed guards refused entry. Come after the conference is over, they barked, staring, as if my left hand was a cathode and my right hand an anode and my body all set to hug and explode a senior Hindu Party leader.

Photos I took in Delhi, old photos of my daughters – these were gone, stolen, apparently lost forever. I had a copy of my engineering research in my office at Cornell and I had printed a copy of the notes and left it in my father's study in Delhi. That loss was reversible. I tried using my cellphone, but the reception was not good, so when I returned home in a moment of panic I borrowed Nelly's phone and called Father.

One must be careful about one's confessions, especially during moments of vulnerability, and perhaps it was not a good idea to share with Nelly that night my other life, something that had become an obsession.

In my free time (on my colleague's and Clara's recommendation) I had started writing science fiction and slowly I found that my notes acquired a real dimension, a tangent line, and it transformed into Professor Singh's story, as if his life was a circle, and by delving into the fog of words I hoped to touch the circle at a single point, a tangent line. How little I knew about him, and I made up a past and made up a future; in that sense I imagined what happened to Nelly and his children after the violence. For me the starting, crystallising image or the 'decisive moment' was the railway platform where Nelly had come to bid him farewell. What happened after the train was no longer visible, when it became two little red dots in the morning fog?

Did my father talk to her then? What conversation brewed? Did he offer her a ride home? I imagined my good father cracking a joke about something. He drops her home. She invites him in for tea. I imagined infidelity.

She listened to me, preoccupied, and before she told me 'nothing of that sort happened', I mentioned the new feeling within me, to determine only the truth, I was on the wrong track earlier. You know in the old version I made you (Nelly) watch the city of Delhi, burning in the fires of hell, from the top of a 120-metre-high water tank. Not so long ago at an IIT reunion in New York I met an ex-classmate of mine, who had watched the city (Delhi) burning from the top of a concrete water tank. I gave you (Nelly) his experience. I made you flee to safety from the barbaric slogans of hate: *khoon ka badla khoon se*. It wasn't just the fire, you see, it was the acoustics. I could not help you then, but in my attempts to exhume and decipher the past, in my note-taking, I am not a coward. I am trying to achieve more and more clarity. The sole reason I go to these inane IIT reunions in North American cities is to recover your traces. Do you understand? Do you?

'Is that why you have come?'

'Yes, to see you.'

'You are gathering material?'

'I need your help. I have a tiny digital device. Tomorrow, if you don't mind may I record you?'

'Why don't you consult the archives?'

'No other story matters to me more than your specific story. No other truth matters. I have waited for over two decades to find out. Where are the children?'

'Let's talk tomorrow.'

'Please . . . where are they?'

She didn't respond.

'What happened to them? You have no photos of your son and daughter here. Why?'

Again she didn't respond directly to my question. Long, viscous silence lingered in the room. The heaters did the usual *kit kit kit*. Expansion, contraction, expansion. Heat has its own rhythm and subtle signals.

'Are you comfortable on the sofa?'

'I am all right.'

'Tonight why don't you sleep on the bed?'

Then: 'I insist.'

She slept on the uncomfortable sofa and I slept on the bed. I didn't fall asleep right away. She was exhausted and snored mildly. I undressed and changed into kurta pyjama. (Normally I don't use pyjamas at night, I sleep naked, but Nelly had insisted and gave me a spare kurta pyjama. White.)

In Ithaca when I read about children dying in Iraq or Afghanistan or Norway or Gaza I go and lock myself in my office. I don't join the student demos on the campus. Even the most familiar tasks appear unbearable then. Self-loathing and emptiness eat me like dimak, and I accuse myself of a crime I never committed. Damaged, I am aware of the reliable disorder in my mind.

Clara, my estranged wife, tried several times to reduce the disorder. During the early days of our relationship, she gave me an anthology of poems. She believes in the comforting power of poetry. The book occupies a privileged spot in my office. The only *freak* on those shelves (as characterised by a grad student of mine). The one time I achieved success opening those pages a line slipped me into a particularly difficult state of mind. A translation of a line by a Polish Nobel Laureate, whose longish name I don't remember, knocked me down. Sparks began to fly. Poetry has never comforted me. To read a poem is a traumatic event. During my difficult spells (triggered by the strangest of causes) I envy Clara, and envy my friend and colleague. He is afraid someone may steal his sports car. Every couple of months he buys a new security device better than the last one. I envy him his little anxieties, and his deep commitment to work. How little it takes to make him happy.

Sometimes I forget my second visit to Nelly's IIT house. Completely uninvited. Eating an orange, I am walking straight from the boys' hostel to her red-brick house. The road is freshly tarred and slowly I'm trying to make sense of a mathematical conversation I overheard not so long ago: in topology it is possible to create a body the size of our moon, out of a body as small as an orange, the mathematician had said, if you cut an orange or an apple properly it is possible, theoretically, to reassemble the pieces to create something as large as the moon. But in reality such cuttings are impossible because we are dealing with a real orange made up of real atoms . . . On the road I whistle a real old Bombay film song 'Chand Ko Kya Malum', and keep dropping the pips with strange abandon. Approaching closer I hear familiar voices, and see them clearly, the children, Arjun and Indira, on the roof terrace. Red and black clothes. Perhaps green and black. He, the real long-haired boy, is flying a kite and she, the real long-haired girl, is holding an unsteady wheel of string, unspooling. Coated with particles of glass, the long, angled string gleams, it glistens. The kite, a little red dot, soars higher and higher, and the girl keeps moving towards the edge of the terrace. I yell. Don't move. Stop. But she inches backwards. Expecting the worst I drop the leftover orange, the peels and pips, the juiciest bits. I run. Close to the wall. I look up. She falls. No, she doesn't. She heard me just in time and froze. Three or four other men, who noticed her moving precariously towards the edge, leave whatever they were doing and rush towards the wall. Never before had I witnessed this human impulse to save a life. The fall would not have killed her. Severe injury, perhaps, but it would not have killed. There is a sudden commotion outside the house, I hear it still. Nelly steps out. The girl, Indira, still frozen, starts sobbing. Her brother starts too, as if competing with his sister.

Nelly climbs up the stairs, picks up her daughter. I climb up the spiral stairs. She has figured out exactly what happened. Nelly kisses my hand. First time such a tender thing has happened to my hand. She invites me to dine with them again that night. The news travels fast to the hostel and to the class. Professor Singh never thanks me verbally, but the gratitude is in his long looks, in his tone, in handshakes. Words, I did not know then, are a defective medium to say what one really wants to say.

Shimla was peaceful that night on Nelly's bed, but my insomnia didn't give in. In the dressing-table drawers I located an album, a compilation of nothing. Only four or five dimak-eaten photos. One of them: Professor Singh, a six-year-old, dressed like a girl. Two braided ponytails.

On Nelly's bed my mouth felt completely dry. The *girl's* photo stared me in the face. Was I doing something terribly wrong? In the dressing-table drawers, more albums. The second one had a yellowing postcard on the very first page, mailed to Mohan on 12 February 1979. Mr or Ms G describes a chance meeting with a creationist pastor, a descendant of Darwin. Mr or Ms G would like to get rid of bad habits and visit India soon. Lots of love, G. I reread the postcard, then lost interest. Engulfed by strange indifference I lost interest. This is not the reason I was in Shimla. Nelly had no idea I was going through intimate materials.

The rest of the album felt insignificant: glossy pictures of birds, and hundreds of sketches. The third and the fourth albums were the same. Part Audubon's field notes, part Hokusai. Real and unreal. I did not even know the names of those birds. A bird caught in rain. A bird blinded by daylight. I stared at them, they stared back at me. Murmuration. A long list of technical words and phrases. I had to look one up in the dictionary. My thoughts acquired an absurd dimension that night, whirling, wobbling, and I thought again about my insignificant affairs and my obsessive–compulsive ex-girlfriend.

Slowly I opened the bedroom door. No matter how carefully, the hinges never fail to be noisy. She woke up, startled, and sat up on the sofa.

'Sorry I disturbed you, Mrs Singh. I feel like walking. I am going to step out for a while.'

What else could I say?

'Dr Kumar . . . at this hour?' She was so formal.

'If–'

'Turn on the table lamp.'

Four or five unwanted insects came to the lamp and started hovering.

I forget many details of the surreal conversation that took place between us that night. I do recall her eyes from time to time gathering moisture and changing colour. She would place her index finger just above her upper lip, a gesture that made her face change drastically: at times she looked more than herself, at times less so. She talked and I listened and all I remember are the birds. The photos, twenty bundles, of birds. Nelly, a collector. No pesky questions, so I shared an old memory connected to birds. I badly wanted her to talk about her children, but there I was talking about birds. I offered an old memory. When I was eight or nine, my father drove me to the highest mountains to see snow. In my mind snow was warm and gluey and hard, something like salt, and I imagined the mountain birds turning completely white in winter. Father took me to an aviary in the mountains and I asked him if it was possible to spend the night with the birds in the aviary.

'Why don't you sit down?'

'No, I am fine.'

She asked me to turn on the brighter light.

I poured myself a glass of water from the jug in the kitchen.

On the sofa she wrapped a black shawl round her shoulders. Orange hem. No socks. In the apartment she rarely wore socks. Her hair looked less grey and brittle in that light. 'Fathers,' she said. 'My dar-ji, too, took me on a similar journey,' she said in a single breath. 'He took me to the aviary. I called him Dar-ji. He would mimic the chatrik bird, who drinks only the swaati droplets that fall from the leaves of trees, and chakors and koels and the flame-throated bulbuls and papihas and sheldrake. Dar-ji would tell me about the trickster bagula and white baaj and egrets, and the migrating cranes. *Ude ud aave se kosa / tis paachhe bachre chharya / tin kavan khalave / kavan chugaave? There are birds, they fly from far far away lands to escape bitter winters, they leave the children behind, who feeds their young?* I would ask him to recite this passage from Gurbani over and over. But how does the bird know that it has to migrate? I would ask. But how does the bird know that it has reached its destination?' Nelly was drifting slowly to some other world, her voice was now coming from somewhere I had no access to. This sudden monologue made her resemble Clara more and more, my wife.

'One of the first lists I made as a girl was the list of migratory birds,' she continued. 'Sarus cranes that come from the edges of coldest Siberia. Curlews, who never lose their

94

breath flying thousands of miles. The geese, who fly like machines, higher than Everest. But what happens to the bird who separates from the migrating flock? Why do some birds turn their heads from side to side several times before flying? Why were the birds in the aviary performing repetitive movements? Something was not right. The more I tried to play with them, the more I frightened them. Even the injured fledgling I held in my hand shrank with fear.'

Sleep was heavy in her eyelids, but she didn't stop, as if rehearsing her retirement speech. When she spoke about birds her gestures returned. She did not notice the magical moment, the phase transition. I saw a phantom wedding ring on those old fingers. If there was still a trace left of the original Nelly I knew, it was visible in those avian gestures. I'd seen those hands before, shelling peas and braiding her children's long hair. Hands that also conveyed an openness, and an exuberant curiosity about the world. I sat down on the carpet. Now I was really uncomfortable.

She told me that one of her projects at the archives was to actively seek material connected to 'Empire and Ornithology'. Nelly was particularly interested in one Allan Octavian Hume, a retired civil servant in colonial India; the white man lived in Shimla for several years, and it was here, in 1883–4, he conceived the idea of forming the Congress Party, which would eventually work towards Indian independence. The Congress was not formed by Mahatma Gandhi or Pandit Nehru, but by an enlightened Scotsman in 1885. Gandhi and Nehru joined the party much later.

Twenty-five years ago when Nelly shifted to Shimla she had no idea that the colonial Hume was different from the philosopher David Hume. Allan Octavian was also a prodigious collector, with eccentrically large trophies of stuffed birds and eggs. The collection arose out of perpetual travel and constant communication with a vast network of ornithologists scattered throughout South Asia. He used his own savings to start a first-of-a-kind journal, *Stray Feathers*, and authored books like *From Lahore to Yarcanda* and *The Nests and Birds of the Empire*. Some call him the 'Pope or the Father of Indian Ornithology'.

For a moment I thought I had learned nothing about the history of my own country from the teachers at school.

She paused. Her left hand cleared cold perspiration from her brow, and her thoughts drifted to a distant tribe in the Great Andamans. The Andamanese believe when

we humans die we become birds, she said. That is why the population of birds is higher than that of humans. The tribe members never hunt birds, because to kill them is to destroy our own ancestors.

Her tone was that of a rationalist, not superstition. How beautiful was this fluidity between humans and birds. How beautiful the semi-permeable membrane between the living and the dead. But a part of me felt that she wasn't interested in answering the very real questions she herself had posed about the migration of birds. How do birds use Earth's magnetic field to migrate? Is there a compass in their eyes? And if they are able to 'see' the magnetic field, then how do they fly at night?

'Mrs Singh, I am an insomniac. When I was a child my father wrote poems about my inability to sleep.'

She, apparently, didn't hear me properly, and her thoughts drifted towards the terns of Havelock Island, and a different tribe. Then towards endemic birds (nightjar? Narcondam hornbill?) on a volcanic island, some hundred kilometres from the penal colony set up by the British.

As much as I wanted the monologue to continue, I recall leaving the room in haste. I put on my jacket, collected the keys and simply walked out of the apartment, perhaps giving the impression that I could stand her no longer. But that was not why I fled.

Once outside I heard sounds unfamiliar to my ears. Snow was falling faintly, but did not settle on the ground. Instant phase transition. The three phases of water, it seemed, found a temporary equilibrium. Nothing was going to change, I thought, trapped now in the city and its cold night. The neighbouring hills looked more alive with dim dots of light. Where are the children? Not a single word about them. Not a single word about God, etc., only the ballistic little miracle of birds. A breathing space, I felt. Birds for her were like tiny healing devices; they were her prayers. Nevertheless, where were the children? Arjun and Indira and? Did our relation-ship lead to something or someone? A new life? Stolen? The laptop, still heavy in my thoughts, sent me purposefully towards the Peterhof. By now I have forgotten the exact details of my slippery, uneven walk. Freezing translucent rain was falling on sinuous streets, on parked army vehicles, on the corrugated roofs, on the nursery school under construction. On the bronze head of Ambedkar. The great leader lost in deep thought on caste and power and utopian hope. Ambedkar, instead of hope, filled me with foreboding. One of the cops posted outside the hotel was peeing against a wall. When I waved he yelled and four or five of his colleagues marched me on crunchy pebbles to their senior officer in the tent. He smelled of betel nut, and demanded my papers, etc., and when I spelled out the details he demanded American dollars, and it was only then I spilled out my father's name, and his ultra-high rank, and the police inspector, not surprisingly, stood up, erect, and saluted me and apologised for his rude behaviour, and added 'sir' to whatever he said, 'your father was/is a supercop, sir', and then he asked me to accompany him to the lobby and 'just point at the man who had last handled the bags, sir'. A few party delegates were shuffling about the lobby. Fortunately the man was still present at the reception. He was explaining a map to a young lady, and the digital clock on the wall was ten minutes slow. That one in black. The officer requested me to leave an address or return the next day and check at the reception. 'We will see what we can do.'

Nelly had moved to the bedroom during my absence, and the door was not ajar. The light in her room was on, and I felt someone else's presence. My Zara jacket was wet and I spread it on the same dining chair where I had seen her clothes dry the first night. She was reading a text aloud. I moved close to the door and heard, it was the same cruel story my father would read to me when I was a child, he would use Kipling to put me to sleep, 'Rikki-Tikki-Tavi'. Father would read 'Kabuliwala' and *Alice* and Dorothy as well and Panchtantra and Lamb's abridged Shakespeare and Grimm Brothers and *Chandamama* and Vikram aur Vetal. Several times I felt like knocking mildly on her door, but I didn't and continued to scan the objects in the living room, the bookshelves, and I happened to discover by sheer chance a large collection of children's books at the bottom. My conjecture was Nelly chose a different book every night and read it aloud to an imaginary child curled up in her bed.

This is how she had maintained her sanity. (I was proven correct a few days later.) How wrong Professor Singh was that day on the train when he said that the three most important questions for us concerned the origin of the universe, the origin of life and the origin of mind. He forgot to add other questions, or shall I say he forgot to ask the three really significant ones: Why do people respond differently to traumatic events? How do we remember the past? Why when 'meaning' collapses in our lives, do some of us seem to locate a new 'meaning'?

My father, after leaving the police force, consciously decided against getting a corporate job or setting up his own security company. He has enough stocks, and lockers in foreign banks. Three generations can live off his assets. In his retirement he has stumbled upon a new meaning. He reads the classics and studies alternative medicine, and sometimes prescribes Ayurvedic remedies to friends, most of them retired civil servants or diplomats and even industrialists, and they spend time in his living room in Delhi, learning the medicinal properties of a rare mushroom extract.

I read some of these details in a letter he wrote to Clara. Everything happened behind my back. I never gave her Father's address, Clara got it from my old passport. She sent him our wedding photo, and he responded on Mother's death anniversary.

Ever since, although they have never met, my estranged wife and my father have formed a mutual admiration club and exchange polite meaningless words every couple of months.

Not so long ago she arranged a Skype call between our daughters and my father. Had I known in advance I would not have allowed any such contact. Clara, during that one and only video call, encouraged Father to teach Hindi to the kids. He was overjoyed to hear those words coming out of the American wife. Conversation turned to *Sita Sings the Blues*. Urvashi and Ursula take immense delight in transcendental animation. Clara persuaded him to tell them the Indian myths. The girls feigned interest when Grandpapa started repeating stories they had already heard from their father. Clara rescued the delicate situation like a true Midwesterner. She printed out the myths and mailed them to Father. In my spare time I had compiled hundreds of them to entertain the girls. It was Clara's idea. She suggested a good and proper translation of those myths (my myths) into Hindi.

Father, it seems, took the suggestion seriously. After all, he is a self-appointed saviour of Indian languages and culture. That night I felt an abnormally strong urge to hurt myself. Once again my wife and I were upset with each other over Father . . .

I am twenty years old. It is my last day in Delhi. The flight to New York via Europe is supposed to take off at the most inconvenient hour of the night. My mother and the maid (from Nepal) have just finished packing my suitcase and I step out on to the lawns and touch trees, shrubs and flowers as if I am going to the moon. Father beckons me. His voice urgent, but lacking in emotion. Son, I would like to have a word. As usual he utters the word 'son' with mechanical authority. Father always has that special 'word' with me at the dining table. No food on the table yet, just salt and pepper shakers. A fat bottle of Kissan lemon pickle. He waits for me to sit down. He, the head of the table, clears his throat. Don't feel bad, he begins. Just answer me honestly. Do you have plans to return? After the studies are over do you come back? We know you keep things deep inside, so answer me honestly. Come on, don't hide. Will you return? The long pause is my fault. I am observing my good father like never before. As if you are not hiding something? I say. Jokes apart, he says. Tell us, will you return? How words betray his gestures. As if subconsciously he has figured me out completely, and doesn't desire my return. Yes, I conceal myself from him. I want to sort this problem out, but Mother is standing by the edge of the oblong table. I wait for her to pull out the chair and sit next to me. She doesn't. She keeps staring at the lemons trapped in the bottle. Of course I will, I say, more for her sake. I will return after the studies are over. But the moment I do so, she weeps more not less. I have abandoned her as well.

Where would we be without lithium? Ever since the doctor prescribed lithium she made no attempts to kill herself. The lithium story freaked out all my girlfriends. So I omitted talking about that element in the periodic table

101

to anyone. Clara has no clue about lithium. I pretended I knew nothing. Now it is too late to tell.

Clara would insist on a short visit to India after we got married. She figured out something was not right. She detected a problem, a 'non-amicable' relationship, something messy connected to my past. No family member of mine had attended our wedding. I could not invite Mother, because she was dead. I never invited Father. Because he was alive. Clara wanted to meet him. 'You go,' I would respond. Frustrated, she would mimic and mock my 'you go'. Between Halloween and Thanksgiving, unfailingly, she would try hard to persuade. But she never bought a ticket.

Why did she fall for me? She fell for her idea of me. My defects. Mathematics. My exoticness. My mild British accent. I don't need an analyst to reveal this. But things were different when we first met. Her presence comforted and calmed me down during those early days. She made me less lonely. And we laughed together. There were heavier things I was unable to tell, things that really mattered. I spared her that. Not telling meant not processing the stuff myself. She didn't sense any major concealment. Let me spell them out clearly – two things I could not share with the woman (who was not yet my wife). The first: my anxiety that she would run away the moment she discovered my ideas about not having children. The second one, more complex, connected to Father. Something wrong, periodically sinister, but I could not bring myself to believe it. So I started concealing it even from my own self. And Clara? Not that I didn't trust her, but I knew the way she was, the way she operated in the world, she would not understand.

The night was dense with its tightly packed shadows. I tried to forget my stolen Mac. Forgetting doesn't come easy to me. Needlessly I tossed and turned on the sofa, now abandoning the pillow, now claiming it back. Then the phone rang. Nelly didn't step out of the room. Reluctantly I responded. Who's this? Call is from Mashobra, said the woman. Who would you like to talk to? Wrong number. The phone disconnected. The woman's voice kept echoing in my ears. My mouth completely dry, and I felt a cold sweat, I felt as if I didn't belong to my body and it was raining inside Nelly's apartment, slowly burying me in thixotropic mud. I cannot say I missed sleeping with Clara. Sex with her always lacked fun and spontaneity. One had to plan days in advance . . . But I have not forgotten . . . She taught me tenderness, and for that I am grateful . . . Soon the foolish hallucination *I will go to the moon*. The ridiculous Chandrayan chant. *No water on moon*. The madwoman's voice transported me to 1982 or 1983, and together, in my hallucination, we watched a Russian film, *Solaris*. Ironically it was that film which had first given me the bug to walk into the crepuscular world of science fiction. On the space-ship there is a library. Not far from the shelves a cosmonaut is alone with his long-dead wife, Haari, his subconscious personified. (In my mind when I think about Haari, I cannot but help thinking about Nelly, and when I think about Nelly I think about Haari.) She sits next to him, Haari, a melancholic, lost in deep thought, almost human. Then: zero gravity. Together they experience thirty seconds of weightlessness. Four flaming candles soar steeply upwards and collide with the sparkling chandelier, a fugue of a chime, and Haari and the cosmonaut levitate like helium, wrapped in Bach's little organ music, an open book (an encyclopaedia) orbiting around them. Five elements, fire, metal, glass, air and wood, come together, and Planet Earth merges via the painting on the wall . . . Human figures, animals skating

103

on snow. Skating, I am inside the cosmonaut's consciousness now, I am witnessing my own childhood memories, a swing, a boy wearing a red cap, red pants, running around in a winter landscape; I warm myself by setting fire to twigs; images of two intimate strangers, my mother and father, and outside the spaceship the colloidal ocean moves vortex-like. Solaris takes over, filling the screen with its mysterious slow eddies. Sound of a flask breaking. The madwoman has tried to kill herself again, this time with liquid oxygen. An echo of a scientist's voice: instead of space explorations, what we humans really need is a mirror.

Next morning when I woke up she was still in bed, the door slightly ajar. Outside the window: membranes of snow. Millimetre-thin layers. *Papadi wali baraf.* I muffled myself and walked to the hotel reception. The Hindu Party had left behind lots of debris in its wake (the 'chintan baithak' over). The cops had left too. Suffocating smell of crushed marigold flowers and sandalwood incense. Ruins (smouldering ash and smoke) of a huge safety hazard of a havan. Wine- and tea-stained furniture. Mountains of discarded styrofoam cups and plastic. At first I didn't recognise the man at the reception; he was no longer in black, there was a red scarf around his neck and his left arm was in a white cast. On his face there were three or four fresh marks of violence. One look and he trembled. 'We found your missing item, sa'ab,' and his assistant literally ran towards me and handed me an object – my muddy laptop.

'What happened to you?'

'Sa'ab, I just fell,' he said. 'I was walking last night with too many things on my mind.' He trembled again, and I checked with him if the wounds were the result of falling or something else. 'Minor matter, sa'ab.' Then I spent some time in the gift shop. Why was he not at home? Did he receive strict instructions? Later when I walked to the exit with my laptop, I turned back one last time. Again the skinny man trembled. Most likely I was the cause.

Back in the apartment a note was waiting for me on the kitchen table. Nelly had stepped out for a morning walk to 'cleanse her mind'. It was her big day, and she had no plans to share it with me. *Why not visit Mashobra today? Hill of deodars. Lush and wrinkled. Go stand on the slopes of the 'Magic Mountain'.* Second time she had brought up that idyllic hamlet, six miles away. Mashobra, the so-called post-colonial wilderness. Less a forest, more the remnant of a forest. Mashobra, the Viceroy's weekend chateau, the so-called retreat; according to travel books during the last days of the Empire Lady Mountbatten had fucked Pandit Nehru there, but the topic is of little interest to me. There is nothing more boring than celebrity political romance. I understand Nelly absolutely does not desire my presence at the institute during her retirement gathering. I brush my teeth with Sensodyne and take a hot mugga bath (flooding the bathroom again) and leave her apartment around nine thirty (as soon as the sirens start wailing across the city, alerting the denizens to begin work) and spend some time at the antique and rare bookshop on the slushy Mall Road. Then I take the bus.

Mashobra makes me feel more and more disorientated. Something deeply unconsolable about the landscape. Every inch, like Shimla, every slope, every tree carries traces of colonialism. The 'magic' is still there, but it is the magic of ruins and destruction. Crumbling buildings left behind by the British and the maharajahs. Private villas owned by the old rich and the neo-rich. Lots of dead and dying trees, a couple of them planted by the Viceroy's old tailor. In Mashobra the rare English oaks are highly stressed and visibly injured. One saving grace, though: the tourists are largely absent, and the deodar forest is dense, tightly packed, sublime, the trees melt into each other like old memories, and they are everywhere, the rhizomes and wild strawberries. A poet or a historian would have liked it. Mrs Gandhi stayed in the chateau there in 1972 when she signed the so-called Shimla Agreement with the defeated Pakistani PM on Kafka's birthday. Yes, there is fresh mountain air in Mashobra, and roofless walls of snow, and unlimited angled views of teacup-shaped valleys, but the fresh mountain air-oxygen and teacups and ponies and sanatorium-like buildings make me all the more sick. Rereading Thomas Mann's *Magic Mountain* is not a bad idea, I remind myself. Magic Lower Himalaya. Then I feel an invisible blow. Whiteness hurts. Whiteness never fails to hurt my eyes. My feet are cold. To warm myself I walk into the stately Oberoi Wild Flower Cafe. By the entrance I find a dark object embedded in snow. The guard at the gates smiles like a mythical figure. Inside it is just the right temperature. Warm, the way it should be warm. I order a latte. With my fingers I clean a dark yellowish metal disc. The object reveals itself fully – a watch without a strap, and only one hand. She is cute. The woman at the table next to mine. Resembles someone vaguely familiar; her sharp features carry traces of my ex-girlfriend. Longish neck, medium-sized breasts, and a young Benazir Bhutto face. Dark brown leather boots, and a deep, deep sexual fragrance. Never before have I encountered such voluptuous calves. In the cafe she was alone (her table touched mine and the thick radiator), reading a Kindle. Such women by their sheer existence make fellow humans happy, and help them achieve that blissful state of forgetfulness. I had a lot to forget. Slowly she crossed and uncrossed her legs and kept twiddling a strand of her hair over and over. To this day I have not understood fully the power of her attraction. For a change I felt no resistance, only a strong urge to seduce or be seduced, hopelessly and instantaneously haunted. The detail that really matters is that we hung out together and those hours bought me rare happiness. Later we shared a cab; and from Shimla bus stand she took the Volvo to Delhi.

Ironically, whenever I think about Mashobra I don't know why I immediately move that happy day into parentheses, not sure if the silencing or the repression is subconscious, or because the details are too improper, too embarrassing to admit. Details that never fail to double my grief. (I will return to Benazir a bit later.)

Nelly was still not back in her apartment in Shimla. Her absence slipped me into a state of disquiet. Then worry. Perhaps it was wrong to make assumptions. But it was around ten at night. Outside the window snow was falling silently. No sign of her, no message. To distract myself I did the dirty dishes, then I read a book for children. *Just So Stories*. I read aloud, thirty or forty pages, and when I checked my watch it was past midnight. The idea of reporting to the police was laughable. I read one last piece aloud. Slowly, I put the large-format book aside and turned off the lights. But doing so only exacerbated the questions floating around. Perhaps Nelly's colleagues had taken her somewhere after the event, perhaps there was something else she didn't want to share with me. Perhaps something happened. Something done by someone, something done by herself. The more I thought the more my anxiety grew. Did I ask wrong stuff the previous night? Was she offended by my project?

Something within me was convinced that Nelly was not going to return that night.

From the window I saw the neighbour's cottage (a young chap shining his shoes). He looked like a man who was watching himself, not entirely comfortable in his body. Most likely he knew next to nothing about Nelly. Perhaps he saw her as an old and redundant woman.

In the bedroom I noticed. She did not go to the institute in the dress she was ironing. She had changed several times before deciding on the one she liked. There was no other clue in the bedroom.

When I returned to the window the neighbour was no longer there. The Observatory Hill. Globes and pinpricks of light, and rising and falling vortices of snow. I see it still. White powder accumulating on the dark tiles and turrets of the institute.

The phone rang. Expecting bad news, I paced towards the instrument, but the answering machine clicked in and I decided not to answer. An unfamiliar voice rippled towards me. The way the caller spoke English with a mild accent, I was able to identify her Spanishness. She wished Nelly all the best on her special day. *Hola. Ciao. Gran abrazos.*

I replayed, checked all the messages on the machine . . . My own, the one I had left right after my arrival in Shimla, was still part of the tape, not erased. Stored, perfectly preserved messages. There were more. All in the same voice, messages from the same man, perhaps he was the man in her life. The greeting on the answering machine had the identical voice. Indian Leonard Cohen. Everything I did that night, every object I touched, felt like a clue to locating Nelly because I was convinced.

I had grown up observing my supercop father. He suspected everything, and revealed rarely his innermost thoughts before resolving an investigation. Now I found myself operating in the same mode.

Only a day ago when I broached the topic of her retirement, Nelly's face had transformed momentarily. To me her oval of a face looked like a phase diagram plotted between fear and shame. A moment later she smiled a thin smile. The face had transformed into her usual expression then.

To deal with my growing anxiety I distracted myself further, and made two calls to Ithaca. November is the month Clara buys leg warmers. This happens after Halloween. Children love the festival. They exaggerate the spookiness of pumpkins. They dress up as dead nerds or dead fashion models. They knock on almost every door in the neighbourhood and return joyous with their loot. After Halloween we celebrate Diwali. Clara has her romantic ideas of India and she clings to those ideas and I am a personification of those ideas. I am not allowed to narrate the dark side of that romance – how ugly the collective consciousness of a nation can be.

My wife (my estranged wife) has this remarkable ability to explain difficult concepts to children, which I admire, which I never developed really. I am too adult-like with children, I believe if the world is not good they should know the details, but she shields them – at times I tell her that they might find out the 'truth' at school and they might find out the 'wrong truth', but at the same time I hope they don't find out. Iraq War, Abu Ghraib, Afghanistan. Tsunami, 9/11, Air India bombing. Clara explains the world to them in small doses, and the girls find this satisfactory. Who is the Devil? the younger one asked. And Clara's response was, The Devil is a character, who makes people do evil things. And Clara has already explained 'evil' in a roundabout way to the girls. So they, especially the younger one, are satisfied, and no nightmares follow. And this is the ability I lack – I end up telling them a lot, even when I confine myself to 'myths', and this leaves the girls confused.

Clara – if she had been born in Nazi Germany, she would have told our children that the Jewish neighbours were really headed to some land of toys and candies. What if one of the kids really took off with the neighbours?

I called home. The girls were about to begin breakfast and I could hear their mother in the background. Clara doing the blueberry pancakes. 'Dad, she asked who is an Egypt?' the elder one said. 'She doesn't even know that Egypt is a country.'

And then Clara took the phone and asked me to call later in the evening (her evening). The girls are going to school today. She, if she could help it, would never allow me to be in contact with the girls again.

Clara is not just angry at me. She is also angry at herself that she is angry at me. She feels emotional excesses are highly contagious. 'Before I met you I didn't know anger.'

I made the second call to my colleague. Before I took off for India we had agreed to work on a book, co-edit an anthology on rheology, and I was lagging behind. Nelly was not responsible for the delay. The real reason? I felt increasingly out of place in my department in my adopted country. The Chair was kind of all right, but the Dean disliked me, and I knew, all the popularity in the classroom doesn't mean much to the university if you don't have publications. The Dean was especially not keen on my area of research because it brought little corporate funding. If he had his way he would even accept money from the tainted Dow Chemicals. Not many people know. Dow bought Union Carbide, the corporation criminally responsible for

110

the Bhopal gas leak. And Dow seems to have no plans to clean up Bhopal. No moral responsibility.

Nelly was not back and I grew more worried. I watered all the plants in her apartment, one by one. I identified them using the Internet. Then I checked my email. Forty-five more minutes passed by. Then without making any sounds I left the apartment and slowly took the steep, dangerous path towards the Observatory Hill. First down on the cobblestones, then up. The neighbour was looking out of the window, the shoeshine man. For me he did not exist.

The Summer Hill train station was bright with moth-like lights. Fresh snow on the tracks, and on layers and layers of open garbage. Snow on the high arches of the tunnel. Ice and loose snow. I walked past a sharp smell of piss. Climbing up the half-hill I felt the city itself was a collection, an archive, a ghostly archive of hubris, greed, neglect and fear. Alongside me walked Kipling's dark wild animals, imaginary cheetahs, Shere Khan, Baloo, Bagheera, Kaa and cruel poisonous nags. How easy it is to read about Kaa and Darzee in *The Jungle Book* from the comfort of a living room in Ithaca. (Not so long ago Clara pointed out that Kipling never managed to create skunks and raccoons, the North American inhabitants. India cast a bigger spell than North America, or even his 'native' Britain.) The more he stayed away from this landscape, the more he wrote about its people and animals. Distance failed to make India disappear. Not the first time someone disappeared from my own life, so many friends of mine made the disappearing act one by one. During my day walks on the same path I'd noticed mysterious local women knitting or sweeping (the Brownian trajectories of rising and falling dust particles, eddies and vortices), but now it was night. The women gone. Ahead of me the incongruous Scottish baronial castle, its menacing turrets. High up on the canopy of trees, nimble monkeys. They knew the double bonds, and made me think of *The Wrench* by Primo Levi and *The Periodic Table*. 'The Grey Zone'. The worst survived, the best all died. Vanadium. After the war a chance occurrence in the paint factory brought Primo Levi into contact with his ex-boss, Dr Müller of Auschwitz. Reappearance. After a long disappearance. *A vast zone of grey consciences that stands between the great men of evil and the pure victims.* Buna rubber factory. Levi was one of the three chemists in the factory just seven miles from the camp. Dr Müller was the chief chemist there. On clear days the flames of the crematorium, the carbide tower, were visible from the factory. After a difficult exchange of letters Dr Müller phoned – 'Could we meet?' So much time had passed by. 'Yes,' said Levi, taken unawares. But the meeting never happened. Eight days later he died, Dr Müller. *Why the children in the gas chambers? (In the letters) Müller's condemnation of Nazism was timid and evasive, but he had not sought justifications.*

The snow-covered pebbles crunched under my feet. The closer I approached the castle the more I felt like a 'native', a 'brown heathen', a petty subject of the British Empire, who by a freak accident managed to sneak out of his shack, duping the guards, climbing up the hill to marvel at the wonders of electrification. How this new force would one day eliminate the darkness that had occupied his land, and send the foreign rulers home. The land of his ancestors, now ruled by those who claimed to be the creators of civilisation. But in reality they had damaged and frightened his people more or less like Attila the Hun. Imperial policies had led to extermination of large numbers of humans in the colonies. 'Auschwitz was the modern industrial application of a policy of extermination on which European world domination has long rested' Sven Lindqvist. One by one I observed through the tall fuzzy uncurtained windows objects that belonged to the Empire, and the new ones. An oak desk. Just like the desk in daylight. But different now. A fluorescent light flickering, irradiating a red sash in the ballroom. On the desk a head. A human head. Was she asleep? The porte cochère, on the other side, fifty metres away, the main entrance half blocked by a huge silhouette of a rusty colonial bell. I woke up the bidi-smoking porter. Once a complete battalion of Gurkhas guarded the place and now only one red-eyed night porter sporting a threadbare baseball cap.

'Madam-ji is locked inside. Hurry.'

The porter shook his head. Bhoot, he whispered the Hindi word for a ghost.

'Archivist madam.'

'Madam who?'

'The librarian.'

'Who are you?'

Losing my patience, I pinched the man wearing a baseball cap and fingerless gloves. His name was Suraj.

Suraj = Sun.

'And who are you?'

Suraj knew I lived not far from New York, we'd had an extended conversation only a day ago. He had saluted me and was friendly and he had shared his own details then in a sprightly voice. 'Sa'ab, I grew up in a village on the high mountains.' His brother and parents were still on the 'high mountains' dependent on a couple of farms and a small orchard. He himself lived with his nephew and niece in a single room in what used to be the Viceroy's horse stables.

113

LIBRARY HOURS
MONDAY TO FRIDAY 9.00am TO 7.30pm
SATURDAY 9.00am-9.00am TO 5.30pm

The kids had moved to the 'big' city to attend school. Only a day ago Suraj and I had talked about his lowly salary; I had even taken the liberty to ask him about his political affiliation, his take on the Hindu Party, and he had said that he never supported those corrupt politicians, and when I had asked 'why', he had explained, Those people destroy what they don't want to remember.

But Suraj was a transformed man that night.

'Sa'ab, the lady is the bhoot of Curzon. Dressed in a white petticoat. We have seen before. She rustles though the corridors. Everyone knows. Sometimes the petticoat hits the old furniture and one hears someone crying.'

'Suraj, Nelly-ji is inside.' I grabbed his wrist. 'She is wearing an orange salwar kameez.'

He rubbed his eyes. 'These, as I say, are manifestations of a ghost,' he said in Hindi. 'Not my job. Are you her husband?'

He wasted five more minutes before unlocking the door, and as I stepped in I felt I was walking not on a soft carpet, but on a sea of freshly molten wax. Everything inside the mansion was mute and dimly lit, the wallpaper peeling as if it were the skin of colonialism, unable to express properly its real purpose or pain. So many of my memories are completely extinguished by now, but this is hard to repress. After the difficult farewell Nelly had stayed behind, she wanted to move the last few boxes from her office to the collection. Took her a couple of hours, then she locked the archives, and her office in the basement. She spent a few moments in the ladies' washroom, cleaning her dusty hands thoroughly, and then moved upstairs and sat at the assistant librarian's desk, and started observing through the glass window a shower of snow, and she had no idea when sleep overtook her. The farewell gathering took place in the Vice-roy's tea room (the transmuted 'seminar room').

116

Nelly requested the porter to show me the debris of the event. She didn't accompany us into the room. So this is where she delivered an improvised speech, I thought. All I remember of that dimly lit room now is the 'original' maple-coloured silk wall-covering and the 'original' but faded, threadbare curtains and the portrait of long-grey-bearded Tagore on the wall facing the Raj-era podium. For forty-five years Tagore had stayed glued to the same colonial wall, keeping watch over hundreds of seminars, panels and workshops, or gatherings of a more private nature. Standing there I could not help but think that in 1919 the Nobel Laureate had returned his knighthood to the British to protest the Amritsar Massacre. For a while I was not sure where exactly I was.

'It is all coming back to me now, Sa'ab,' Suraj said. 'You a New Yorker.'

Suraj and I stepped out. Nelly was in the lobby (with its infinitely high ceiling). She looked up. She was staring at a black dot, which swelled as it flew right above us . . . Skilful user of a sonar device, the gliding dot of a creature knew how to avoid collisions with big objects and the walls. The bat shrank and swelled again passing right above us, and moved without disturbing the air, without producing any audible effects. Suraj, no longer afraid, claimed he knew how to take care of chamgadars. I will see to it, he reassured her. The porter's eyes glowed as if he were a modern-day Kipling, as if after dealing with the bat or chamgadar he was going to sit down and write a book for his nephew and niece. *Namaskar, madam-ji.* He didn't wish me goodnight.

On the way home she walked slower than her usual pace, and Nelly's beautiful face looked sad and exhausted, and she mentioned next to nothing about the event. The real reason – as I found out later – was shame (and she didn't want me to play the witness). I cannot even begin

117

imagining what she experienced being in the same room as the man who destroyed the life she had assembled, everything that was meaningful to her.

How does one look into the eyes of someone who ruins one's nest? What else, if not shame? She chose to tell me ghost stories instead, fear and fantasy floating around at the institute: a research fellow who finds the quilt on his bed neatly wrapped every morning, an illiterate dhobi who mutters a line or two of perfect Victorian English and calls himself Cyril Radcliffe, and that no matter how many locks are used on the Vicereine's bathroom door some mysterious figure always manages to take a hot shower.

She stopped and took a deep breath.

'Are you all right?'

'Small thing,' she said. 'My foot is hurting.'

She offered the details herself.

'A heavy box fell . . . and I tripped down the stairs.'

'Is that true?'

'Small thing.'

Her response carried an echo of the response I got earlier in the day from the trembling lips of that receptionist, the man in black. I asked again and when she nodded I noticed for the first time a black eye. Someone had punched her hard. Perhaps in that darkness I wanted to believe that someone had punched her, and punched again.

'Should we get a taxi?'

There were no taxis around. We stood in the middle of the road, where only sixty or seventy years ago some of our liveried compatriots plied foot rickshaws. *Jinrickshaw*, the colonial terminology. Kipling's characters rode them, sahibs and memsahibs. Every summer they came to 'Simla' to 'forget India', but India always tagged along, showing its dirty feet. The same feet and hands pulled brown sahibs and memsahibs

118

up and down the hills, including our brown leaders, who arrived by train to hold 'round table' talks on freedom.

'Should we go to a doctor?'

'No.'

The rest of the way, awkwardly, I held her hand. Soft and scabrous at once, her skin. Her handbag dangled in my other hand. In the cold and crisp air our words generated plumes of white smoke. No, not an apparition – Nelly, walking beside me, was real. She was hiding something, and that, too, was real. It took us almost an hour. Back home she spent a long time in the cold bathroom. When she stepped out her limp was more pronounced. I made her hot tea. She asked me to serve it in the bedroom.

'You would like to know,' I disclosed finally. 'The laptop is back.'

She displayed no surprise. Only a thin smile.

She sat on the bed and requested me to cover her feet with the quilt. Grotesque swelling on her right toe. Purple or faint blue. I turned on the heaters as well. She smiled again and unribboned and unwrapped the farewell gifts. Two red mugs. A miniature bronze woman, reading a tiny bronze book. The surface rough, but shining. Someone at the library knew her passion. Two Oxford India paperbacks: *The Birds of Eastern Himalayas*, and a veteran ornithologist's memoir, *The Fall of a Sparrow*.

She didn't volunteer more information about the farewell or the black eye, and I didn't persist. Something was not right. Inside the bathroom two or three drops of blood. Outside the fog grew thick like an unknown animal. I knew it was not a good idea to start investigating blood. So I asked her if she had more old photos.

'Most of them were destroyed.' She requested me to open the upper chest of drawers and retrieve an album. I found two old postcards from Cornell (mailed to Mohan) and only one photo, a girl. Braided hair, ribbons, frock.

'This is my son,' she said. 'You met him.'

'Arjun?'

Shaking mildly I turned on my Mac. She put on her reading glasses. Nelly didn't reveal much emotion while scanning and scrolling the photos of my research lab, and photos from my student days at IIT. Once or twice she tapped her fingers on the flickering screen. Then I showed her the photo which had gone through so many reflections and refractions, the railway station group photo.

'Mrs Singh, you took this photo. Remember?'

'I see,' she said.

I felt she was staring at my father.

The following was recorded with Nelly's permission.

Please, Mrs Singh, what happened that day after our train departed?

I took a three-wheeler to my friend's place.

Your friend's name?

Maribel. She played me her favourite song. Do you really want to know?

Yes . . .

She was excessively funny that day. Maribel grew up in Mexico thinking that we Indians have eight toes on each foot and eight fingers on each hand! Señor Weinberger, her uncle, told her that in India people have white shocks of hair until thirty, and at that precise age the hair colour begins to turn black! She played me her favourite song. One of José Alfredo Jiménez's, sung by Maria Dolores Pradera. I have no idea why all this has stayed in my mind . . .

Who is she?

She worked at the Mexican High Commission. We had met at the International School six months earlier in 1983. Our children were in the same class.

What were their names?

My son, Arjun, and my daughter, Indira. They were eight and seven years old. You know this.

After the High Commission you returned home?

Yes.

How did you first meet Professor Singh?

Mohan and I had an arranged marriage. You know this.

No, I don't.

I see.

Eventually did you fall in love with him?

Love? Not the way it happens in Hollywood or Bollywood. Mohan didn't talk much about his past. Whenever I raised the question of his childhood he would not give a proper response. Evasive is the right word. By and by I found out.

121

By and by you found out?

He was born in a village called Toba Tek Singh, named after a compassionate Punjabi man who distributed free water to travellers. Mohan's grandfather, an independence fighter, spent time in jails, and later his father was shipped to Kala Pani, or Black Water, the dreaded 'Guantánamo Bay' run by the British. His family had no problems with the colonial administration before the Amritsar Massacre. Mohan's mother turned 'half mad' – at least that is what the relatives said, and when the partition was announced in '47, despite several attempts, no one was able to locate her, not even close to the waters. He had just joined a school where classes took place under a 200-year-old fig tree. Then the violence flared up. At the refugee camp (in Toba Tek Singh) he was adopted by a

school headmaster, and they made it safely to the Indian side on a special military escorted train.

Mohan told me bits and fragments of this when we visited the Golden Temple after our wedding. We were circumambulating the sarovar and he recalled how when he was four or five he had made it safely to the Golden Temple. Later he showed me a couple of photos from that era, his hair braided, ribboned, the boy looked more cute than a girl. First his mother and then the headmaster's wife dressed him up in colourful frocks . . .

He was terrified of trains, I know you don't know this. Whenever possible he avoided taking the train. Every couple of months we would take the bus to Amritsar. Sometimes we would change buses two or three times. Sometimes we would combine the bus with a short train journey from Delhi. Slowly I helped him overcome his fear.

He was extremely fond of the children. I remember the first time we took them to the Golden Temple – Mohan showed them the museum, toshakhana and the reference library. In the museum there were huge paintings of the enlightened ones; I recall Mohan telling the children about Guru Nanak and his walks. Nanak was a saint and a poet and he walked around twenty thousand miles in forty years, all the way to Ceylon, Tibet and Baghdad, a figure as important as the Buddha, and aspired to eliminate caste. Nanak rejected Brahmanical Hinduism, and untouchability. He rejected the authority of priests, and pointed out the injustices committed by the powerful rulers of his time ... The word 'Sikh' means 'student' in Sanskrit, and in a way all Sikhs are students for life. Mohan and I took the children to Jallianwala Bagh Memorial, the site of the 1919 Amritsar Massacre. Arjun noticed a squirrel and parakeet and a pigeon dining together in the garden! Back in the temple complex we sat by the shimmering waters and listened to Gurbani. Often I think back to that day. Mohan dazzled the kids with more stories about the life of Baba Nanak. The melancholies of the saint, his udasis and the art of travelling long distances on foot. Once Nanak walked all the way to Benaras and waded through the Ganges and there he encountered a cluster of sham holy men. Unable to comprehend why the Brahmins were splashing water, he asked the usual question. What is the purpose? Clever, as always, the Brahmins replied, We are only sending holy water to the sun. The souls of our ancestors live there, screaming with thirst. Nanak questioned the sham logic with a precise action, something beyond words. He turned 180 degrees and started sending water in the opposite direction.

What are you doing? The Brahmins tried to stop him. Listen, brothers, said Nanak, the wheat fields of Punjab are really dry . . . But your water will never reach the crops, the Brahmins mocked him. Brothers, spoke Nanak, if your water is able to flow all the way to the sun, which is millions of miles away, then sure my water will fall like a heavy monsoon shower over the fields of Punjab.

My family had agrarian roots. My father was the first one who attended university. He got a doctorate in botany and taught at the agricultural university in Ludhiana. I grew up listening to Partition stories. Every time he would tell a story my hand would automatically rise to my mouth. Stories that informed me that the Punjabis and the Bengalis did most of the dying. The so-called 'azadi diwas' was really a 'barbadi diwas'. The holocaust could have been avoided, if only Lord Mountbatten and our leaders had chosen to act differently . . . Two million people dead, twenty million displaced. Women raped. Tens of thousands of children became

124

orphans. We Sikhs were separated from most of our historic and cultural centres. The birthplace of Nanak and the place of his death are now on the wrong side of the border. The Partition dead were never mourned properly, so much was suppressed, the government built no memorials, for so many people life continued amid the ruins as if *nothing* had happened. To build memorials is to acknowledge not just what 'they' did to us, but also what 'we' did to them.

[Pause.]

It is painful for me to continue.

[Pause.]

One day my father informed me over dinner that an IIT professor who knew even the tiniest details about the big bang and other theories of the universe was interested in me.

[Smiles.]

You were considerably younger?

Yes, and I was notorious for rejecting men my father would introduce.

Mohan was in town to deliver a lecture at the local engineering college. I attended the talk, and was mesmerised. I requested my father to do everything in his power to invite Mohan home! Our first conversation was not about food or weather, but about work, about the archives. I had done an advanced course at the National Archives in Delhi. He asked me about my thesis. I had completed two projects. 'How Outsiders Have Looked at Us Indians', and 'Nehru's

Prison Letters to his Daughter'. I never managed to finish my report on textile dyes. 'Indigo' in particular.

Mohan asked if I was interested in the Punjab as well. I recall mentioning the Russian prince Soltykoff's 1842 travels to Ludhiana in 'Punjaub', as he used to say. Soltykoff wrote: I am able to see the Shivalik mountains from Ludhiana. Mohan found this particular line strangely amusing and smiled.

And then I asked him my first question, about his projects, and he said: Only one. Helium.

He played bridge and tennis. I had no fondness for tennis, I felt more at ease with badminton and its feathered shuttlecocks. He presented himself as a cosmopolitan, sophisticated reader, who liked Musil, but stayed away from Maugham. I liked Virginia Woolf and Dickens and Hardy and was oddly indifferent to Maugham. Both of us had read Bhai Vir Singh's Punjabi Renaissance novels in translation. *Soon my knees will fail. Will you marry me?* This is how he proposed! Yes, I said. Then he recited from memory a translated Turkish poem by Nazim Hikmet.

Our wedding took place in a gurdwara; we spent our honeymoon in Kashmir in a houseboat called *Neil Armstrong*. Mohan, I soon found, was a bit like my father without his defects. This made him slightly less interesting. He had a tendency to make everyone happy, so life with him was less dramatic. After our honeymoon we visited a relative in Amritsar. My new husband knew that auntie-ji and uncle-ji didn't approve of husbands doing the laundry. So: Mohan washes our clothes including the undergarments in the bathroom, and asks me to go and hang them to dry on the clothes line.

Harmandar, the way we refer to the 'Golden Temple'. It was just after our honeymoon, I still remember. My husband and I were circumambulating the shimmering pool in the Harmandar complex, and he commented on the orange haze of a blob, the reflection of sun in water, and he started describing the surface of 'helios' to me, our sun's mysterious core. His one obsession was 'Helium-3'. Thermonuclear equations, etc., etc. I phased out for a while, and don't recall how our conversation turned to 'neutrinos'. I knew neutrons. But *neutrinos*? Was it a diminutive? Mohan explained they were particles that go right through you. No charge. No mass. Ghost particles, Nelly. Going right through you and me, Nelly, and those beautiful marble inlays and the waters and the unrusting dome of Harmandar. They are all around us, invisible, dancing, a movement you would have never known. They come to us from deep inside the helios. Millions and zillions of them, passing through. For neutrinos there are no walls, Nelly.

Harmandar has no walls. I almost levitated while saying this to Mohan. It is open to all the people in the world, the entire human race. He looked at me with deep affection, and it was at that precise moment I think I fell in love with him.

Indira Gandhi is no longer your hero. When did she cease to be so?

[Pause.]

Would you like to say something?

When I heard the news of her death I wept. But the Congress Party didn't allow me and so many others to mourn her. On the TV we saw the close-up of her face (her body lay in state at the Teen Murti House), and the soundtrack on the national TV was the music of the mob – inciting people to kill all the Sikhs in the country. The Information and Broadcasting Minister responsible for the

127

telecasts was later rewarded by the new Prime Minister, Indira's first son. (The minister, H. K. L. Bhagat, was also the ex-Mayor of Delhi. Hundreds of eye-witnesses and victims accused him of mass murder in '84. How strange he was born on the same day as Goebbels.)

You have not told me much about your daughter. You rarely mention her.

She was born a year after my son, and they were so alike and so different. She was not shy like him, she would go to people, make friends, she learned everything faster than him, she learned to walk before him, talk before him, and she never once said those hurtful things my son would say: I will make you unhappy. But why? Because you didn't do this for me or you didn't do that for me.

She got this home assignment on flags . . . The teacher had asked her to select the map of a neighbouring country and write twenty lines about the country, and my girl was disappointed. She wanted to write twenty lines about Mexico, but Mexico was not our neighbouring country – she had two hundred lines ready on Mexico, on Oaxaca. She loved the way it is pronounced, Wah-ha-ka. She opened the atlas and looked at the maps. Of all the neighbouring countries she chose Pakistan, our official enemy. Why? Because I have to play, I don't have much time, and the map of Pakistan is the easiest thing to sketch. She drew the map and used green crayons and asked me to help her write those twenty lines, but I really didn't know how to begin telling her the story of that complex neighbour. Nepal or Sri Lanka would have been easier, even Bhutan.

The children were extremely fond of my friend Maribel. She said her name was made out of two words, Maria plus

Isabel. I met her at the IIC library, where I worked in the archives section. She worked in the cultural wing of the Mexican High Commission. She was curious about Octavio Paz's days in Delhi (when he was the Mexican ambassador to India). We had invited her to the Diwali dinner six days earlier and, while the children ignited the firecrackers and sparklers, I told her the joyous reason why Sikhs celebrated the festival of lights. She asked me then about the difference between the Sikh and Hindu ideas on reincarnation. Whenever she said 'cows' it really meant 'chaos'. She had given beautifully illustrated books (by an artist called Posada) to my children; one was on the Mexican Day of the Dead. I checked if the books were appropriate for children – my daughter and my son were impressionable, and they would find it difficult to sleep if they heard a frightening ghost story. Maribel said, 'In Mexico the Day of the Dead is the most joyous and festive day . . . And she invited us to a gathering at her place. What is the party about? OK, we will call it a "Diwali fancy dress" party,' she said.

Maribel . . . The Day of the Dead . . . Dress . . . We introduced her to my tailor-master in Khan Market. My son and daughter and Maribel and I had gone to get our costumes made. I had no idea. Vaquero dress for my boy (and her boy), and Maharani for my girl (and her girl). The tailor-master handled Maribel's body differently, he touched her inappropriately and I scolded the rascal until he trembled, and when he took my measurements he was extremely cautious, maintaining five inches of distance with his so-called inch-i-tape, and my son laughed and laughed until he was on the floor. I often forget how much we laughed in '84.

How eerie that day was when Maribel picked up her glittery new dress and she resembled my mother as a young woman. She had her long hair braided – she told me it's called *trenzas* in Spanish. She told me more details about the Day of the Dead, the way the Mexicans cele-brate it; they cook for the absent ones, she said. The dead 'eat' on that day food they liked when alive. And the living eat *pan de muerto*, freshly baked bread shaped like an assemblage of bones, and sugar skulls. In Mexico, the Day of the Dead is celebrated with jokes, marigold flowers and laughter, Maribel said. And lots of alcohol.

And my children (Arjun and Indira) tried the dresses on. They had grand plans to go to school decked up in their new clothes on 14 November, Children's Day (and Nehru's birthday). Maribel and I had our own private plans for 14 November. We had tickets to attend the Nehru Memorial Lecture. Octavio Paz was going to deliver the lecture that year.

On 30 October I dropped Mohan at the train station. (I had packed his suitcase the previous night, and I had

130

forgotten his toothbrush.) From the station I took an auto-rickshaw to the Mexican High Commission. Maribel served hot chocolate and churros and played me her favourite song. Later I collected my children from school and we took another auto to stay at my brother's place in Greater Kailash. My brother was a wing commander in the Indian Air Force, he had fought the '71 war with Pakistan, which got him the Maha Vir Chakra from the President on recommendation of Mrs Gandhi. He had also participated in Operation Meghdoot when India took control of Siachen Glacier in Kashmir. His house was filled with sparkling medals and trophies. And knick-knacks from Russia. Bust of Yuri Gagarin. On 31 October when we heard the news about Mrs Gandhi's assassination we didn't eat. My brother played the saddest classical music on his HMV player, I remember his little dog stopped barking when it heard the music. Next morning I didn't send the children to school. They did their homework, and later they were eager to try on the newly stitched costumes and I gave them permission to do so only in their room. It was my daughter's idea to swap the costumes. We had a light lunch, and soon it was time for evening prayers. We washed our hands, covered our heads and prayed. During prayers my left eye kept flickering.

And then: a knock on the door . . . I will never forget those five minutes. Three hundred dreadful seconds. We never believed that any harm would come to us. My daughter kept saying she had to finish her homework. I forced the kids to hide under the bed upstairs. My brother loaded his pistol and he asked the Congress thugs to disappear and he even fired in the air. It was then the cops appeared and they said they were going to take away his weapon and they were there to protect us. My brother was not going to but I forced him to listen to the police inspector. As soon as the police disappeared the mob reappeared and they dragged my brother out and made him sing the national anthem and bow before a calendar image of the goddess Durga and cut his hair and his beard and cut his penis and cut his testicles and doused kerosene on him and burned him . . . and then my daughter, no, my son . . . my daughter saved me . . . she saved me . . . she was dressed like a boy, she had seen so many things . . . she is the one who went to the neighbours and because of her three or four women came and they formed a chain around me and would not give me up . . . Leave my mother alone, she said . . . and my son, that idiot, came down as if he was competing with his sister to save me . . . Give us your son, and the Congress thugs picked her up, took her and smeared her with a white explosive powder (as if they were playing holi) and burned her . . . phosphorus, I know it was phosphorus, Mohan had shown me phosphorus in the lab . . . we will burn your daughter as well, they said . . . but they fled with the loot, including the war medals and the colour TV . . . the screams of my 'son' . . . she never once said that she was a girl . . . sometimes I think if they had taken my real son I would have behaved differently.

[Pause.]

I helped them kill my own daughter.

You didn't go to the police?

Barefoot I ran after them . . . holding my 'daughter' tight I ran after them. Most of the Hindu men in the neighbourhood did nothing. Some applauded. It was not clear if they

132

were applauding me or the killers or the cops, who did nothing. I asked the cops for help, but there was no help. I ran all the way to the main police station and the SHO didn't register the preliminary FIR report ... He refused to file a complaint. 'Same thing will happen to you as happens to other Sikhs ...' At the police station there were other women as well. Similar stories. To stay there would have meant rape ... sure rape ... The sub-inspector didn't allow us to leave. Then a man showed up, God knows from where. He said I was his wife. He said I was not a Sikh, that I was his half-mad wife who had run away from the house taking advantage of the 'riots'. I didn't trust him, but I decided to trust him as it was the only way out of the police station. At that point I just wanted to save my son and I didn't care for the other women. The man took us to his big house and put us in the tiny room, the barsati on the roof terrace. He locked the barsati – he said this was for our own safety. There was no bathroom. My son clung to me tight. Two days later the man unlocked the barsati and drove us to the relief camp. He said Sikhs were really Hindus. He said the violence was wounding the Temple of India. On the way to the camp I kept saying to that good man, What have you done to my daughter? He looked at me with incomprehension. Then he wept.

At this point did you know anything about what had happened to Professor Singh?

No. From the camp I called home several times. But no one picked up the phone. I called the IIT Chairman. He didn't pick up the phone either.

Where were you?

133

I should have called Maribel earlier from the camp. But I was shocked and paralysed. So many women had been raped ... and two of them noticed that the same Congress leader, H. K. L. Bhagat, who, according to witnesses, had ordered his men to kill thousands of Sikhs and rape the women, was now there in the camp distributing blankets and food. The women had seen the Congress leader before. They pounced on him. Eighty-year-old Sikh men were crying like babies in the camp.

Just like one cannot forget Einstein's face, no matter how distorted, I am unable to forget the face of that monster H. K. L. Bhagat. Member of Parliament. Cabinet Minister. Ex-Mayor of Delhi.

I called Maribel and she came right away in a diplomatic car with security guards on four motorcycles. *Guardias de seguridad.* Maribel installed us in the High Commission. I simply can't tell my husband that I have lost my daughter. You tell him. Maribel, you are not allowed to tell him she is no more. Half a day later Maribel brought back the news, she was in tears, she said it is best I tell you now that your husband is no more. Don't lie, Maribel. The IIT Chair had accompanied her. He was waiting in the living room, and I refused to see him.

I slipped into a vegetable-like state. My son was playing in the other room. I asked Maribel not to tell him that his father was no more. My son had already observed a lot. He sketched a lot, and wrote a lot in his tiny journal. Circles, triangles, straight lines, gibbous eyes. Some of his images were right out of Maribel's book – imaginary insects and a profusion of strange saffron yellow flowers. Cempasúchitl.

But something had changed in our relationship. I was not able to touch him after that. I have not been able to touch anyone since November '84.

For a few days we played this grand elaborate game for him, as if all the violence was a game, as if it was really part of the Mexican celebrations. I told the boy his father had taken his engineering students to a factory in a foreign country.

What happened to your things at the house in IIT?

Maribel. She fell while retrieving the things. She broke her tooth. *Me quebré un diente!* she said. Charred LP player. The molten records resembled a Dalí exhibition. Most of the books that burned were our copies of Ramayana and Mahabharata and the Bhagavadgita. My husband had a twelve-volume translation of the Rig Veda. Half of these were reduced to ashes. So many other books were destroyed: *The Temple of the Golden Pavilion* by Yukio Mishima, two translations of the Adi Granth, *Orlando* by Virginia Woolf, *Shame* by Rushdie, *A History of the Sikhs* by Khushwant Singh, *Pale Fire* by Nabokov (first edition), a copy of the Bible Mohan purchased at an antiquarian book fair in Ithaca, an anthology of Punjabi Dalit litera-ture, *Dubliners* by James Joyce, poems by Shiv Kumar Batalvi and Dhani Ram Chatrik, *Correspondence Between Tolstoy and Gandhi*, Feynman Lectures, *El Llano en Llamas* by Juan Rulfo, *The Man Without Qualities* by Musil, *The Little Prince*, two books by Jean Amery, *The Moon and Sixpence* by Maugham, P. G. Wodehouse, Borges.

To come out of my vegetable state Maribel suggested trav-els. She was the one who got us passports and visas and I withdrew most of the money in the bank and my son from school and I flew to Italy. Professor Singh had already planned the trip, and we were waiting for our savings to build up …

Then we took the train to Milan and from Milan the train to Switzerland. The Alps. And Zurich. All I remember of Zurich are the roasted chestnuts we had after not eating for two days. On the way back we spent two nights at the Milan railway terminal, we had no more money left. That is where during a vulnerable moment I told my son that his father was no more. In that fascist train station (built by Mussolini, as I found out later) my mind and my body overflowed with suicidal thoughts. My son didn't believe his father was dead. He said he had seen him yesterday. Where? Behind the train to Zurich. On the train to Basel. I believed his fictions. Both of us started looking for his father in that fascist terminal. At first I thought he was an apparition. A chance meeting at the terminal, someone I knew was walking towards us. He was the chief librarian at the India International Centre, Delhi, and he was in Italy to attend a workshop on the Medici collection.

As long as you are alive your story is alive, my senior told me.

And he is the one who got me this position at the institute archives.

Any trouble here at the institute?

The director has been good to me in his own way; I have improved the archival collection. This is what I am good at and it kept me going. Ironically, it is in the libraries where I have always felt free. Another reason I continued is that my son knows I am always involved with the libraries and archives, and if he really wants to come back to me he knows where to locate me. But of late I have been losing hope, and the reason I decided to retire early is because I have lost all hope of his return. Over the years I have saved some money and I would like to start an oral history project. *As long as I am alive, my story is alive.* I cannot forget the unbroken voice of that woman who lives in the slums in Delhi, she lost twenty-six members of her family in a single day. *As long as I am alive I will feel ashamed to call myself an Indian,* the woman had screamed. At the end of the day all she had was her husband's leg, half eaten by dogs. *Agar Angrez hotey to hum bach jatey. In British-ruled India we would have survived.* That woman who held on to Gagan Singh's amputated finger. She doesn't know how to read or write but she carries an entire archive inside. I would like to locate all of them, and interview all the survivors. That woman whose fasting, mourning husband was burned before her eyes. Where is Nanaki Bai now? Does she comprehend the 'abnormal' better now? That girl with two ponytails, who did not speak for three months? What happened to that mourning tongue? Where is she now, the three-year-old who screamed at the peace marchers, *meri mummy ko mat maro, don't kill my mother?* Mira Bai? *Tin dhiyan si mayriyan. Lash vi nahi milee. I had three daughters. We couldn't even find their corpses.* I would do anything. I would locate, too, the stories of the dead. Stories of those who saved lives. Countless unsung heroes, Hindus and Muslims and Christians, who risked their own lives to save lives. This is going to be my monument to them all, and I would like to work without institutional interference. Do you understand?

Where is your son?

[Pause.]

Do you really think he is alive?

Who?

137

Your son . . .

Of course. He is waiting. Waiting for the right moment to surface. To come back to me. When we returned to Delhi from Milan the immigration guard gave him a dirty look. But after our return my son wanted to go back to the camp . . . He said he was sure his father was in the camp . . . Again I found it easier to believe him . . . So we returned . . . and there were so many helpless people there, so many jumbled emotions . . . those who had survived due to the kindness of neighbours, those who had been savaged by neighbours, those who had seen senior Congress Party leaders like Kamal Nath directing, inciting the mobs close to the parliament building . . . lament, helpless anger, lament, helpless rage . . . How roles had reversed in the camp. Men behaved like women and women like men. Children kept saying to phantom parents: *Take us home* . . . Maribel sent her own driver with us to Shimla . . . My son did not want to join the new school. I insisted. One day he didn't return home. He was only eight then.

Do you believe in God?

I used to. And now I only believe in music. Even now during my darkest moments I find myself reciting *pavan guru pani pita mata dharat mahat, divas raat dui dai daya khelay sagal jagat.* But I think God doesn't exist. All we have is music.

*　　*　　*

This recording I have heard more than twenty times by now. It always stops. Stops with a loud pounding sound. They were the monkeys on the roof in Shimla. I spent the rest of the night listening to her breathing punctuated occasionally by the sounds on the roof. One question not part of this recording: *Did you do anything to get justice?* Nelly didn't say anything. Outside the window snow kept falling. I knew at some point it would stop.

My name doesn't matter. What matters is my age. Soon I will turn fifty-six and I don't even have a house of my own.

I have lived in the mountains for twenty-five years now. For twenty-five years in this 'approximate' hill station. I love the crispness of the air here, and recognise the sounds and silences of this town, the bells and whistles. At nine o'clock the last train will roll into the Summer Hill station, I will hear the rumble and its echo, and around two in the morning a platoon of monkeys will climb up the roof of my rented apartment and cause a minor geological activity. They know I live alone and that is why they never fail to put on a special performance. After they leave all I will hear is silence. Andhera. Khamoshi. Once in a while the leaves and the fluttering of flags in the wind.

...

There is a reason I didn't remarry. A man was persistent, but I refused. To get married at this age, he said, is for companionship and to lie next to each other on the same bed, if not sex, for touch. I am afraid of being touched, I told him. Ever since I was little I have not been touched much, I lost my birth mother and birth father very young and Dar-ji didn't touch me at all, he would not even embrace or hug, and whatever I learned from my husband I seem to have forgotten. These days the only things I touch are books and even those, distantly.

...

Raj believes me when I say that I have given up all hope. How could a mother give up hope for her son's return? I would like to hug tightly my boy one last time. Every day I chart out

139

hundreds of thousands of different paths he would have followed. I write letters and emails to known and unknown individuals on those paths. Some respond with materials, which break my heart, and make me go through helpless rage. This is how I am assembling the 1984 archives.

He didn't come home from school, he took the toy train to Kalka, then the night train to Delhi, and from the railway station he walked to the so-called 'relief camp', but there was no camp any more, so he took the DTC bus to the IIT campus. Walking around, he felt hungry. His pockets empty. No more money. He felt like crying, and walked all the way to Bangla Sahib Gurdwara. I have charted hundreds and thousands of paths Arjun would have followed.

Morning brightened the mountains. Snow on all things living and dead. But it didn't last long and vaporised without melting. Then it rained hard. When it stopped raining the city erased its memory of snow. I found the drops of blood had disappeared in the bathroom. She had obviously noticed, and wiped them clean. I made tea. Nelly came to the living room sobbing. I gave her my shoulder. You didn't ask me a few things, she said. The most important one you left out. When I packed Mohan's suitcase that night, when I forgot to pack the toothpaste (Promise toothpaste) I was wondering what Mohan was thinking.

Nelly realised she was sobbing, a belated awareness, and tried to stop. You didn't ask about the night of packing. Not everything was at peace despite his good spirits. There were the usual tensions at work, rivalries, and a difficult situation that had cropped up at the hostel, something between a student and a Dalit employee, said Nelly. But I was thinking that night about what Mohan was thinking about me. In August '84, two months after the attack on the Golden

Temple, Mohan and I had gone to Punjab to attend a cousin's wedding. I still recall the sombre mood during the ceremony and the reception. The boy's father didn't show up, he had opposed the wedding because the girl was a Hindu. Something about that atmosphere was stifling, the August heat stifling. What does it matter? I said to a relative. Of course, it doesn't matter to you. Because you are a Dalit.

This had never come up before. Of course she didn't say 'Dalit', her tongue used a more derogatory word. But the certainty and uncertainty of the revelation stunned me to silence, said Nelly. Some relatives standing around us rushed to denial. No, you are not impure. You are different. You are also very fair ... The relative who revealed the secret raised her hand to her mouth. I shouldn't have, she said, said Nelly. No one knew the details about my past, no one was able to guide me to the unknown. My own memories, if I ever formed memories of my early years, were virtually non-existent.

In Delhi I asked Mohan if this mattered to him. Why should it matter to me? he said. We were in the kitchen. He was doing the dishes and I was drying them with a cloth. But if I had grown up in an impoverished Dalit family, we would not have married. But you didn't grow up in a Dalit family. I mean if I had, let us just assume? Mohan was silent. Both of us felt like orphans that night, said Nelly. For more than a month or a couple of months I didn't feel like sleeping with him. We did not sleep in the same room. It is all coming back to me now. When my father would tell me about birds, he once said that I, too, had come to him as a bird. My father never told me about my adoption. Often he shielded me from his relatives. I know it must have been difficult for him. He was very bold, now that I think about it, he was also very wrong. All my memories of my birth mother and birth father are

141

totally expunged. Why was I adopted? Is it because my biological parents disappeared? Always I shudder when the thought crosses my mind, said Nelly.

Were their Dalit bodies set on fire the way upper castes often do? Or did they merely endure the 'normal' invisible everyday violence?

Caste, said Nelly, how ironic. It is embedded in all organised religions. Even those with aspirations to eliminate it.

The day was progressing quickly. Outside the window the clouds were low, but the sun had started to play games. Fresh light as it fell on fresh snow on the mountains had the feel of Japanese prints by Hokusai. In one of his notebooks, Hokusai writes about breaking the rules set by old masters, and I don't know why while listening to Nelly I thought also about Hokusai. So much information had erupted in such a short span of time. Unable to absorb it fully, I felt a knot in my belly, a choking sensation in my throat, as if I were standing on the summit of an eight-kilometre-high mountain, looking down. Inside that safe room I experienced vertigo. Some feel vertigo in their calves or groin, I always get the sensation in my chest. I sat on the kitchen chair to recover balance. When I recovered, my eyes opened to the rectangle of light pouring in through the window. Outside, the city was mute, gleaming in the sun. Soon after melting the snow, I thought, the sun would heal the grass and the oaks. My healing, too, was connected to Nelly's healing, I thought. She had cleared blood from the bathroom, and she limped when she walked. Something was not right, I knew then.

During breakfast I asked her more about her adoption. She raised her voice (so unlike her). Then a phone call. I think she was expecting the call. The wrinkles on her face moved like minor mountains as she spoke. Briefly I phased out. The sun disappeared again, but I knew it was only a

142

game. Nelly was on the phone for a long time. The door-bell rang. Perhaps that is what brought an end to the call. The postman came up. She collected the parcel. The package was not addressed to her. 'For you,' she said.

It was an overnight delivery dispatched by Father. The khaki package heavy. Momentarily I thought all his awards and medals were inside.

Medals were awarded in '85 to police officers for meritorious, distinguished or gallantry work performed in 1984. 'Meritorious' is the code word for mediocre losers, Father told me once. 'Distinguished' means the officer is just about to retire. The 'gallantry' medal is the only real medal. But then I don't know why Father received a gallantry in '85, his third 'real medal'. In '72 he got a gallantry because he nabbed a gang of dacoits. Again in '79 he received one for rescuing a kidnapped child. This was reported in the papers, and it raised his professional profile. He was treated like a real hero because he had injured himself during the rescue mission. Father fell from a horse, fracturing both his arms. The only time I saw him grow a beard. During those days when he was in the hospital ward, I would stand in front of a mirror at home wearing his police hats.

What was in the package? I need to explain a few things. Without informing Nelly I had called Father and politely asked him to help locate Arjun. The old man, retired now, still knew how to pull a few strings within the police force, and I provided all the information to help trace the missing boy, who (if alive) was now a man thirty-five years old.

Nelly was hiding something important from me. Arjun never attended that school in Shimla. The headmistress of the school told me 'no one with that name was enrolled in our school in '84, '85 or '86'.

143

I must mention that I was not expecting Father to respond so quickly. In fact when Nelly said 'the package is for you' I imagined a collection of papers from my colleague at Cornell. Or papers connected to Dow Chemicals acquiring Union Carbide and the latest soil and water report on Bhopal. What arrived instead was a package containing the Hindi 'translation'. Clara had suggested the project to Father during the one and only Skype call. He had not been able to expunge the contents of the call from his memory, and translated almost all the myths for my daughters.

Almost all of them. For he had ignored a few. He neither acknowledged nor translated the 'modern myths'. No handwritten note fell out of the package explaining why he ignored the five new myths I had formulated for my American daughters, Urvashi and Ursula. Five myths connected to violence in post-independence India. One of them involved November '84. A father and son walk on corpses, burning carcasses. Stumble upon piles of hair, burnt rubber tyres, amputated limbs and ash. The son asks his father about those men, who returned home after setting bodies on fire, men who returned after rape. What did they tell their children and wives? Did the wives go to bed with them that night? The father doesn't respond. He continues to listen to his son's strange questions: Were there women who denied sex to their husbands? For how long did they refuse to make love?

Father's translation or rather 'lack of translation' distracted us. Instead of helping me persuade Nelly to reveal details about her adoption, we got sidetracked. Nelly had just begun telling me about the origin of the word 'caste' when the package arrived. How the Portuguese seafarers saw social relations in India in the fifteenth century . . . I must have been completely out of my mind. I told her about the details, the 'translation'. Now I know I committed a big faux pas by handing her the package.

Nelly read the untranslated passages silently towards the end. After she was done I murmured a few incomprehensible words. She didn't ask me to repeat or explain; slowly the disturbance within me dissipated on its own.

She was not mad at me, but she gave me an interrogative look. 'Instead of composing these absurd "modern myths" why not write about the boy who didn't return? It is not just your father who is living the lie, but you as well.'

'Me?'

'Yes, you.'

Now that you have shown me these pages, and before this asked all your schoolboyish questions, let me ask you my own, said Nelly. Not that they are significant, not many things in my remaining life are, but they might be to you.

145

I know the answer, and perhaps I am right, but I would like to hear it from you, said Nelly. (Some of her old gestures returned, and her hands were shaking.) That answer is more significant than any real or imaginary drops of blood you happen to have seen now or twenty-five years ago . . . You were Mohan's favourite student. In his eccentric scheme you were placed at the very top, special. You knew this, the entire class did. Mohan rarely invited students home to dinner, not even star students, but he made an exception. The star students would come to tea (two or three times a year) and my interaction with them was minimal. Open the door, make tea, serve snacks, then disappear to my room. It was useless eavesdropping. After the students left he would tell me about them, what he really thought about them despite the grades; at times he would pronounce harsh judgements.

You were an exception. You came with exceptional talent, a 'model', an 'ideal', and you were well grounded in the arts. It was possible to have a real, intelligent conversation. He made a judgement about you as well – the difference is that he made the judgement before inviting you to our place. I was curious. When you first came to our house I was not taken by you. You were shy and did not say much, and you were in awe of your professor. Mohan looked visibly pleased with himself. Then I looked at your sandals, the black sandals and they made me laugh. The sandals didn't match your body, you had a strange aesthetic sense . . .

Twenty-five years later you did not have to come back to tell me that you had joined Cornell. I checked the website. Over the years I have learned to use the Internet. I had gone to the university website to check if Gergina was still there. She was Mohan's first love (before he met

146

me), a fellow graduate student, and he had broken her heart. I wanted to tell her that the person she had loved was dead and gone. Gergina was there on the website, a full professor now. A distinguished-looking woman ageing gracefully. And your name was next to hers. And I didn't send her an email. How does one explain something that cannot be explained? In her mind the man she loved once was still alive (and also dead). Most likely she had not heard. I thought it was perhaps for the best not to disturb her peace.

One by one all the star students of Mohan wrote to me. To this day I don't know how they got hold of my address, but the letters arrived here in Shimla, and they all made it within three or four years; the last one arrived in 1989, when the world was going through massive upheavals. That wall crumbled in Berlin. I say 'last', because I was not expecting a letter from you. A visit, yes. In fact, till the beginning of '89 none of his students mattered; even you, who were so important, ceased to matter.

You talk obsessively now about that railway platform photo, but have you forgotten the photo we never took? I wish I'd had a camera that day. On the surface it was an ordinary day, but before it ended it revealed all that was carefully concealed. Mohan had invited you to yet another dinner. His ex-room-mate from Cornell, an Italian American, now a professor of literature, was in town. I cooked Bengali-style fish. Our guest is magnetically drawn to Mohan's 'dancing girl' and 'priest king', the Harappa artefacts. His eyes pop out as he rolls in his hand the Indus seals. A script impossible to translate. It is best certain things never get translated, he says. He, our charming guest, holds court that night, delights us with short bios of authors we never heard of before. We have only one bottle, but the

147

wine is good. Conversation moves to a book, I remember, by Moravia. Our guest recites a fragment that has been troubling him, and because of that passage he finds it difficult to read fiction. All fiction. Technically it is a simple situation. X invites Y, his best friend, to dinner, and while X (the host) disappears for five minutes to the basement to get wine, X's wife leans towards Y and kisses him. What should Y do? No matter what choice he makes he is doomed. Should he tell X? Not tell X? Will X believe him? Even if X believes him how will the telling affect the friendship? And what if Y chooses not to tell? Then the Italian American pauses, and for a brief moment there is absolute silence around the table, and then everyone laughs.

You were the only one who didn't laugh. I had observed you while the Italian American was narrating the story. The way your body shrank. Your face transformed, and its colour. As if you were not there. You concealed yourself. I had no idea – I still don't know – if the others noticed.

When you recovered you told a horrible Sikh joke as if you wanted me to dislike you. You knew I hated those jokes. (Repelled by your 'surd' and 'sardine' I made you stop.) When you left you didn't even bother shaking hands with me that night. You made yourself repulsive and vanished. And a few days later I heard about your jaundice. At first I doubted the sickness was real. But I didn't want you to die. When I was a girl the rickshaw-wallah who took me to school died of 'pilia', his eyes had turned yellow before he stopped coming. For a month you vacated the IIT hostel and moved to your parents' house. Mohan was the one who encouraged me to go and see you. I called you. Mohan was the one who gave me the phone number. The maid picked up. She gave me the address. I changed city buses twice and made it to Amrita Sher-Gil Marg. You

148

know how difficult it is for women to travel on those buses. I took a day off only to find out that your parents' house was not far from the International Centre. Because it was an elite neighbourhood there was no trace of slums. The houses were bigger and more majestic than ours. Outside your bungalow on that billionaires' boulevard real cops were posted, loaded with carbines. Two or three black cars and a jeep chaotically parked just outside the gate. I presented myself to the guards, they didn't frisk me, they were respectful. There was no one on the veranda. I walked in. The bookshelves and other objects in the house suggested this family was steeped in deep knowledge about the world. It appeared the place had several servants, but at that time none visible. Service people cannot afford such places, such a house comes to one as inheritance or through high levels of corruption. In the kitchen I found the old maid in a sari. Your parents were not home. She told me you were fast asleep. She had gone to your room. I heard the conversation. You didn't want to see me. Absolutely not. You commanded the maid to get rid of me. I overheard just enough. On the way home it occurred to me that something was keeping you from introducing me to your parents. Certain things don't need proof.

Later on the railway platform you pretended this episode didn't take place. You relied on ambiguity. But you never introduced me to your father as your professor's wife. I could have been anyone. Someone's mother. Thirty or thirty-one boys on the platform. All your father saw that day was the wave of my hand, farewell to you all. All he saw was a lie.

3.

Particles

I don't know what she meant about the lie, but I moved out of Nelly's place and got a room in a hotel. I could see pain and outrage accumulating inside me, but tried to stay calm. The most difficult thing was the mirror in the bathroom, completely unnecessary. I taped three or four sheets on that clumsily polished surface. It was a four-star hotel, on the highest mountain in the city, with angled views of young chir pines, walls of deodars and swatches of green, and comfortable. I spent two continuous days in my room, unwell, filled with a kind of nausea not experienced for twenty or twenty-five years. On the wall across from my bed there were huge black-and-white photos of colonial tiger hunts, and the constant gaze of white sahibs stirred strange, uncomfortable thoughts within me.

On TV the main news items (regardless of the spin) highlighted the occupation of Kashmir, its alienated youth. The last two decades had left 90,000 dead. Thousands had disappeared. Women had been raped, entire villages, by men in uniform. Abuse. Torture. Mass graves. Despite that, the armed forces and paramilitaries enjoyed absolute impunity. Equally disturbing was the ongoing tragedy of Kashmiri Pandits living in exile. Local news focused on the collapse of a bridge in the Commonwealth Games complex. Twenty-five years ago there was only one state-run channel; now in 'new and shining India' 136 channels were telling the 'truth' in a babel of voices.

For a long time I stared at the empty, redundant swimming pool outside the window, and for some unknown reason thought about Father's swimming pool in Delhi. I

don't know when exactly I called the bookshop downstairs to ask if they had stories set in Shimla. The bellboy got me every single forgettable book by Kipling. Nevertheless I flipped through those collectors' editions. Kipling still had power over me. Buying the books, sa'ab? Get me three bottles of wine instead, I said. Sula. Worst in the world.

Nelly didn't call me either, I was the one who did, but something kept her from returning my calls. I felt I had perhaps offended her by not saying much. I had not uttered a single meaningful word.

My father, too, hunted tigers. When he visited Jabalpur to attend a police conference he developed a passion for the wild. He got lucky and shot the big cat 'Surma'. The tiger was processed by the taxidermist in Calcutta. Once a year men in our house in Delhi would spread the skin (and the attached head) on the lawns. Burning bright, flames of winter sun would dry the kill. Inside, displayed on the wall, the head gleamed at night. When I was a child the tiger would create extreme emotional upheavals within me. I was proud of my father, and also hated him. 'Dislike' was not a strong enough emotion. In all he hunted thirteen tigers, I don't know where the other twelve are. In post-independence India more than nine thousand were eliminated by foreign and indigenous hunters. Ironically, it was Indira Gandhi who imposed a so-called ban in the early seventies. One by one I consumed the bottles of horrible Sula red and then switched to beer. I heard inter-mittently the occasional whistle of a train. Long, long, short, long. Thick clouds galloped towards my window. Yes, long ago, an extremely strong and beautiful woman had stirred a powerful attraction within me that is hard to articulate. The whole thing started as pure lust, I remem-ber still the dizzy feeling, the cloud of confusion, the delirium. The jacaranda earrings I made for her. How fool-ish and bold of me to make earrings out of seed pods which essentially look like vaginas. Nelly wore them only once, in his absence, and that is not a lie. I thought then that she was the love of my life (whatever it meant) and that is not a lie. But the truth is that I was really afraid. Afraid that

155

day on the railway platform. I didn't act, I could not, not because of the reason Nelly implied. Yes, indeed, long ago, in my wildest thoughts I did wish my professor dead once or twice (just as I wished my father dead when I was very young). But the wish was not real. Nelly didn't understand me completely. She, too, knew the truth partially, and that is not a lie. Fear had penetrated my bones, and paralysed me, that is why I did not try to save him on the platform. Not because I wished him dead. I know now any action on my part would not have helped. I regret it though; if only I had tried (regardless of the consequences) I would have been hurt less, and by now I would have figured out a way to heal the wound.

You are living a lie. Nelly was mad at me.

Bubbles in a glass of beer grow twice as big by the time they rise to the very top. Students almost always get this wrong: Why is the diameter of the bubble at the bottom of the glass half the diameter of the one at the top? A simple calculation shows that pressure-induced size reduction is no more than 10 per cent even in a very tall glass of beer. So, what is the real reason?

While rising, each bubble acts as a typical nucleation site. Moving up, it gathers dissolved carbon dioxide, which causes expansion. Size change also changes its speed. But that is a separate question, a separate set of equations.

My cellphone was ringing.

The IIT Chair's name and number stared at me. I let it ring. I was done with helium. I had no idea how to introduce Professor Osheroff. Helium-3 was not even my area. And I was also done with my area as well – rheology.

Rhea is the second largest moon of Saturn.

Wispy and full of icy cliffs.

The only moon with rings around it.

The Rings of Rhea.

Beautiful and melancholic like Saturn.

Rhea is also a bird.

Unable to fly.

A distant cousin of the ostrich.

Both the moon and the bird were named after the 'daughter of sky and Earth' and the 'mother of gods'. Rhea is a myth. Rhea is the wife of Time. And Time, back then, was a myth. 'Time' or 'Cronus' or 'Saturn' ate his own children. Rhea hid a newborn in a cave and gave Cronus a stone wrapped in a rag. Cronus ate that stone. In ancient Greek *rhea* means 'flow' or 'discharge'. *Panta rei*, says Heraclitus: 'everything flows'.

What appealed to me about rheology, at least during those early years, was its focus on deformation and flow of materials. Anomalous ones. Materials which betray Newton's laws. 'Thickness' or 'viscosity' fail to characterise them fully the way they do with air and water and even honey. Blood, clay, toothpaste, biological molecules, liquid crystals, foam, paint, menstrual blood and lava are non-Newtonian. Anomalous equations guide them through various incarnations.

A spider crawled to the bottom of my beer glass and slowly moved up. I surveyed the curious movement of its small wriggly legs on glass. Detecting trouble or 'instability' it returned quickly to the base. 'Nature is altogether out of it.' I couldn't but help think of the one student who had tried to 'save' Professor Singh. At least he made an attempt while I stood on the platform numb and paralysed. What did he get in return? An iron bar that missed his head, and hit his shoulder instead. He fell on the platform and wriggled. Then he got punched in his mouth. Blood gushed out of him. He was not even a friend of the professor's, not a favourite student, not an exceptionally bright student. No one thought he was 'brave'. We all used to call him an expert masturbator. But when the need arose this mediocrity acted 'brave'. He deserved a gallantry medal for trying. But he too ran away after blood gushed out. He kept running and never looked back. He is now a professor at Clarkson (Potsdam, New York). I traced him through the alumni association, and drove to his place and stayed with him. Tactfully over a drink I brought up Professor Singh. I saw him turn numb. Terrified. Now after so many years it was his turn to grow numb. He urged me not to open up that can of worms. I remember nothing, he insisted. His voice broke down. Nothing. I told him clearly about my project, also the fact that I was going to mention him for the sake of posterity. He raised his voice, which kept breaking. Is this why you have come? His wife shoved him into the study. Then she asked me to pack all my things and leave as soon as possible. On the way back I had thought and thought a lot about India and my father.

When I was eight or nine my father took me along to the remote areas on the so-called 'police inspections'. Together we travelled to the high bur-fi-lay mountains. He drove the 4x4 jeep himself. Our luggage included his hunting gun. I sat in the front, since Mother was not with us. The driver sat at the back.

Father drove to Kalka, Solan and Shimla, and continued on the road to Kullu-Manali because he wanted me to see (or rather hunt in) the highest mountains. The road was a marvel of high-altitude engineering. He drove all the way to Rohtang Pass, 3,978 metres high. Rohtang, he explained, means a 'pile of bones'. He was right. The pass resembled a Yeti's icy knuckle.

We stood looking down. Cold wind struck our cheeks. I thought my cap was going to fall off, and all I saw was rock and road and no trees. Shivering, I returned to the parked jeep. Father encouraged me to take pictures. My hands shook when I used the metallic camera. Then we drove through a thin veil of clouds to the origin of Beas, the river water white and foamy, roaring and kicking and galloping towards the plains. We drank tea directly from the Thermos, and walked a mile to the base of the glacier, where we found a mountaineer's shoe, and a minute later a perfectly preserved body no longer attached to it. The mountaineer's face was well preserved too. Father and I hurried back to the jeep where the driver was waiting, a lump of snow in my hand. The lump melted drop by drop through my fingers, giving me immense pain and pleasure, both at once.

Father got directions from the nomads to the police check post, where he alerted the saluting, trembling havildar on duty about the body and then we were on our way again. During the descent, we encountered more nomads and flocks of sheep. The animals slowed us down, and when the jeep finally picked up speed I had to put on a thick sweater and zip up my jacket.

Those days Rohtang Pass (or Rohtang La, in Tibetan) was not connected to Leh. Father had promised to show me the semi-arid Leh. So he called a few important friends from the local police station, and from the valley on the other side of Rohtang a helicopter picked us up and spiralled to Ladakh. There we saw snow and a desert, and Father did some hunting, but what took our breath away was the chiru antelope migrating. In Leh we also bought three or four shahtoosh ring-shawls for relatives.

The same helicopter, a couple of days later, dropped us at the base of Mount Affarwat, 4,143 metres high. Father told me that he thought it would be a good idea to climb that beautiful mountain. He gave me a little test. You must learn to take only the most essential things along, he said. What would you keep and what would you discard? I told him it was not a good idea to carry his gun during the climb. Father patted my back, thrice. He left the gun with the driver and we hiked up extremely light.

From the summit of Affarwat we could see that 8,126-metre wonder of the world. The mountain looked semi-naked, and I was not surprised when the local police officer told us its name. Nanga Parbat, or the Naked Mountain.

In my hotel room I thought over and over about our journey to the 'highest' mountains. I know Father has not forgotten the journey either. He rarely forgets. Our house in Delhi is filled with paintings of Nanga Parbat. He commissions his favourite artists to do a 'Nanga Parbat' for him. He loves the magic of mountains and starts glowing when someone mentions Kipling, Kim, or K1, K2, K3 . . . I still remember that beautiful story he told me, the tiny myth about the origin of mountains . . . The police helicopter was flying over Affarwat when he told me about the mythic orogenesis.

Once upon a time elephants were able to fly. Completely white and delightful, the flying creatures also destroyed a lot of objects, houses, and trees. One day a fatigued elephant perched on a big tree. The tree fell. On several children. So, with a single thunderbolt, the gods cut off its wings ... Collective punishment ... What we see as mountains now are really those elephants without wings, and the ever-thickening clouds hovering about the upper slopes are really the detached wings. Together, the clouds and the mountains mourn their loss, and what comes down is rain.

The next few days it rained in Shimla and in the overheated hotel room I drifted in and out of a kind of dizziness and nausea I rarely experience. The white elephants remained invisible most of the time. Several times in my room or in the hotel lobby I heard sounds of bells wafting in from a faraway school or a temple.

When the rain stopped, I stepped out for an aimless walk, and spent some time browsing through dusty volumes at the rare bookshop on the Mall Road. The owner had a tiny TV and was watching a documentary on the Siachen glacier. Utopian proposals to build a 'peace park' at Siachen were being discussed. I bought a bottle of mineral water from the chemist's shop, where, quite unexpectedly, I ran into a vaguely familiar nocturnal figure, the night porter wearing the same threadbare baseball cap. Suraj. He was sleep-starved, and informed me that he was heading to his village later that evening. Every year he was allowed a month off.

161

'Who will take care of your nephew and niece?'

'My sister-in-law is here,' he said.

Suraj inspired me to do some planning, and that evening when he took the bus to his village in the high mountains I accompanied him. As the bus gained elevation he opened up, and even told me how he dealt with the chamgadar, the bat in the library. But my mind was elsewhere. I found it difficult to talk, and difficult to listen, especially to human voices. I yearned for silence, not absolute silence, but the silence of the high mountains.

The bus driver, speeding on that narrow, unsafe road, steered wildly like Captain Billions-of-Blue-Blistering-Barnacles in *Tintin*. Through the window I saw the abuse. Fewer trees and animals. That old magic of the landscape had vanished for ever.

Suraj drifted into deep sleep; he leaned against my shoulder for an hour, then woke up rubbing his eyes like a child, and asked me a sudden question, which left me unsettled.

'Sa'ab, do you suffer from a pain?'

Unable to respond, I looked out the window.

Nelly's pain was real. My 'pain' was merely a fantasy. I indulged in pain. I had no pain really. I had no guilt. Yes, there was shame. But shame is not the same thing as pain.

Yet I was unable to answer Suraj. He had used the Hindi/Urdu/Pahari word 'dard' for pain, and for some unknown reason that four-letter word cut right through me.

'Why do you ask, Suraj?'

Intuitively he had understood something about me. He never invited me, but it was implied that I would stay at his place. His brother was away as well. When we looped up the narrow, numinous path to that log cabin of a house,

Suraj used a key. Then he ran to the shop to get provisions and fixed us a meal. While eating he mentioned his neighbour, an old man who knew how to get rid of 'pain'.

'Perhaps tomorrow.'

Later that evening we dressed warmly and he took me on a short familiarising walk through his village. Now and then he described how a snow leopard skinned a musk deer. It struck me that Suraj's own pain had abruptly ended because he was no longer in a big city. He walked 'naturally' here, a walk he was unable to walk in Shimla. Here, I was the one who felt unnatural – here I had to relearn the 'walk'. Suraj pointed his index finger towards the neighbouring mountain. Slowly my gaze moved in that direction. The slopes were black and purple (the incline over sixty degrees) and the dead trees on the slopes vertical and horizontal cylinders of coke and coal, some still standing. That ruined, blackened brick building standing on the ridge, Suraj said, used to be a sanatorium.

Then followed a long, almost inchoate monologue.

'Sa'ab, I was five or six years old when that mountain lit up so bright it was possible to find lost objects inside our house.

'I have not been able to forget what happened when our village for the first time ever decided to celebrate the festival of Dusshera in that grand, spectacular way by burning effigies of the demons. I have no idea why the elders chose that mountain and not this one. The fire started not by lightning or by a bidi or an electric wire. The demon figures were burning and exploding at the base of the mountain by the river . . . Fortunately, there was no one inside the old sanatorium at the top, otherwise there would have been more casualties. The sanatorium had been long shut down, and other than old furniture there was nothing

163

inside. To this day, sa'ab, I remember the sound of fire-crackers . . . and the sounds of fire and the terrified animals.

'The colour of the sun changed. For days on end the air smelled of smoke.'

I wanted to stop Suraj midway during that near poetic moment of recall, and I wanted to urge him to speak directly to the recorder. But I knew that even a flicker of an interruption ran the risk of making him self-conscious, so I refrained. I listened carefully to him and his hypnotic account of fire that engulfed the forest. Now I don't remember half of the words he spoke. Some of them stir me still. 'Aag'. 'Agni'. 'The god of fire has two heads, and

three legs and seven tongues'. The effigies, he told me in Hindi, stood by the river on the lower slopes of that mountain, and once the big sparks touched the firs and pines everything grew agitated, the fire spread like mad, sweeping, combing the entire slope. I don't know if Suraj knew that if the festival effigies had been planted on the ridge, at the very top of the mountain, the fire would have been contained. But because the effigies (with ten or twenty demon heads) stood on the lower slopes, the hot air moved up like a leopard, facil-itating combustion.

164

Suraj's neighbour, the pain doctor, used to work for the TB sanatorium before it was shut down. He had no proper medical training – he used to work as a dhobi at the sanatorium. Nevertheless, villagers travelled many miles to the dhobi's place to get rid of their 'pain'.

Suraj narrated an ensemble of success stories, and he was not pleased when I declined the offer to consult the doctor. I knew my response offended him.

I decided to spend one more day and then return. That day, in search of silence, I walked, and the more I walked the more the place looked familiar. Like a dog I tried to sniff out the place. Like a dog I anticipated the hot spring (rather the 'thermal spring') long before I found myself by the banks of the river in its fog.

Water at a near boiling temperature gushed out of an orifice and merged with the cold glacial meltwater of a river.

I saw not a single tourist, and was certain that most religious festivals were over. There were no more than three or four villagers bobbing up and down in that safe confluence where the water temperature was thirty to forty degrees Celsius, and there was fog.

It was all coming back to me now. Father and I had come to this exact place many years ago. We dived in and quickly moved to the warm zone in the middle.

I removed my clothes and entered the river.

Feet first.

Father and I had come to this precise confluence of hot and cold water. Then snow started falling . . . I dipped and ran my fingers in eddies and vortices. Snow settled on

165

Father's face and his thin moustache and snow settled on me, and everything around us was mute and vibrating, both at once. Warm vapour kept rising, melting the snow on us into drops, but new snow kept falling, accumulating the muteness . . . and the highest mountains up the river resembled a giant writing desk that belonged to the gods. From where we were submerged in warm water a distant mountain looked like a woman who had just washed her hair and turned her neck . . . a frozen wave . . . a smiling Yeti.

Fog.

I thought about thermal gradients and brought to mind the rheology of molten rock, and I thought about the real reason our mountains were formed – to cool the Earth. The mobile plate tectonics are merely a response to the extreme heat-transfer problems that take place inside the belly of the Earth. And that extreme high temperature and pressure flow of that complex, extreme heterogeneous fluid beneath our feet is also responsible for Earth's magnetic field, a field which helps us find our way, and helps birds migrate, and protects our planet from harmful radiation that comes from the sun. Without that invisible flow, our Earth would die more or less like Mars, I thought.

Soon, I thought, in 25 million years, the waters between Australia and Asia will move elsewhere, and the two continents will merge. Now it was all making sense. Everything flows. Nothing is constant. India was once a part of Africa, and India separated from Africa, turned and moved and turned and moved and collided with Asia. India was never constant, and its Himalayas were never constant, they are still growing, and undergoing toroidal motion, and after all the growing they will shrink and turn and shrink and turn again. And then I thought: What holds things together is more important than what separates them.

We slept in a damp dak bungalow that night, Father and I, and shared a quilt as damp as the room, and despite hundreds of embers in the brazier, the room was very cold. Before going to bed he cleaned and oiled his gun and read a book he always carried along. Nehru's *History of India*.

On the bus to Shimla I thought a lot about Nehru's *History* and I thought how limited our understanding of time is. So many moments have vanished for ever . . . and by the time we made it to the bus terminal the only question on the tip of my tongue was: How would Nehru (who died in 1964) write about 1984? How would the great man formulate the missing chapter on the deeds of his daughter and his two unworthy grandsons? And: How will I write about my father?

Back in Shimla, by strange coincidence, I got the same room number in the hotel. 48. In the overheated, pine-smelling room I pieced together everything Nelly had told me (directly or indirectly), even through her silences. I was not going to dwell on the distant past. Nelly required my assistance, but was reluctant to ask. Something didn't feel right. Something didn't make sense. An idea plants itself, tucks itself inside one's head. All the little jigsaw pieces that presented themselves to me during that brief span of time in Shimla suggested that someone was hurting her.

For three nights I slept with the windows open, and thought about her and thought a lot about my father.

Four days later she called. We agreed to meet in the lobby. The wound was healing, her limp was slightly better.

Now it was possible to take courage and be more direct.

I didn't tell her about my trip to the high mountains this time, we only talked about her. The scar on Nelly's cheek was from long ago, she said. When I insisted, she explained that it was almost twenty years old. In 1993 just before the so-called inquiry into the pogroms, a lawyer had approached her at the institute. (The National Archives in Delhi, harder to penetrate than Kafka's Castle, and the Police Archives had destroyed many files connected to the violence, but because of work done by several human rights organisations, a huge non-governmental archive had assembled itself; Nelly's effort at the Institute of Advanced Studies was a small but important contribution.)

'The Doordarshan TV Archives either destroyed the tapes connected to October/November '84 or put them away in boxes that would do Stalin's Russia proud. Or so the lawyer told me,' said Nelly. 'During our many conversations he urged me to travel to Delhi as a witness against the man under investigation. At first I said "yes" and then "no". My body responded in a strange way at the mere thought of travelling to that city. In '84, from the upstairs room in my saviour's house where we had initially taken refuge, I had witnessed two women being raped. No clothes on, dishevelled hair, the women completely exposed. Four men discharged their hate into those two one by one, then again. Children were made to watch the spectacle, and I had witnessed it all from the barsati. I felt like screaming, I felt disembodied. The lawyer later made me aware of the silence and denial around sexual violence. Sikh men chose silence, Hindu men chose complete denial. The loudest denials came from those who had committed the crimes. He begged me to say "yes" and gave me the other option – if you don't feel safe travelling "home" then our organisation could be persuaded to send a legal team to Shimla. Maybe we will succeed this time to get the rape trials started.

'Next week a man came to the library. I was alone in the photocopier room, about to copy a long article on "Churchill and the Bengal Famine". He entered without knocking, and sealed my lips with his filthy hands. I felt cold metal on my forehead, then against my cheek. "One word," he said, "and you are finished. No one will remember you any more." The institute director's office was right above us, and next to it was Lady Curzon's boudoir.

'While he pressed me against the staircase,' she continued, 'and punched my lower body, I saw her clearly in her Victorian costume, Lady Curzon's hat at an angle. The Vicereine gave me the courage to scratch his skin with my nails. I managed to injure him a bit.

'Then he hit my chest with his elbow again and again and then hit me one last time on my nose and was gone. I stared at the few drops of blood on the wooden floor. Drops of congealed blood, no longer mine. It is so easy to make that red thing flow out of our bodies. With my chunni I wiped it.

'When my body started hurting badly I thought all the best our civilisation has to offer in the form of books and all the worst (in the form of that filthy man) had converged for five or six minutes in the photocopier room of a crumbling building filled with apparitions of some other empire. The lawyer returned. I refused to record my statement. I followed yet another inquiry.

'Nothing came of it. Nothing. So many other bolder witnesses were there too. One had refused an offer of thirty million rupees from the perpetrators and inciters. Two retracted their statements under pressure, and turned hostile. Two were killed. Some Sikh leaders sided with the perpetrators. Some shameless Sikh men became rich doing the dirty work for the Congress, pressurising the witnesses. All charges against the accused Congress leader were withdrawn. He was promoted to the rank of a cabinet minister. The inquiry and many other inquiries and committees resembled a farce.'

Nelly's cheek and her forehead carried traces of what I had noticed on the face of someone else, a 73-year-old man. Five or six years before, during a flight to Europe, I found myself sitting next to him as he flew from the US to Delhi to be a witness at another so-called court. Of course he didn't disclose the exact reason. I found out about it later in the papers. The justice system protected the criminals and punished the victims. During that flight the elderly man did share some of his painful memories. A fellow passenger, sitting across the aisle, asked him gently: 'Why don't you Sikhs forget what happened a long time ago?' The elderly man paused for a while and said, 'For the same reason we Indians don't forget British colonialism, the Amritsar Massacre or Mahatma Gandhi's Dandi march. We don't even forget mythological events like Diwali and Dusshera. And you want me to forget something that happened as recently as in 1984? Did you do something wrong then? Is that why you want us to forget?' The elderly man's wounds had become scars, but inside he was still deeply disturbed, unable to achieve equilibrium.

Over time Nelly's wound healed, but it triggered PTSD, an acronym she didn't know then.

When I met Mrs Singh after a long gap of years the first thing I noticed were the scars, even before I noticed how much she had aged. The scars for some reason also reminded me of an exhibition by an artist in San Francisco. In his paintings, white people had proper faces, and black people were simply dots or smudges. In the hotel lobby

170

Nelly opened up, sharing fragments from a long-concealed past. She ordered her coffee black and added no sugar. The waiter, in his early twenties, dressed in beautifully embroidered Pahari clothes, kept staring at her cup. What she told me left a chill in my limbs.

The second time she decided to record her statement was on the insistence of a female lawyer. It was 1997. Two days after she agreed to do so, someone threw concentrated acid on her neck. The man was waiting outside her apartment when she returned home from work. He was arrested. He claimed he was her *lover* and he had thrown acid on her after a lovers' quarrel. A portion of her neck simply melted away, and she spent months afterwards undergoing treatment. The doctor who first examined her thought she must have jumped up during the attack because the acid was most likely meant for her face. Nelly had to put on a special cast around her neck. That is how most staff members at the institute remembered her past: *An irate lover threw acid on the beautiful 'Sikh librarian'.* She had not remarried, and people invented her sexuality. They called her the *librarian* because they knew no difference between the library and the archives.

Not many staff remembered the day Nelly first joined the institute. Not many knew about her son, or the fact that she had prolonged periods of memory lapses during the first eighteen months of her arrival. Time when she assumed complete silence. The director tolerated her symptoms. Two months after Arjun's disappearance, she experienced the darkest period. Sleeplessness, nausea, a dull crackling silence. Discontinuous screams. Counting something mentally. For a couple of months Maribel moved to Shimla. Maribel bathed Nelly, combed her hair. Nelly did not eat, she resisted the plate on the table, and

Maribel would tear her roti into small pieces as if feeding a child. Every meal took over two hours. Frustrated, Maribel started reading books aloud (half English, half Spanish). She thought listening to stories would make Nelly accept food. The only stories that worked, though, were stories for children. When Maribel read *The Jungle Book* or *Alice's Adventures in Wonderland*, Nelly accepted dal and roti from her hand. Nelly started making alphabetical lists of all the children's books in the world. Lists of various themes in fairy tales. The Mexican visited several times, occasionally unannounced, and she reintroduced Nelly to yoga, especially the breathing exercises. Yoga filled her with life. Yoga in thin mountain air was different.

People talk about the healing power of a landscape. The high mountains also started curing her, providing a balance between left-brain time (time = discrete units) and right-brain time (time = continuous flow). More than anything else 1984 had damaged this balance, and the walks through the 'hill station' (as if by osmosis) began repairing that loss. Nelly's condition improved, but even then, once in a while she would sit down on the stairs outside her apartment and hit her forehead with her right palm. *Nothing makes sense. Nothing. No sense at all. Nothing.* She would walk for days on end, aimless walking, and return with no memory of her outings. She would spend time at Summer Hill train station, waiting. The walks and waiting and children's stories ejected her out of an uncanny darkness outside the realm of language. During one of her stays, Maribel asked Nelly the Punjabi word for *denial*, and Nelly was unable to recall the equivalent. She searched the bookshelves all day long, and later in the library she used a fat dictionary. She became obsessed with the Punjabi word, wrote it down on a sheet of paper, and requested her special friend to quiz

172

her about more words. Nelly bought a primer for children and started learning/relearning her mother tongue. *Urah, ehrah, eri, sasa, haha* . . . the alphabet, and each new/old word started expanding what she called 'islands of memory' and 'what I had forgotten', 'what I was like as a girl', 'who I was as a woman'.

She recalled even the darkest times as patches of a strange and intimate language, her husband saying over and over *dhundhla dikhda hai* about Partition (*all I see is fog*), and her son saying over and over *saah ghutda hai* about the pogrom in '84 (*I'm choking*). It is impossible to translate, no equivalents exist in English. Shimla, instead of allowing forgetting, imposed more and more remembering. Shimla became her Harappa and Mohenjodaro. Shimla was Excavation.

Then the unexpected happened. In February 1987 a Burmese scholar arrived at the institute, who started enquiring about the history of the Indian National Congress, and while assisting her, Nelly by sheer chance came across the Hume Papers. The Hume Papers, like Maribel, helped heal Nelly.

Grandson of the founding director of the East India Company, Hume, this most unlikely agent of healing, sailed to India in 1849 to work as a civil servant, and witnessed first hand the 1857 'War of Independence', which left a deep impression on him. When he arrived the young, twenty-year-old bureaucrat was just like any other Scotsman who had been sent to India to do the dirty work for the Empire. But years later, quite ironically, he wrote, 'No earthly power can stem a universal agrarian rising in a country like this. My compatriots, the British, will be as men in the desert, vainly struggling for a brief space against the simoom.' Hume became a vegetarian and more and more outspoken with time. But his mind was essentially

173

the mind of a collector; not many know today that he was an amateur ornithologist in contact with a vast network of bird-men.

Allan Octavian Hume presented most of his collection (over 80,000 birds) to the British Museum of Natural History before he died at the age of eighty-four; his ashes are buried in Brookwood, Surrey, England, where he shares space with John Singer Sargent and M. F. Husain. Born 6 June 1829 – Died 31 July 1912. The British Empire considered this dignified, avuncular man 'seditious'. On 18 March 1894, when he left India, Hume called himself a 'failure'. No memorial was built, not even by the Congress Party; his residence in Shimla lies in utter ruin, only the shell remains. We now know from innumerable diaries and memos Hume's favourite quote from Schiller: 'Worth is the ocean. Fame is but the bruit that roars along the shadows.'

Going through the files, Nelly became obsessed with Hume's prodigious collection of the birds and eggs of India. She started collecting artistic representations of Indian birds, calendar art, modern art, miniatures. Etchings with metal, galvanised eyes. Flamingoes. Pelicans. Peacocks. Little egrets. Purple herons. Black ibis. Scaly-breasted munia. Common tailorbirds. Baya weavers. Nelly sketched them all with exaggerated detail. Not a trained bird artist, her sketches for the first few months were raw and naive. Swarming, building, preening. Never in flight. Birds on paper as if myths. Birds as reflection of her altering moods. Diving. Darting with suicidal thoughts. Crying like a limpkin. She read more and more about the colonial collector and his birds. Flat, macabre, skinned, archived. Birds of the Andaman Islands. Birds of the Western Ghats. Birds of the Himalayas. Titmouse. Stonechat. Eurasian hoopoe. Black-winged stilt. Asian hornbill. Saras cranes in pairs. Nicobar pigeons. Hovering kestrels. Painted storks. Hume's whitethroat. Shaheen or wandering peregrine falcon, Northern goshawk (also known as a baaz), and the red-legged partridge, chakor, who can't stop gazing at the moon with intense longing. Some twelve hundred avian species. She spent her free time drawing, one finished drawing a day. She would only do birds. Endless variations, daily exorcisms. Those drawings of hers are marvellous expressions of grief. Eyes out of scale, immensely expressive, pools of dense concentrated madness. Nightmarish bills, feet and necks. Stiff, silent, baroque, speckled – English words fail to do justice. 'The days I didn't sketch, I felt dead.'

She would wake up early to create in a dizzy state. Then she would eat and go to work. That is when the problem of destruction or decreation arose. Nelly destroyed her work by stabbing the sheets with a 6B pencil, or by tearing them to pieces. To deal with the impulse to destroy, she decided not to look at her creations. She would drop the 'daily exorcisms' in a box and try erasing the bird completely from her mind.

Ironically, the ghost of Allan Octavian Hume helped her bounce back, by giving her a new obsession. This work

175

filled her with life and lightness. But it in no way prepared her for the attack in the photocopier room, or the concentrated acid. Both times, in addition to bodily pain, she suffered from PTSD, and both times the director was helpful in his own way.

Evening had descended and the light outside was dim and very pale. A guest in the hotel lobby was looking for her badminton partner and briefly Nelly turned her gaze in that direction. Perhaps she simply wanted to pause for a while. Most likely the hotel complex had a full indoor court, but the exact location was a mystery to me. Nelly was looking away and it seemed I was still playing badminton with her in IIT. (She holds the racket differently each time she changes side. Her long black hair is wrapped in a neat bun. The poles are black and the netting, too, is black. We win and lose, dressed in white. Singles on Tuesdays, doubles on Fridays. I can still play. I can still play, even outdoors in the wind. Sure, it is not going to be easy.)
    'Stay . . . Dinner?'
    'Some other time. Now I know where to find you.'
    She made it to the revolving door, driven by a sudden need to be alone. As I watched her dissolve into the city below, I understood.
    How we had shared our worlds then, our little anxieties, and how I used to yearn to be alone with her. Every word she uttered would wrap me for days on end, and I would fill every random gesture of hers with supreme significance. After badminton she would return to those interstitial spaces of life that I had little access to. I recall conjuring her up more sad than she really was.
    Fridays we played doubles. Her partner, a woman with very dark skin. My partner, a fellow hosteler. Joint Entrance

176

Exam, All India Rank: 28. He would hit the shuttlecock gently and carefully towards Nelly, but applied all the Newtons of force available in the world while sending it towards the dark-skinned woman. Nelly complained, and I confronted him back in the hostel. You don't expect me to play like a gent with that sweeperess, he said. Nelly is a proper lady, but that other woman is an impure achhoot, he said. What struck me was that he was not even a member of some extreme right-wing, fascist organisation. The prejudice deeply internalised in every single bone of his, a mind otherwise so bright. Nelly still doesn't know his response. Perhaps she guessed. Why I stopped bringing him to the courts as my partner. So much I could not share with her then, even when I got some more access. And I am still not able to.

Arjun and Indira, her children – I called them Space and Time. Both prone to hyper-imagination, the boy less social, the girl making a special effort to reach out to others. Both affectionate and treated me like family. The boy's face and especially his eyes resembled Nelly's, and the girl looked more like her father. Once in a while (purely by mistake) they addressed me as 'Papa'. Curled up on the bed, Nelly would reward them by reading aloud stories about Siberian tigers.

Part of me felt that, by living in America, the distance would help erase that beautiful time, but distance, ironically, had the reverse effect. Ithaca was not a solution. Especially when I felt like an outsider or was made to feel like one, I would enter the house of the 'past', and the 'past' would enter me like a veil of ash. I would drive to Seneca or Ovid or go to the stunningly beautiful gorges and lakes and swim and camp there or sleep in my car. Or I would listen to Carl Sagan talk about the cosmos in one of those Cornell auditoriums. But memory would refuse to become memory. Like a boundary-layer fluid, memory would gush or ripple towards me in widening circles, an interference pattern whose wavelength I could not determine. What was its amplitude really? And frequency? I would feel I was not normal, not even anomalous. As if I were a stuffed animal and in my cracks lived a beetle or a moth or some other creature constantly eating the fluids of my brain.

Nnnnn

Eeeee

Lllll

Lllll

Yyyyy

Something was not normal – once again.

She had not offered the details on her own. It was a topic that often ended with long pauses. And averted eyes. The retirement event. She was hiding something. The Internet was helpful. I Googled.

I used several sources to locate the missing information. At Nelly's retirement event the chief guest was none other than one of the ministers accused of conducting the November 1984 pogroms. He was accompanied by two foreign delegations. From Germany and Austria.

When I looked at the photo of the 'chief guest' on the Net it produced a sickening reaction within my body. His designer khadi. Plump and sleek, swept-back hair. A mere photo had a strong effect. Finally the horror was in the palm of my hand.

Today in the library I spent the last few hours helping my assistant shelve books. Then I instructed her to take a tea break. Madam, aap chai nahin lengey? she checked. No, I said, I've had plenty of tea today, and after she was gone I gazed nostalgically at the books in the poetry section and felt like making an ironic declaration, but my inner voice interrupted again: *You have been tricked. Are you ready to undertake enormous responsibility? How will you conduct the oral history project without institutional support? Delhi is the city of goondas. Are you out of your mind?*

How will you return?

That city will kill you again.

So engrossed was I in my thoughts that the book by Mandelstam, the one in my hand, fell, and just when I picked it up and wiped it clean with my chunni I heard the director's footsteps. He wears army boots. *Namaste*, he said, and walked unbearably close to me and asked if he could have a word.

'There is one thing I forgot to tell you, Mrs Kaur.'

'Oh, the gathering?'

'You see, I would like to invite an important government official to honour you.'

'No need.'

'You see, the minister is, as it is, coming to the town, and he will be attending.'

'No need to make it so pompous.'

'He will come anyway.'

'Who?'

The minister's profile flashed before me. Murderer. His face on postage stamps. Plump and sleek, swept-back hair. The way he smiles and folds his hands in a mythical *namaste*. His designer khadi. The way he steps on people as if they were beetles or cockroaches.

'Not him,' I said. 'Why don't we cancel the retirement party?'

179

'I didn't invite him, Mrs Kaur. He insisted. He would like to take this opportunity to show our institute to important foreign delegates.'

The director well knows that many years ago the minister along with many senior Congress leaders conducted a genocide. I felt like reminding him of the details. But then I thought it was inappropriate to do so. How could he ignore the recent news reports –

'Not him.'

'Move on, Mrs Kaur. Will you? He is no longer the man he was and you are no longer the woman you were.'

'I am definitely no longer the woman I was . . . But don't you dare say – MOVE ON.'

'Tomorrow take the morning off. At 3 p.m. I will send my own car to pick you up.'

Even if I try hard I can't despise the director fully. All these years he has allowed me to work here without trouble, he has helped me during my moments of panic, moments when I saw dust gathering on the shelves and the orange curtains and the fire that engulfs us all. As I heard his footsteps departing the library my mind was filled with so many poisonous thoughts.

On 28 December 1945, Primo Levi, after surviving the Buna-Monowitz camp, wrote a poem. The poem is titled 'Buna'. *With what kind of face would we confront each other?* The Nelly in my notes knows this last line. Her favourite line in the poem, however, is neither the first nor the last, but line four: *A day like every other day.* The real Nelly perhaps never read the poem; and she would not allow me complete access to her inner self. But I know this for sure. A lot was going on in her mind that day when I located her under the tulip tree by the crumbling colonial mansion. Escape? Revenge? Nelly sends me ten miles away to Mashobra. She 'forgets' her speech at home. She wanted me to read the speech. She didn't feel like delivering the speech at the retirement event. All the little facts and little actions led me to the following conclusion. There was someone else. Something larger at stake. Someone who was forcing Nelly to deliver that particular speech.

She sends me to Mashobra that day; she wanted to keep me away. Reluctantly I took the bus. At the Oberoi Wild Flower Cafe I met the Benazir Bhutto lookalike. The young woman was sitting at the table close by, reading, or trying to read, her Kindle, unable to focus, distracted. She, in a black kurta, colourful Sanskrit mantras scrawled all over, and need I mention again her most voluptuous calves? She was reading the flickering page and I was trying to begin the book I bought from the antique shop, Maria Brothers, in Shimla. On her table a large plate of exotic green salad.

'What book are you perusing?'

Scarcely had I finished the question when I realised how many times in the past those five words led to an answer that transported not one, but two people on a long journey. She was reading *Men in the Off Hours*, a title I had not heard of. She returned to her Kindle as soon as she uttered those words, giving me the impression that my interruption was really an ill-timed interruption. Women in the Off Hours.

Twenty or twenty-five minutes later she opened her handbag and dug out a cellphone. From what I could make out she called her driver, and the man's loud Pahari voice said that the car needed repairs. From that moment on she was unable to sit still. She applied a coat of raspberry lip gloss and surveyed her face now and then in the reflecting surfaces around us. On her dry hands she applied a Vichy moisturiser and massaged it into her skin.

'Excuse me.' She looked in my direction. 'I did not mean to be rude. What book are you perusing?'

I had picked up an old volume from Maria Brothers, a rare book on bird etchings. She flipped through it and said something that has stayed with me. Birds, she said, the more you look for them, the more you see them. Her thought was not original, but she ended up articulating something true.

With every passing second she looked more and more familiar, but I could not place her. She could have been the one at the student's party who was studying attentively the nude Radha and Krishna.

I moved to her table. We shook hands.

'You look like an artist.'

'Yes, I sketch birds,' I lied.

'What kind?'

'The ones that live inside me. I need to draw every day. My daily exorcisms.'

'You appear to be an intense man.'

The waiter, a long shadow, appeared with the menu as soon as I installed myself.

She took a while. I ordered Earl Grey tea.

'Viennese,' she said. 'Without cream.'

The young man blinked, a puzzled look on his face.

'Something wrong?'

'Then it is a black coffee, ma'am.'

'What do you mean?'

'Viennese without cream is "normal" coffee, ma'am.'

She worked as an interpreter for foreign tourists in Delhi. Slowly it emerged that she did several other

182

part-time jobs. She was also trained (the way she phrased it) as a 'past-life regression analyst'. Obviously she had made an error about my occupation! But I was immensely attracted and chose to play along. Occupations like hers were new in the new India with its teeming middle class. Part of my attraction to her was connected to this newness, this transition I'd missed. But, in certain ways, she was more North American than me. Fuck, she said. Viennese coffee! He thinks he knows more about coffee than me! What if? I asked. What if you are doing a past-life regression for a client and determine that three or four centuries ago they murdered you? Will you go to the cops? What will you do really? What if you determine that it was you who murdered the person standing before you? Fucking brilliant, she said. Fuck, I never thought about this! She applied more of her Vichy moisturiser. An hour later, when the driver phoned, she invited me 'home': her retired father's cottage. She was in town for two days 'only'. Mashobra was cold, and Mashobra was covered with pure walls of melting snow. During an erotically charged moment I kissed her lips; she told me, 'Forget it, buddy', she was seeing someone, the person was a consultant in the music business, and this person paid the rent. Forget it, she said. 'I can't do that thing with you.' No, I don't think I will be able to do it, she said, and pushed me aside. From the beginning I had anticipated this situation, for she was young and I was not young any more. Racism can be overcome, but age is more of a challenge. I kissed her again, this time on the left cheek. Help me forget something, I said. Only you can help me forget. I would like to forget myself and this shitty world. Murderer! she said. We settled on oral sex. One thing led to another. To be honest, for a while I

183

felt my father had paid her the money to help me forget something. But it was a passing thought. We made what some people call 'love'. Several times. Thrice in two hours. There were no condoms, we did it unprotected. We mimicked the Viennese waiter, never have I laughed so much, a deep belly laughter. What was I? A wild animal in AD 1060, an ant in 1214, a parrot during the times of Sikandar, and a moth when the Bamian Buddhas were being carved out of live rock. Fucking brilliant! Two full-length mirrors in the room, and they, too, saturated with our release. Afterwards her brown belladonna eyes became moist and she played some Arvo Pärt, the Estonian composer, and smoked cigarettes. How much money do I owe you? I checked. I am not a whore, she said, smiling and sobbing. She told me she got the biggest scare of her life when she had unprotected sex with a guy who revealed later that he had herpes. I hope you are free of diseases? she checked. Suddenly her nakedness felt exposed, and I, too, felt exposed. I used a few unprotected words. Raised my voice. Why didn't you tell me about this beforehand? Why did you not tell me that you had slept without a condom with a diseased man, you cunt? She pounced on me and bit my ears. It happened so long ago, sweets . . . let me reassure you I got myself tested and I didn't pick up the disease. But are you sure you are free of germs, you prick? I lit up a cigarette. After so many years of quitting I felt like a smoke. The ashtray on the study table was full. The desktop computer next to the ashtray had no screensaver. She mentioned the ashtray belonged to her father. He is in Shimla at the moment, she said. Next to the ashtray, four or five luminous apples. Almost all the cigarettes had been extinguished in a peculiar way. The ashtray reminded me of an old friend of my father's, a senior civil servant. He would extinguish exactly like that. He would smoke only three-quarters of a cigarette and drop it. The cigarette would then extinguish itself, but it would retain the original shape, a perfect cylinder of ash.

Following our so-called after-play she ran to the kitchen to get us warm milk. During her absence I went through the dressing-table drawers. Whitening serums. Facewash. Magenta-coloured moisturiser bottles. I thought of Clara, and had the urge to check my emails. The keyboard, stained, carried a slim layer of dust, black on the edges. The desktop was unlocked. But the mouse was not connected. It took me three seconds to reconnect. Unreal. What I saw was a bit shocking. It didn't take me long to understand. There was no need now to check my emails.

Before me was a single folder called *Hindu Rashtra*. I clicked and entered. Image after shocking image. Pictures of a crumbling, national historic building – a 500-year-old place of worship that belonged to a minority community. Being destroyed by tens and hundreds of men in saffron. Being reduced to rubble by men in khaki shorts. I clicked on the folders within the folder. Deep inside I found links to acronyms like RSS, VHP, BD. Rashtriya Swayam Sevak Sangh. Vishwa Hindu Parishad. Bajrang Dal. These were extreme fascist organisations, which used the Hindu Party as a political front. Each one more eager to establish upper-caste supremacy. Each one preaching more patriarchy, hatred and violence. Collectively the group was known as the Sangh Parivar.

I heard her. She was headed to the bedroom with milk. Quickly I shuffled away from the desktop. She entered with a silver tray, two tall glasses. She didn't take long to realise what I might have seen. After a brief conversation

185

she stared at the screen and turned off the machine. Tactfully I restricted our conversation to computers. How I almost became a software engineer. She didn't ask a single question. I squeezed her tremulous hand. She didn't withdraw. A dog came from a different room and sniffed me. Out, she said, and it disappeared. She had not used the dog's name. 'Why are you not carrying your laptop?' she asked. There and then I shared the details. My laptop. Stolen and recovered.

The 'Peterhof?' she checked.

'Yes, the Peterhof.'

The hotel has many past lives, I didn't say.

'Ugly architecture,' she blurted out. 'Sweetie, it is a cross between—'

'The Hindu Party organised a chintan baithak there.'

'As a delegate?'

I missed my chance to lie. 'As an observer.'

'I see,' she said. 'My father, too, spent two days at the Peterhof.'

'Recently?'

'Recently.'

'Is he a member?'

'Say that again.'

'Member of the Hindu Party?'

'He is a doctor.'

'How old is he?'

'He is retired. But now and then he acts as a locum for the hotel emergencies.'

'Does he know?'

'Say again.'

'Does he know what the party is all about?'

She paused for a while. 'What do you mean?'

'Does he, too, believe in Hindu supremacy?'

186

'No,' she said. But after a long pause.

There were photos of her father in the glass cabinet, and one of them similar to the photo I had seen in Nelly's albums, the photo of the man who saved her life by locking her in the barsati upstairs. I extrapolated the man's 'old face' from his 'young face' and came to a conclusion. Nelly had called him 'my saviour'.

She had used the phrase three or four times. Unable to hide that something was not right. Every mention of the man made her uncomfortable. As if he were nearby in the same room floating around as a shadow.

In Shimla that night while waiting for Nelly in her apartment I used the Internet to locate more information about the 'saviour'. What I found perturbed me. At a certain point in his life, Benazir Bhutto's father had started defending the pogroms conducted by the Hindu Party. In 2002, Muslims (and not Sikhs or Christians or Dalits) were the target. The 2002 pogrom took place in Gujarat.

That such a man existed and was able to breathe like any other ordinary human being really upset me. Whatever limited hope I still harboured about the inherent goodness of human beings imploded. That night after recording my interview with Nelly I sensed truth in that cliché (now or never), I knew I had to pose real 'pesky' questions. She had already spoken a lot, and I could hear exhaustion in her voice. Possessed by unknown energy I pressed on. She grew more and more uncomfortable and agitated and literally ordered me to turn off the recorder, which I did. Now there was no gizmo between us. But our face-to-face talk grew more and more awkward and she switched to complete silence. That said: it became possible to see what cannot be seen. Outside the window snow

187

kept falling and when it stopped she spoke again, giving well-rehearsed answers to my questions. But why? Like a difficult thesis adviser (or rather, like my father's supercop persona) I would not let her go. Mass murder. That is what we were solving. Something more complicated than a typical problem in engineering. I even dropped 'Mrs Singh' during the exchange.

'You must be going through stress. I understand. Too bad you have started smoking.'

She said a friend had visited.

'This is perhaps none of my business, but is this person by any chance your saviour? You must have kept in touch.'

I stared at her.

'Yes,' she said.

Something eerie about her response, I felt. But she was not lying.

'Did he attend your retirement party?'

Long pause.

'Yes, he did.'

'But first he showed up here?'

'Yes.'

'Later you two walked together to the institute?'

'No.'

'How did you go?'

'I took a taxi.'

She dug out a receipt from her handbag.

'He attended?'

'Yes.'

'Who invited him?'

'He invited himself.'

'Did something unusual happen during the event?'

'I forgot my speech at home, I almost panicked, but I managed. Why are you asking so many questions?'

The speech. I had read those nine printed sheets. She had planted the quivering pages on the kitchen table. My fingers still remember the texture and edges of that yellow legal pad paper. Small, baroque handwriting. No corrections. The speech was based on facts (I verified them later). I understood why she didn't want to deliver the speech (although the most probable explanation didn't occur to me right away). Obviously she didn't want to embarrass the director of the institute. What I didn't understand was why the saviour hit her.

The 'saviour' made one last attempt to persuade her. She expressed doubts all over again, so in a cool and calculated manner he hit her. Perhaps he did so after the event, because she failed to follow the instructions.

'You didn't fall. That man hit you, didn't he?'

She was stunned and silent.

'This has happened before?'

'Never.'

'It must have.'

'No, it was all my fault.'

The saviour pressured her to deliver the speech (the one he had composed). Papers, media. This was the best way to warn the rival Congress Party: don't investigate the 2002 pogroms conducted by the Hindu Party, otherwise the party would insist on further investigations of the 1984 pogroms conducted by the Congress Party. A strange balance of power: Gujarat brought back the ghosts of Delhi. Gujarat ended the long silence. Pogrom One absolves Pogrom Two and vice versa. Such was the perverse logic in the so-called largest democracy. How reassuring the knowledge must have been for the Hindu Party that its rival had indulged in a similar, if not identical, orgy. Dangerous and perverse.

'Did he hit you before or after the event?'

Long ago I felt paralysed at New Delhi railway station, and now that fear was gone, the paralysis was not there. In my hotel room I felt like doing the right thing. The most rational thing was to arrange a meeting with the saviour right away. I had to warn him in no uncertain terms that the beatings must stop.

So many died in '84. She will compile a list. Julio Cortazar died on 12 February. Ansel Adams died on 22 April. Lee Krasner Pollock died on 19 June. Michel Foucault died on 25 June. Lillian Hellman died on 25 June. Truman Capote died on 25 August. François Truffaut died on 21 October. Martin Luther King (Senior) died on 11 November. Faiz Ahmad Faiz died on 20 November . . . Michael Jackson didn't die then, but he burned himself in 1984.

Throughout my childhood days a different woman (Indira Gandhi) was my inspiration.
    How wrong I was, she says.
    Indira was a harmful heavy metal. Indira was radium. She made clocks gleam, and then killed the very women who painted the dials.
    These days if I consider someone close to being a hero I can think of no one other than Aung San. I know I am right this time.
    Like Aung San I would like to go 'home'.
    Delhi, the wounded city, the psychotic city, the city of 12 million unfinished histories. Delhi, the city of human unsuccess. Soon it will turn a hundred years old, the Imperial New Delhi, but it will refuse to narrate those stories of FIRE. Dilli, the miserable city of collective amnesia.
    If I go back to that discarded city, it will tear me apart. With its amnesia.

190

Next morning the mountains awoke slowly in angled light. The air was damp and cold, the sky blue and bright. From the hotel lobby the distant villages visible for the first time. Cheap and hasty constructions. Corrugated tin or asbestos roofs angled just like the light. With some effort I was able to detect the Chadwick Falls in the gap between two sheer cliffs. In the early sun the parabola of widening water resembled molten iron. Without warning the receptionist, I walked past the glinty skating rink all the way to the bus stop. The wait was not long. On the vibrating bus my body acquired a strange momentum, and for a change I overcame the usual feeling of worthlessness. I had a mission now, knew exactly why I was headed there. Most passengers were simple hill folk, local Paharis and Khadus, one carrying a glinty metallic object, and after some hesitation I checked if he would be willing to sell it to me. The man panicked and moved a few seats away. A rifle is more impersonal, I thought. The bus followed the serpentine road, making me think about Father's 44-calibre rifle, the one that terrified me as a child. I wish I knew more about weapons. The bus dropped me at the slushy stop. What looked like a boulder from a distance were two stubborn yaks. I walked towards the solitary optician's shop. The vehicle disappeared with a strange sense of urgency after dumping a vapour of diesel in my face. The dense deodar forest, entangled in low ribbons of clouds, appeared more tranquil than last time. The snow gone, high walls more or less at an equilibrium, and I was struck again by the sublime beauty of bare, leafless trees and apple orchards.

He was a retired golf-playing oncologist in his late sixties with a Chekhovian goatee, and charming. Very charming and clear-sighted and more youthful than I had expected. His Leonard Cohen voice different from the way it

191

sounded on the answering machine. He spoke Mayo College or Doon School English, and wore tweed, and didn't smoke all the time. He smoked only two cigarettes during the fifty or sixty minutes we spent together in his Hindutava living room. He began with the Great Trigonometric Survey conducted by the British in the nineteenth century, but soon drifted towards Vedic mathematics. He spoke about a root borer, the beetle that was destroying the trees in his orchard.

How India had a large 'treasonous minority' (the Muslims), the enemy within. Dalits were 'Hindus'. Sikhs were 'Hindus'. All non-Hindus must acknowledge their Hindu ancestry. Failure to do so would mean no voting rights. I had heard that before. Humans for him were no more than communal categories. The codling moth is another pest we would like to eliminate, he explained. The bookshelves next to me had complete works by Shakespeare and Naipaul. Two walls were crowded with luminous photos of mythological characters, independence fighters, genocide-denier Narendra Modi, accused by national and international human rights organisations as the chief architect of the 2002 pogrom, and muscular-looking men. I kept my jacket on.

He asked me to relax and offered a cigarette.

'But I no longer smoke.'

'May I?'

'Of course.'

Before I reveal the details I must confess that a part of me derived enormous delight out of the conversation. His right-wing views, contradictions, and attempts to explain himself in a frank, open manner carried a literary potential. His profession (oncology) made him all the more exciting. The man recalled a book I had read in Ithaca on a friend's recommendation, Bolaño's *Nazi Literature in the Americas*.

'Did you sleep with her?'

'No, sir.'

'Good. Now we can talk.'

Rarely had I experienced such direct, no-nonsense dialogue with a lover's family. So far my 'meet the parents' encounters had turned out to be disasters because the heart of the matter never surfaced, was never allowed to surface. Concealment was the guiding principle. My younger years were filled with offensive overtures delivered by testy mothers or fathers.

'You see, sometimes my daughter just gets carried away.'

Other than wood burning in the fireplace, the cottage was perfectly quiet – a silence unknown in flatlands or even in Shimla. The dog came and sniffed me. Tactfully his master shifted gear. He really wanted me to dislike her.

'You see, she kept telling me. For ten years.'

He roused my curiosity.

'Only women turn me on, she kept telling.'

'Until she met me?'

'I am glad. She is not averse to men.'

The silence that followed was natural.

'What caste are you?'

'What if I am not the right one?'

My response didn't go down well.

'Oh but why are we talking about this? You have come for the Kindle. Haven't you?'

When I called Benazir the previous night she reassured me that she got the tests done at the Apollo Clinic and the doctor found no disease. Great news, I said. You prick, she laughed. Fucking brilliant, I said. I have forgotten something in the heights of Mashobra, she said. And I don't want to buy a new one, I am very attached to my old one. When do you visit Delhi? Visit me, honey! Bring me my Kindle.

The saviour's cellphone rang. Faux-patriotic ringtone. He got rid of the cigarette and hurried slowly to the adjoining room. Although I couldn't follow, it was clear he switched languages several times. When he returned the phone was still in his hand emitting a strange bluish light.

'Sorry for the interruption.'

He settled down. Still fiddling with the gizmo.

'What were we talking about?'

'Kindle.'

'Her Kindle.'

The servant served tea and spinach pakoras and dropped more wood in the fireplace. The saviour sa'ab gave instructions, and sent the chap to the bazaar on a longish mission. For a brief second my eyes rested on spilled ash.

'What are you hiding from me?'

I knew the effect my entirely unexpected curiosity would have on him. The oncologist asked me to repeat.

'Did a human being do that to you?'

'No. This is what an animal did.' He pointed at his face, drawing attention to his black eye. The left one. I had noticed it right after entry into the cottage, but felt it was impolite to pursue the cause-and-effect questions without proper reason.

194

'Looks like an animal punched you hard.'

'Does it appear that bad?'

'Just curious.'

'Bloody monkey.'

'Fuck,' I said.

He turned his fascist gaze towards the shelves. Right above the poetry and fiction section there were hundreds of medical textbooks, and right above the medical section there were medieval weapons and rifles on display. Of course the man was a villain. Although the servant was no longer at home, I felt we were not alone. There was a small movement. The curtains flapped.

Without my host's permission I shut the window. 'What are you doing?' I didn't use the curtains to make a rope. The sash cloth on my sofa came in handy. It was bound to happen. The saviour protested as I tied his ancient hands to one of the wooden columns in the room. I didn't seal his lips because that would have made it difficult to hear his responses.

'You must have hit her first. She must have done it in self-defence. Please, why did you hit her?'

He stared at me. 'What is the good engineer talking about?'

'What are you hiding?'

'I am hiding nothing. I can even show you the place where the incident took place.'

The dog came running. There was a black sock in its mouth. Benazir had warned me that the dog loved playing with socks and brassieres. 'Leaves them lacerated.'

This is painful to write. The old man struggled to free himself. 'This is a mistake,' he said.

'Listen, Mrs Singh didn't send me here, I figured it out all on my own.'

'I have no idea, my dear, no idea, my good engineer, what you are talking about.'

195

'The beatings must stop. My father is a supercop, and if you continue your ways we will make sure you get arrested. You will spend the rest of your days in Tihar jail. She doesn't owe you anything. She doesn't owe anyone anything. Understand? She is the one who decides. You will break all contact with her. Now, where is *the* Kindle?'

Benazir's father, beyond a shadow of doubt, was not the 'saviour'. I was on the wrong track. My aversion to right-wingers made me commit a serious error. Right-wingers do not just screw the world, they screw logic, common sense and imagination. And: I was not myself then. Something was wrong with my state of mind in Shimla, everyone around me seemed to be a suspect. The world I inhabited consisted of no fixed laws, everything looked more confused and complex than it normally is.

Slowly I was walking, and someone was following me.

On the Mall Road, rather late in the chilly evening, when I turned back for a brief second I noticed a mangy dog. With its cracked skin and diseases it came very close. Foul odour. I changed my pace. The dog continued to stalk, adjusting quickly to my speed. From a certain angle it resembled Goya's dog, and when I heard the whimpering sound I was reminded of the dog in the Russian film, *Stalker*. Although not completely black, the resemblance was astounding and so was its mysterious appearance, as if Tarkovsky's dog had moved to Shimla after surviving Chernobyl. From another angle it revealed large protruding eyes, and disproportion-ately large ears. I could smell its gutter smell. The creature following me was more or less a blackish mound of shov-elled snow. Yet, it was grotesquely beautiful. I stopped at the chemist's shop; the dog stopped, I stopped at the newspaper kiosk; the dog trotted a little ahead, and stopped. Just then a couple overtook me. I sensed a tense quarrel, the woman kept saying na, na, na, and the man alternated between foul words and charm-coated words of gentle persuasion.

I followed them for a while, but the gluey dog walked next to me. The couple stepped inside a cafe. It was basically to get rid of the dog that I, too, took refuge in the cafe, planting myself close to the window. From a high stool I observed people passing by. I read local papers. Especially the ones in Hindi. A police jeep passed by. In the wake of that sarkari automobile there was a familiar figure. Slowly she was approaching the cafe.

At first I thought the man walking beside Nelly was not with her at all. But they were together. No loud quarrel ensuing, and they walked in intimate silence and that silent intimacy, at least to me, revealed enormous tension. With a newspaper I shielded my face. By the time I stepped out of the cafe they had already melted away in the crowd.

The man walking beside Nelly was the one I was after. The way to resolve this mystery was to have a direct word with Nelly. But I wanted to respect her privacy. I had already gone overboard the previous time.

On Monday I planted myself behind the tall oak trees outside Nelly's apartment. Serrated oak leaves, still and silent. Unshaking. I had no idea about her new schedule. She stepped out at around nine, and that is when I thought it was safe to enter. The keys were still with me. She had not asked me to return the keys to her apartment. Soon I dashed inside like a thief. Everything looked the way it was. I checked her landline, the answering machine. No new messages. Something she had said about the saviour kept coming to me. I sat at the kitchen table. No handwritten messages on yellow legal paper. But she had forgotten a significant object I was not even looking for. Her cellphone on the table. I hesitated for a minute. The phone: unlocked. I went through the text messages. They convinced me beyond doubt that someone else was the saviour, the man walking intimately beside her. The nagging feeling within me was correct. I had his phone number now and this simplified the job. Human problems, just like engineering problems, are amply simplified by numbers. Sitting at the kitchen table I was afraid, though; she may return sooner than expected. If she returns to pick up the mobile, I will simply surrender, no, I will not hide in the closet or under the bed, I said to myself. She didn't return. Although I felt the neighbour's eyes on me, the skinny man packing a duffel bag. I used the bathroom and left the cellphone at its original location. Then I locked the apartment.

The real saviour also lived in Shimla. Not far from the Railway Board Building. I called him. To get advice on books on Hindutava. How to save and defend 'our religion'. How to publicise and spread our cause in North America. He said there were already agents in both America and Canada involved with the diasporics. Of course he was gauging me. Our phone conversation dragged on; he mentioned briefly our national 'traitors' and invited me to his place during the weekend. Before I met him I thought it prudent to call Nelly. I apologised for having forgotten to return her keys. She met me briefly at the Mall. She looked more calm and collected than I had expected. In her hand a book as usual. She had just finished reading. She was carrying it around because 'a part of me is still stuck inside'. This is the way she put it.

That is how I came to borrow *The Fall of a Sparrow*, which Nelly received as her retirement gift. While going through those pages I found myself looking for birds, and I found them everywhere.

Saturday, I decided to visit the real saviour. But the moment I stepped out I had a distinct feeling that I was being followed. Someone was keeping a watch on me. On the way to the Railway Board Building (for he lived in the vicinity) I mailed a postcard to my daughters. If something happens this would be their last gift, I thought. Instead of reporting my well-being I wrote in capital letters how much I loved them, and sketched a small flame-throated bulbul for Urvashi and a hornbill for Ursula.

The saviour's house had a sentry posted outside. The place itself was modest compared to that cottage in Mashobra.

I was led to a special room. For five minutes I sat alone before he appeared. The man was not as tall or youthful as the oncologist. The tartan silk scarf on his accordion neck could have belonged to a Scotsman. My visit lasted no longer than thirty minutes. He didn't offer tea. I didn't tie his hands with a rope. But being in the same room with that man stirred a storm within me and made my pulse go quicker. The beatings must stop, I warned him. This one more forceful than the previous; at the same time it carried the air of theatre. Air of repetition. He denied any wrong-doing more or less like the oncologist. But he also tried to play a dirty game. Our conversation ended with three questions, and an answer.

'Your father. What is his good name?'

'That man, your father?'

'Do you know what you have just revealed?'

'You, sir, are the unfortunate son of a mass murderer.'

Second time in my life I felt like spitting in someone's face because of a dirty game. But my mouth was dry. I slapped his shoulder. He lost his balance, but recovered quickly, the way mediocre singers do.

The path from the saviour's front door to the main road was very slippery. As I walked to my hotel room I felt an immense need to hear the madwoman's chandrayan chants. *Go to the moon and tell them about you.* But she was nowhere around. The one question on the tip of my tongue, the one I didn't ask the saviour, was the question about his transformation. How come after saving Nelly in 1984 he beat her up in 2009? How come after saving lives during November 1984's Bigger-Than-Kristallnacht-Barbarity he supported the 2002 pogrom in Gujarat? I had left this question for the very end, but the way our meeting ended, I felt he simply snatched away my right to pose these questions. He played real dirty.

Don't worry, he said as I was leaving. I have not told her about your father.

Back in my hotel room I tried to read the book I'd borrowed from Nelly: *The Fall of a Sparrow*. But I could not focus. So I tried to think about Father. But I could not. I returned again to the book. Instead of birds or the ornithologist, Salim Ali, my mind drifted towards tigers and jungles and young Orwell, a colonial police officer in Burma, and I thought about his essay 'Shooting an Elephant', and I

200

thought again about Father. I could not focus no matter how hard I tried, so I thought again about Nelly. Seeking clarity I waded into dense fog, and waited. When I recovered consciousness I found myself skating on memories. No ice. Sand and soil and grit and green grass. That day Nelly and I, after a game of badminton, had taken the bus to

Jantar Mantar. All along I had a feeling someone was following us. Jantar Mantar, the eighteenth-century observatory, reminded her of a painting by de Chirico. Giant stone machines built by the Maharajah to forecast eclipses accurately. We stood by the sundial. A police jeep passed by. Slowly it was making its way towards the Imperial Hotel. It was Father's jeep.

She had watched me watching the jeep longer than necessary, but ignored it. What is wrong with you? Tell me what is troubling you. You will feel better. I was about to tell her a few facts, but changed my mind. There, leaning against one of the measuring instruments, she took it upon herself to cheer me up, and told me she was a Pisces. What sign are you? *The red disc of the sun was about to set, we also saw a flock of birds, a murmuration, although I didn't know the word 'murmuration' then. Standing so close to each other our lips quivered. My hands remember still the warmth, the texture of her skin. Dark and soft, which produced a burning sensation. I have my period, she told me, and the lights that night were dim and low and yellow.* Back in the campus we walked all the way to her place. Professor Singh's Fiat, I see it still, parked outside the garage. She didn't invite me in. The door slammed shut, and I stood by the gnarled bougainvillea hedge for a long time hearing voices. About to leave I heard the voices grow louder. I froze and listened. Neither Punjabi, nor Hindi, nor English, as if the two of them had invented a private lingo.

Back in the hostel I imagined a major quarrel brewing between the two of them. Unable to study or sleep in my room I decide to jog towards the Wind Tunnel, and when I was done with jogging and sweating I started worrying for her and a couple of hours later drove to their place. (Those days I used to take lessons from one of my father's drivers. The chap would show up every alternate evening, and after the lesson he would park Father's black Ambassador outside the hostel.) Carefully I drove the car with the big Learner's sign, although there was no need for a car; slowly in the mottled night towards the faculty residences beyond the Solar Building. I turned off the headlights long before I arrived. All the lights of their house were on, and as I walked closer to the thorny bougainvillea, I heard a crackling sound. The living-room windows were open, curtains flapping, a stack of vinyl records by the turntable. The song is still embedded somewhere deep inside me.

Frank Sinatra's 'September'. Warm September of my years. A man is in step with the song. He is alone, wet in his sweat. I would like to believe him 'sad', I would like to see him alone, but he is neither sad nor alone. Nelly is is is with him. Extremely close. Entangled, in slow step. Not bhangra, not gidda. But another private invention. The man is exuding the kind of tenderness I had not associated with him. The kind that comes when one feels absolutely secure. His loose blue jeans rolled up to his knees, nothing on his chest, only long hair, curly and wavy, which had tumbled down from his head. She is bonded to his body and mind via a mecha-nism I understood (and yet I didn't and still don't). The slow, crackling September fills the space around them. For a second I felt and still feel Nelly was aware of my presence that night. But the second melts away. And the slow, non-bombastic, melancholic melody continues on and on and on tearing my eyes.

I called Nelly. She was pleased to hear from me. But expressed reluctance to send me to the institute director. Why do you need to take a look at the archives? All you need is in these disks. You don't really need to go, I have digitised everything.

She had 'everything' on disks. I insisted on consulting the originals anyway. Something real about holding a twenty-year-old sheet of paper. Yellow and brittle, I wanted to hold the documents of crime. Smell the micro-organ-isms. Touch the coffee stains, and wipe the dust that might have settled on them.

The director, an enlightened squire of a man, had no problems with me going through the files. His well-preserved face seemed to say, Look, I am an important man. So don't waste my precious time. Did he suspect I was gathering evidence? He had too many things on his plate. His grand second-floor office, adjacent to the curi-ous turret, used to be the Viceroy's opulent study (his residence was still called the 'Squire's House'). He offered me a cushioned chair and a glass of water, but all along I felt a fine mix of suspicion and hyper-alertness directed towards me. His tone gave one the impression that the man's sole job was to protect the dusty archives from any human activity. Why would someone with your background need our services? Because I am researching colonial science. The moment I used the word 'colonial' he decided I was safe and became friendly. He offered me tea and asked hundreds of questions about Cornell. 'My daughter is applying for admissions abroad.' After tea he beckoned the clerks to make a temporary card. The babus could barely operate in English, but they used the language anyway. I spoke in Hindi, they responded in English. Finally, after a couple of hours, I received the typed permission. *With reference to your letter on the subject cited above, you, Dr R. Kumar, US passport holder, and university ID card bearing number 250111/95, is hereby allowed to consult the material inside. <u>No borrowing outside premises</u>*. The new archivist, however, was unable to locate the information I was after. We possess nothing on 1984, she clarified. The only listed files are connected to a mini crisis within the Institute of Advanced Studies. 'Yesterday when I took charge from the director,' she said, 'I was made aware of the details. In '84, a group of people signed a petition to shut this institute, and another group tried their level best to keep it running. It is a miracle that this place is still running.'

So where were Nelly's original files, the ones she had digitised?

The new archivist checked boxes and thick rotting files connected to Indira Gandhi and her sons, Shree Sanjay and Shree Rajiv. Nothing.

I understood then. Nelly had either destroyed or hidden the files. She had started assembling material long before she had access to new technologies. Did she destroy the files recently after creating the CDs? But where were the files before she started digitising them? She must have hidden them somewhere in the building. But where?

Where would I hide the material?

A man in khaki entered with a note. The new archivist walked out of the room as if it was an emergency. The man stared at me. Then he too was gone. Waiting, I paced up and down and counted the number of handcarts. I don't know why. I started a brief conversation with two other fellows in the room. One of them, a young chap, was collecting material on Lady Curzon's boudoir, the Bengal famine, the colonial census, and Dalit literature (topics so disparate), and the other on Hume, Allan Octavian, the selfsame founder of the Congress Party. The researcher, however, was focusing on records connected to Hume's work as an ornithologist. In 1885 some twenty thousand stuffed birds, part of the prodigious collection, were destroyed in Shimla. 'Twenty thousand birds,' he exclaimed. Something I didn't know.

Hume Papers
Box I, Box II . . . Box XX.

Box XIX had many files labelled '84'. The year 1884 had been shortened to 84. Box XIX had twenty-seven files that had never been touched. And that is where I found Nelly's 1984 papers. She had taken precautions.

Papers, diaries, letters, postcards, photographs, children's sketchbooks, ration cards, passports, fragile clippings, cuttings of interviews with a few survivors (and the injured and the displaced), lists of the guilty citizens, bureaucrats, diplomats, judges, cabinet ministers, industrialists, politicians, media personalities and senior IPS police officers.

206

The Prime Minister. Then it dawned on me: the Congress Party had conducted its first major genocidal pogrom exactly ninety-nine years after it was formed, and exactly one hundred years after it was conceived in the hill station of Shimla.

*   *   *

Father's name was not on the nefarious list. Only his rank. He was involved. Beyond doubt. He enabled the pogrom, I thought. Father was one of the most senior IPS officers then. Part of Delhi Police. Unable to deal with the shock, I booked a cab. Towards Delhi. I knew it was time to confront him.

The traffic moved slowly that day. Now and then I saw hawks and vultures hovering over deep ravines and burning garbage. An unknown bird, perched on a pile of asbestos sheets, looked at me with large perplexed eyes. Another with a long tail flew wave-like from branch to branch until it disappeared in the mist along sharp, faintly metallic sounds. Just outside Solan, workers were widening the highway, and the air smelled of molten tar. Mile after mile of excess. Mindless construction by so-called developers. On the way to Delhi we stopped in Le Corbusier's city of concrete: Chandigarh. I asked the cabbie to make a detour to Sector XIV, and he drove slowly inside the university campus.

This is where my father studied anthropology, and this is where he was based when he applied for higher studies at Harvard. (He always avoids the topic. His move from Chandigarh to the US and back. Father never finished his grad work at Harvard. I don't know why he discontinued.)

The cabbie drove me slowly to the Gandhi Bhavan, then around the city, and for some unknown reason I started taking pictures of all the concrete buildings designed by the architect who had erased the past. The grids, the modules, the ramps. Massive spatial and formal disconnection. Le Corbusier's architecture produced my father. This new vision, this idea of modern India, produced him.

From Chandigarh I called Nelly. And apologised for my abrupt departure. 'Is your father all right?' she asked in a heavy voice. No, I think I am the one who is not all right. This I didn't tell her. I could not.

Soon the cabbie parked in front of the Rock Garden. I wandered through the surreal 'outsider art' garden for a long time. Then I sat down on a bench and gazed at the objects and figures Nek Chand, the designer, had assembled out of shards. Broken bangles, broken plates, broken china, pottery, old tyres, scrap metal – he had filled them with a new meaning without destroying the old. Nek Chand's dialogue with the past was a perfect counterpoint to Le Corbusier's architectural cleansing, I thought. Le Corbusier's 'open hand' tried to 'purify' the past; Nek Chand, on the other hand, celebrated 'impurity'. Le Corbusier considered 'past' as waste; Nek Chand embraced 'waste'. Broken washbasins, urinals, electrical sockets, tar drums, limestone. Nek Chand connected the modern with Harappa, with Mohenjo-daro. Man is a collector, and man is a builder of ruins, and man is a teller of tales. Man is not modular. Man is not a machine, and his house is not a machine, and his city is not a machine. By constructing the Rock Garden 'illegally' Nek Chand subverted Le Corbusier's vision, I thought. As if a bomb had been dropped overnight over that arrogant vision. It was like saying: No head=No heart=No balls=Le Corbusier.

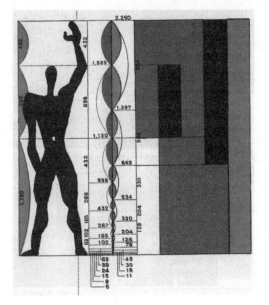

For a strange reason, it seemed, Le Corbusier was responsible for all the troubles in the world. His architecture would have meant something different if only my father had acted differently. Or shown remorse. I extended my stay in Chandigarh. The cabbie drove me to Sector XVII. Reluctantly I ate a Maharaja at McDonald's and consumed a local 'chil(le)d' beer, and just outside Neelam cinema an angled voice (originating from a hole in the ground) made an urgent request. The disembodied voice froze me, and then two hands grasped my leg. Only then I noticed the shoeshine boy. On the pavement. Threadbare black shirt with white embroidery – triangles and stars. Perched on concrete, he was one among many, glued to a tiny wooden box. *Paalish, sa'ab! Shinning!* I had not even made eye contact. So why me? People better dressed walked ahead or behind, but he chose me. *Shinning,* he pointed at my shoes. The leather looked unrespectably filthy – coated by layers and layers of mountain dust and ash, traces of my long walks. No one else in that busy zone outside Neelam cinema required the service as badly as me. He grabbed my stiff leg and put my foot on a wooden crate and started. It was my first time. Public shoeshine. The boy, no more than thirteen years old, possessed unbelievable strength. His eyes huge as if waiting impatiently to absorb the whole world. After a split-second decision he started unlacing my shoes. I was in no hurry, he noticed, and unlaced the right one first and lifted it up like a mirror, and his head oscillated like a pendulum following the motion of the brush. I stood on a small, flat piece of cardboard, observing, and recall his Robin Shoe Polish and Crown Eagle shirt. The only words we exchanged during those five unsteady minutes, 'Where are you from?' *Bhopal, sa'ab.* A chill went through my spine. I paid or overpaid hurriedly and wandered into a bookshop in my black shoes. Half hallucinating I flipped open three or four translations in the fiction section. One of them done by someone I know intimately. Someone who has failed me, but thinks that I deserve blame.

Clara, my estranged wife, is also a translator. She translates from French to English, and asks her authors lots of questions. She fusses over precision and accuracy for days on end. Clara, my red-haired wife, is forever locating the 'echo' of the original, forever locating the 'author's intention', she wakes up in the middle of the night anxious she has made a terrible error. In French the word 'mouton' means 'sheep', but it also means 'mutton'. She fusses over 'tu' and 'vous', and spends sleepless nights getting the emotional impact right. Once she drew me on a sheet of paper her major approach: if the original text is a circle, then the translation ought to be a tangent

210

line to the circle. Clara participates in scholarly conferences on gender and culture. She is the one, an angel of history, who made me aware of how the colonial powers used translations to tame the 'natives' and perpetuate domination. At a conference she met a Cree translator, who told her how the prejudiced missionaries translated the Bible into the Cree language. Long chapters (not originally in the Bible) were added denouncing Cree rituals and culture, calling their potlatches and their way of life and their creation myths ignorant and sinful, literally commanding the so-called heathens to convert in order to save their souls.

As I walked out, hallucinating, I felt the gentle touch of 'early' Clara. Not far from me a boy was eating ice cream from a cone, licking the rivulets of melting fluid. The boy's father – a vaguely familiar face from a different season. But this man could not have been Mr Gopal because he looked twenty years too young. Mr Gopal, my father's close friend. No idea who failed whom. Their friendship had ended abruptly for some mysterious reason. Mr T. Gopal. IPS. Gopal Uncle. He lived in Chandigarh, I found his phone number listed in the yellow directory.

She answered the phone, cold and indifferent. Mrs Gopal. I insisted on speaking to Gopal Uncle. He is in the shower, she said, and put down the phone. Twenty minutes later I called again. He has gone to the Reri Market. An hour later she didn't even bother to respond.

I called at eight in the evening. He is taking a walk. She gave me his cellphone number. Son, why don't you come tomorrow? he said.

The living room was spilling with tablets and bottles of alcohol and ample revelation of an agitated mind. His hair: grey and brittle. I don't have long to live, he said right after we hugged. It is cirrhosis. His wife was in the kitchen, and didn't rush to receive me. In olden days I would call my mother 'ma' and I would call Mrs Gopal 'badi ma', big mother.

Are you married now?

The room had two or three mirrors, but I couldn't see myself in them. Elliptically, I told him how happy I was with my marriage. My lovely wife. I told him the names of my daughters. Perhaps this steered the conversation to his own daughter. Trained as an economist, she had ended up becoming a visual artist in the US, he told me. She switched from a comfortable World Bank job to the precarious life of an artist. Gul had also done photo essays depicting the lives of immigrants, and this had won her a couple of major international awards. We knew each other as children; I recall helping her make a periscope in grade seven. Gul is my real past, my real regression, I thought. Perhaps I should call her.

Despite his failing eyesight and vodka, Gopal Uncle was ploughing through a thick hardback, a biography of the philosopher Wittgenstein. For a while now I have devoted myself to studying this genius, he told me theatrically, just like old times. Whereof one cannot speak (he quoted Wittgenstein), thereof one must be silent.

And both of us were silent for a long time.

Son, what I admire about Wittgenstein is that the man gave away his wealth. His entire wealth. He was an engineer just like you. We Indians call ourselves spiritual but we never give away a single rupee. We produce Tatas and Mittals and Ambanis and polyester princes and mining millionaires – while 500 million lead lives more impoverished than the most wretched in Africa.

More silence.

Mr Gopal poured me vodka on the rocks. The level in his own glass was alarmingly low. Once when I was very young and he was mildly inebriated I had asked him about

212

1*	Die Welt ist alles, was der Fall ist.
1.1	Die Welt ist die Gesamtheit der Tatsachen, nicht der Dinge.
1.11	Die Welt ist durch die Tatsachen bestimmt und dadurch, dass es a l l e Tatsachen sind.
1.12	Denn, die Gesamtheit der Tatsachen bestimmt, was der Fall ist und auch, was alles nicht der Fall ist.
1.13	Die Tatsachen im logischen Raum sind die Welt.
1.2	Die Welt zerfällt in Tatsachen.
1.21	Eines kann der Fall sein oder nicht der Fall sein und alles übrige gleich bleiben.
2	Was der Fall ist, die Tatsache, ist das Bestehen von Sachverhalten.
2.01	Der Sachverhalt ist eine Verbindung von Gegenständen. (Sachen, Dingen.)
2.011	Es ist dem Ding wesentlich, der Bestandteil

the meaning of a new word I had come across. 'Revolution,' he told me. 'Revolution means revolution.' His old sayings were all coming back to me. 'We are really one of the most violent countries in the world. But we tell a different story about ourselves to foreigners. We use Mahatma Gandhi as our poster boy.' The sayings. 'We are a country with a bad memory,' he blurted out once. 'We are good at forgetting. And we remember mostly the wrong things.'

Gopal Uncle topped my glass up, sat next to me and continued his strand of thought.

You see, son, what we need in this country are lots of Wittgensteins and not hideous, vulgar palaces built on land grabbed from orphanages. What we need, my dear son, is an end to further destruction of our land, rivers and air – an end to further plundering. How is the vodka? It is very good, I said. It better be good, he said. You see, son, the world continues to believe that the genius of our great country is spirituality . . . Our genius is that after throwing

213

the British away we have colonised our own people. *Shining India* works for a small minority. The history of our country is the history of one wrong after another.

Shall I pour you another?

Later.

Our national genius, my dear, is to make poor men, women and children defecate on the roadside. Six hundred million don't have proper toilets. We build tens and thousands of cheap, tasteless monuments to Nehru and Gandhi, and we name every single airport and bridge and street and market and ship and roundabout and school after that woman who imposed the dreadful emergency and censorship and forced vasectomies, or we name every single museum or hospital or flying school or market square after Indira Gandhi's son who banned a book by a writer like Salman Rushdie. This first son of hers, Rajiv, was our leader during the biggest massacres in the country. Bhopal, too, happened during his regime. Why was the CEO of Union Carbide allowed to flee India scot-free after the disaster?

He was breathless after the long impassioned monologue. It appeared to me as if he had lost his entire skin. Gopal Uncle had not changed.

'Whereof one cannot speak, thereof one must be silent,' I said.

Long silence.

I broke the silence. Finally, I said something direct, I urged him to talk about that man.

'Who am I to talk about?'

'You know things I don't.'

'Whatever I am going to say, remember, your father didn't start out that way.'

'I know.'

214

'You don't know much. Do you know how your parents met?'

'It was an arranged marriage.'

'Then you know nothing.'

Mr Gopal stared at his glass.

My body became absolutely still.

'Imagine this situation,' he said. 'Right after our training, your father and I, two eligible bachelors, worked in the office of the Police Chief in Delhi. It was a brand-new building. I was in your father's office, when the Chief walked in unannounced. We stood up. Saluted. He shook our hands and politely asked me to leave.

'I know about the first posting. I know Father worked at the headquarters.'

'But do you know what happened behind closed doors?'

'Papa didn't talk much about his job.'

'But this involves you, son. My friend and your father told me afterwards. That night we went out for a drink at the Imperial.'

Mr Gopal kept staring at his glass.

'He was something of a playboy, the Police Chief,' said Mr Gopal. 'To use that old-fashioned word, he *ruined* many young women. That day he was in your father's office to request him, beg him, or rather command him, to marry a woman five months pregnant. Abortion was not a possibility.'

'And I am that child?'

'Son, please don't leap to sudden conclusions. After the wedding your mother delivered a child who didn't survive more than a few hours. You were born a couple of years later. By the time you were born your father had already received two quick promotions.'

My eyes filled with a sadness I had not known before.

'I don't think your father cared for those promotions. I

215

think he genuinely wanted to help your mother. I think in his own way he fell for her.'

'They had a difficult marriage.'

'All marriages are difficult. Together these two produced you. So in a way their union was a success!'

I couldn't control my dark laughter.

'Your father was a graduate student at Harvard University,' he said, 'in the anthropology department, when he took the Civil Service exam. This has always remained a mystery to me, why he chose to do so. He was at an age when idealism infects the young. But really, why did he abort his studies at Harvard? A broken love affair? Culture shock? Or simply the winter?

'Or was it the Vietnam War? This last one is the "exact reason" he himself provided. The protests at the campus against the war. Now I know better: the exact reason is not always the exact one.

'Your father takes the Civil Service exam. He ranks number 24. Which means he is allowed to choose the most coveted Indian Foreign Service. He doesn't. Because those buggers are liars of the first order. That is what he said. Diplomats are the most fraudulent of all human beings, said your father,' said Mr Gopal.

'He opts for the Police Service (not even the second-most coveted Indian Administrative Service). All he told me was "I like a good game of chor-sipahi". What do you make of it? We grew close during training at the Police Academy in Hyderabad. The training, your father perhaps told you, is not just ideological, it is also physical. Perhaps you know. Morning PT, military drills, firing. Now that I think about it human bodies start transforming when they have to learn to assemble parts of a gun and shoot a target within nine minutes. Rigorous training is essential, I am not questioning. *Roznamcha. Nakka.* Do you still remember the words? Your father consistently scored well. Especially in papers that had to do with the Indian penal code, sociology, psychology and problem solving. After training school our fraternal bond became even stronger, because we were from the same state, the same cadre. A few years later we picked up our selection grade the same month. He was sent on a deputation posting for three years to the border zones, as you know, where he fought infiltration. What really happened in those zones is another mystery of cyclonic proportions. Men, weapons, narcotics. The kind of money he made. Don't quote me on this, son. Several complaints were also lodged by the rights organisations against his "interrogation methods". We kept in touch through letters, but he rarely wrote about his job. I had no idea then that our friendship would last exactly nineteen years . . . "Chaurasi," ' said Gopal, 'was a turning point.' He used the Hindi word for 'eighty-four'.

In '85, a few months after the pogroms, when the new Prime Minister presided over a special function, T. Gopal had refused to shake hands with the great man. They transferred him overnight to a Central Reserve Police Force battalion (fighting the Naxalites), and started a ridiculous 'misuse' inquiry and that is when he started studying law. Soon he chose to resign and moved to Chandigarh to practise law.

To be honest, he said, I didn't want the government to reward those who had enabled the massacres. Your father received a medal for the 'commendable work' he did and was promoted, and my career was ruined. (In '84, you see, our friends, the senior officers in West Bengal, didn't allow a single citizen to be harmed.) In Delhi, your father got a gallantry medal. The PM had won his own medal, his party won a landslide election victory. The pogrom, it seemed, was essential to become the leader of the country. And, rather than punish, the PM rewarded the guilty. Son, does this astonish and perturb you when I say that the massacres took place because the PM himself gave a nod? There is no paper trail, but the PM had a direct phone line. The Home Minister had a direct phone line. (The police were under the direct control of the central government.) These two – at the very top – allowed the state to collapse for over seventy-two hours. The senior cops partly followed, partly anticipated the command from the very top. They could have refused. Please forgive me, son, for I don't speak of your father in a positive light. I was his friend, not a chamcha. A silvery medal was pinned on your father's chest and it glowed with a strange hubris and a complete disregard for human lives. No matter what your father says now, he belonged to the school of thought that 'Sikhs ought to be taught a lesson' . . . All these years I have thought it over and I know the overall responsibility is that of the astonishing Congress Party. Congress made that orgy of madness possible. You see, for every Sikh who was saved, equal numbers were handed over by the neighbours. Some well-educated people said, *Maza chakha do Sikhon ko*. Ordinary citizens were mere bystanders; they watched the pogroms the way one watches the Republic Day parade or a cricket match. And yet nothing was spontaneous. As witnessed by thousands of human and animal eyes it was largely a Congress Party affair. As if the party set out to eradicate an entire people. A thousand Sikhs were killed every day in Delhi alone. (Ironically, most of the contractors who constructed the imperial city of Delhi a hundred years ago were Sikhs.)

No, I am not completely out of my mind when I tell you that public buses and trains were used by the State to transport paid 'mobs'. Voters lists were provided and Sikh

218

homes and businesses were marked overnight. Cops disarmed Sikh citizens if they happened to be armed and aided the 'mobs' perform their operations seamlessly. No it can't be true? Most victims, my dear boy, were burned with the aid of oil or a white inflammable powder, the mobs were given instructions-money-liquor-kerosene by senior leaders who belonged to the astonishing Congress Party, some of them Doscos, educated at the elite Doon school, my own classmates, sinister ringleaders, who guided the mobs just a kilometer away from the parliament. The Home Minister, another real hero, sat on his ass while Dilli turned into a killing field my dear son. Untold number of men were set on fire in more than 40 cities throughout the country. Thousands were massacred in Uttar Pradesh, Haryana, Bihar, Madhya Pradesh, Maharashtra . . . There was a massive cover-up; we are still counting the dead.

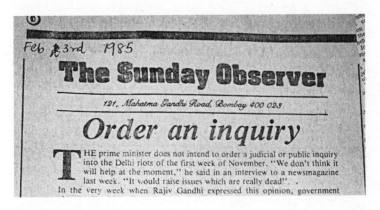

Feb 3rd 1985

The Sunday Observer

121, Mahatma Gandhi Road, Bombay 400 023

Order an inquiry

THE prime minister does not intend to order a judicial or public inquiry into the Delhi riots of the first week of November. "We don't think it will help at the moment," he said in an interview to a newsmagazine last week. "It would raise issues which are really dead". .
In the very week when Rajiv Gandhi expressed this opinion, government

The archive says:

I	Prime Minister Rajiv Gandhi enabled the pogrom.
I.I	His crime was as big as the crime of Home Minister Narasimha Rao.
I.IOI	As IAS officer testified: 'A group of us went to Minister

Arun Nehru, demanding the army be brought out. His demeanour was frighteningly casual . . .'

1.11   So many prominent citizens and lawyers begged Rajiv to stop the unspeakable massacres; he did nothing.

1.12   His MPs argued (something to the effect): *More Sikhs killed in my constituency; I am more important to the party. Make me a bigger minister.*

1.121   According to human rights reports and eye-witness accounts some of the MPs were senior Congress Party leaders and cabinet ministers: H. K. L. Bhagat, Kamal Nath, Lalit Maken, Sajjan Kumar, Jagdish Tytler, etc., etc.

1.13   National TV channel, Doordarshan (the only channel in the country at that time), used to incite ordinary people. The print media by and large collaborated with the state.

1.14   Hospitals like AIIMS refused to admit victims. The Fire Brigade refused to save Sikh homes and businesses.

2   The police were under the direct control of the central government. In November 1984 the Chief of astonishing Delhi Police was Shri S. C. Tandon, IPS. His actions (and non-actions) will outlast him. To this day he has never been held to account.

2.16   The police did not register most reports of murder, mass murder, rape, looting, attacks on photo-journalists.

2.161   The police spread vicious rumours about the Sikhs, and in certain zones actively encouraged the mobs to kill.

2.162   Sikh police officers (20 per cent of the force) were removed from active duty because they planned action against the arsonists.

2.163   Men in khaki directed mobs to houses where the Sikhs were hiding. *You have three days, do whatever you want.*

2.1631 The only people arrested by the police were the Sikhs. Or the police took away weapons from Sikh civilians and armymen trying to defend themselves, and paved way for mobs of trained killers to do their job seamlessly.

2.164   Low-ranking officers who defied the orders were immediately removed from duty and penalised.

2.165   Delhi Police's astonishing slogan to this day gives most citizens goosebumps: *With you, For you, Always.*

3   This kind of coordination of the state apparatus to kill its own citizens in such large numbers was unsurpassed in Indian history after the 1947 Partition.

3.1   Anyone who happened to be a Sikh was the target, doesn't matter if they were Independence fighters, industrialists, scientists, farmers, politicians, diplomats, journalists, soldiers, cooks, mechanics, teachers, taxi drivers and, ironically, 'People who had voted for the Congress Party'.

3.11   The poor suffered more than the rich, and this is an understatement.

3.12   Women were raped and their children were forced to watch the rape. Human body parts were sliced off and left for the dogs.

3.13   Although this was 'mass murder', each Sikh body was dragged out of a house or a shack or a hiding place and burned individually.

3.14   A famous Sikh writer took refuge in the Swedish embassy. 'I felt like a jew in Nazi Germany,' he said.

4   Not one but two prime ministers enabled the pogrom. Narasimha Rao, the Home Minister, also became Prime Minister a few years later.

4.01   When the obituaries of these two chaps were composed (several years later), most editors simply forgot to mention mass murder.

5   Prime Minister Rajiv Gandhi covered up the rapes and massacres, and rewarded the conductors of the pogrom. His is the beautiful face of extreme cruelty and injustice connected to November '84.

...

Sikhs ought to be taught a lesson (continued Mr Gopal). Your father was part of this mindset. He and other senior officers in the police force colluded with the government and ordered the force to behave criminally, unconstitutionally. Your father was an overnight hero, and he was not alone. Son, schoolchildren, today, do not read about the glorious work of astonishing beauty performed by these men because the story is not part of their textbooks ... The state has tried to wipe away this dark memory ... When the parliament reconvened the government never once mentioned the horrific carnage directly. When schools and colleges reopened the headmasters and principals completely forgot to mention those four days the city had just witnessed. The state, like a true criminal, took further advantage of the carnage. The astonishing Congress Party spent millions on an ad campaign, which vilified the minorities. The subliminal message of that PR campaign was that

the pogroms were 'natural', 'spontaneous', 'legitimate', 'outbursts of anger', 'inevitable', 'logical'. An entire community with a deep sense of belonging to India and Indianness was constructed by the state as the 'other'. Part propaganda, part justification, the ad campaign is largely forgotten today, but in '84 the Congress milked the pogroms to win an important election and retain power. The ads portrayed Sikhs as the enemy from across the barbed-wire fence, and the 'strong' Congress Party as the country's most trusted 'saviour'. Soon afterwards our colonial-style justice system took it upon itself to protect the guilty. Calling a public inquiry is not prudent, ruled the High Court judges of 'democratic' and 'secular' India. They were promoted to the Supreme Court, one was made the Chief Justice. Names are important. Have you followed Justice Ranganath Mishra's glittering career? Later, one farcical commission

after another essentially gave the Congress Party a clean chit. Whereof one cannot speak, thereof one must be silent, he said.

No one should be assassinated, but assassinations don't change how one lived one's life, continued Mr Gopal. Mrs Gandhi more than anyone else corroded the institutions of our democracy. The reason the violence against the Sikh citizens took place so efficiently, in such a coordinated fashion, is proof that she left the institutions rotten to the core.

In 1981 Mrs G refused to implement the recommendations of the National Police Commission. The commission after many years of hard work proposed a method to reduce the grip of the party in power on the police force. A thick report was presented to Madam, which also covered reforming police training, so as to inculcate the 'supremacy of law' and 'human dignity'. Madam treated the report like crap.

She started the mess in Punjab. That is a complex and tragic story, topic for a thick book, a separate one. The book would also narrate the lives of Sikh leaders, some of them no better than self-serving pigs . . . Anyway . . . Let us not digress. We must learn from the damaged pages of history. How central this one thing is to that entire era. Mrs Gandhi, the so-called saviour of India, bought into her own 'great leader' myth: *Indira is India and India is Indira*. Myths can be dangerous. That one ruined her and millions of others. I hear a film is being made on her life and on her death. Soon they will worship her as a devi in temples.

The silence between us grew louder and, perhaps to forget it all, we began dozing and fell asleep for an hour. In my dizzy state I noticed a slightly peeved Mrs Gopal, in a green sari and chappals, clearing the table. I stood up and wished her namaste. She didn't hug me her usual way. The years had created an enormous gulf between us. Before you go away there is something I must say. She didn't sit down, but spoke candidly. It might comfort you. Something about your mother. I listened to your conversation with my husband (from the kitchen) and that is why decided to tell you. Under normal circumstances this is not the stuff an aunt tells her nephew. Mrs Gopal literally stammered as she called me her nephew. This might provide you some comfort, she repeated. I turned towards Mr Gopal. He was fast asleep, snoring mildly. On a certain day and at a certain hour, she said, your uncle and your father stopped their friendship and they asked us, the women, to act likewise. Did you? I asked. Well, we tried,

224

but we couldn't and we didn't. Both of us, your mother and I, found a way around the closed doors and continued seeing each other. We stopped sharing confidences for a while, but it started again. If this comforts you to hear then you must know that your mother 'denied' your father after November '84. Denied what? I asked. She denied him sex. This continued for several months. I can't tell you more. And don't ask me for more. Mrs Gopal returned to the kitchen with her eyes moist. Later, when he woke up, Mr Gopal dropped me at the train station.

We were on platform number 1, waiting. I can't forget the operatic cacophony of birds. Tens and thousands of them perched right under the corrugated-metal roof. Perched on trussed structures right above the tracks, diminishing the evening light. Hundreds of them on electric wires and distant carriages and water pipes . . . The station felt like a grand bustling chiria-ghar, each one of those creatures emitting sounds as if hopelessly lost and disorientated, with no sense of distance or direction or purpose. A loss incomprehensi-ble to me, and it hurt my ears, the out-of-tune orchestra, wave after amplified wave assaulting my ears, showing no signs of dampening. The chorus: much larger than the sum of its parts. Why were they there? Why were they indifferent to those thousands of mango and guava groves in the vicinity? Perhaps they were simply waiting for food. Perhaps a railway station is the safest place to roost. No predators. It was all a deafening mystery. What birds are these? I asked. Have you forgotten? he said. Mynahs, the common hill mynahs. Mr Gopal put his courageous arm around my shoulder. He smiled. Thank you, I said. He didn't hear me. Forgot to mention some-thing. His voice louder now. Have you heard of Ved

225

Marwah? IPS? He is still alive, a fine man, but he missed a beautiful chance to become a hero. Ved Marwah, several years ago, after pressure from human rights organisations, was brought in to conduct an inquiry by the authorities, and suddenly he was asked to stop. Ved, you see, had made no attempt to save the guilty. He was not allowed to table the report. Your father and other senior officers and bureaucrats and senior Congress leaders concerned, including that failed aeronautical engineer Rajiv Gandhi (Mr Clean), and all the ethnic cleansers, simply wrecked the inquiry. *It would raise issues which are really dead*, emphasised Mr Clean. He, for his special talents and exemplary deeds, was showered with the highest civilian awards, including the Bharat Ratna, whereas Ved has been hounded for the last twenty-five years. A number of cases have been filed against Ved on flimsy grounds.

The train started rolling as if on Teflon, and soon it began to rain. The mynahs far away now, absolutely silent. Who in this bustling world would be cast to play the role of the great leader Indira Gandhi? I thought. How will the poor woman prepare for her role? If I ever write a book on this topic I will send the actress (my character) to the Indira Memorial in Delhi. She will go there and pay special attention to the polished surfaces, and all the missing bits, all the silences, loud and not so loud. What is absent will teach more about the so-called great leader than what is present, I thought. The great leader's actions and the actions and inactions of her sons will teach my actress more than those four or five hagiographies, categorised as biographies. She will soon realise that her body is not passing through a Memorial, but really a Forgetorial.

She will notice the conspicuous absence of certain citizens and question the state's guided tour, and reject all the propaganda pamphlets. She will question the definitive versions of 'What to remember' and 'How to remember'.

She will pose tons of questions about the Indian state, which organised, incited and carried out the genocidal violence.

The train was moving faster than the front of clouds. Outside, a woman was sitting on a fence scrutinising an undulating green field, tall pampas grass. All I could see (and still see) is a beautiful vortex of hair. She's watching. She is watching a house. She is watching a house that is burning. She is watching a house that is burning in the rain. She draws cold water from a well (and it is still raining) and washes her sultry face. The image has deep subconscious striations, and this is a problem. Emblindened, she washes her hair with a dark textured substance that resembles henna ... Who is this person?

The Russian actress, Margarita Terekhova, would be ideal for the role. She is a proof-reader running towards the printing press in Stalin's Soviet Union. Breathless, in a state of panic, she runs in her unbuttoned overcoat; the dirt road is covered with crunchy autumn leaves. She enters the building through heavy security and runs to her office ... *The evening edition ... The special edition ... No edition should have misprints.* The supervisor rushes the proof-reader to the printing zone amidst a loud hum of machinery, the two women in such a scurry as if paper unspooling out of a giant cylinder ... She checks the proofs ... Outside the window gusty, watery turbulence ... No, she has made no error, and she starts crying ... Her supervisor warms to her, lights a cigarette.

227

But what was the word? I asked the grown-ups over and over while watching the film. Why did the woman whisper the word? Why were we in the audience not supposed to know? My mother put a finger on her lips. Shh! It was 1975. After the film we ate in the International Centre tea room. T. Gopal had just returned from an official trip to Russia. He ordered goulash for all of us, including his daughter Gul. During the middle of our meal he noticed we six were the only ones in the place, and at that precise moment he explained the 'whisper': the misprint 'S(r)alin' means 'shit'.

Mrs Ghandi imposed her Emergency in 1975 and Tarkovsky's *Mirror* was also released in 1975. She claimed she was a mirror that allowed dishevelled India to take a peek at itself. She was India. So she screwed and embogged India extravagantly. During those days of censorship my father read five newspapers, and they all read like exact copies of each other. Perhaps that is why he used them to kill mosquitoes.

In Delhi, go to Jantar Mantar, and then the Lodhi Gardens, said Nelly on the phone, when I called her from Chandigarh. Stand in front of neem and tamarind and peepul and blood-red semal, gulmohar, amaltas and a purple jacaranda, and recite Ghalib and Paz. Then go to Bangla Sahib and Sis Ganj gurdwaras and listen to Gurbani. You will hear more verses there, and if you are lucky you will hear them recited in thirty-one ragas. Only a gesture will allow you to express your true feelings. Sometimes I miss the old city, its walls and exaggerations, its smells, its 12 million people. Those narrow fissured lanes of Chandni Chowk. For my sake: take the train to Delhi. For I have forgotten what it means to travel by a train.

228

In Delhi, go to my favourite bookstores, especially in the maze of Khan Market.

Your presence helped a lot, she said. After Maribel moved back to Mexico I thought I would fail to make it on my own, she said . . . Our walks through Shimla during a particularly difficult time also reminded me of my walks with my father when I was a girl. How keen he was that I learn my 'mother tongue' properly, and I don't know why I resisted then. I see myself listening to Darwin, Partition stories and God, and I see myself asking him questions while watching *Nanak Naam Jahaz Hai*, the film in which a man's blindness is cured by miraculous force.

It was a superfast Shatabdi train, meals on board. Tomato soup saturated with salt and pepper. Samosas and ketchup. Fish curry was the only dish I liked. The mineral-water bottle on my seat smelled of organo-chlorines. Not far from me sat two obese and expressionless Wisconsin tourists and an army general in a thinking-man pose. To this day I don't know what his pensiveness was all about; he seemed to be enduring a bunch of college students, whirling around, exuding incessant silliness. Cellphones kept ringing, and people kept consuming spicy thalis, and cockroaches kept doing their work. At Panipat station two banias entered the carriage and their chatter and petty business deals overwhelmed the whole vibrating compartment. *Wire ki length ki lambai kitni hai.* I was retracing a journey that has haunted me all these years. But on that train it really meant nothing. Half an hour before Delhi most passengers clogged the aisle, unafraid of injury to themselves and others. Then a high-pitched pre-recorded voice announced 'You are requested to destroy the mineral-water bottles' and a chill went right through me.

I was the last one to disembark the train at New Delhi station. Platform number 1. Flickering soot-coated neon signs. UPPER CLASS WAITING ROOM. Smell of human shit, peanuts and marigolds. There I felt a burning sensation. On the train the coffee had burned my tongue and my upper palate. Nothing else. I bought a couple of papers from Pankaj Bookstall, and instead of heading towards the station exit, on the spur of the moment decided to get a haircut from the station barber. Military-style crew cut. The barber made me repeat my request, sensing a disconnection between my words and thoughts. Towards the end his strong fingers massaged my bare head with coconut oil. During the haircut a chill went through my spine, and I thought about my Sikh classmate at IIT. That entire time came back like hard foam and slapped me. It was the 18th or 19th of November in 1984 when *his* hair was being removed; he had shut his eyes tight, and the crackling of the transistor radio could be heard in the barber's shop and Prime Minister Rajiv Gandhi's voice: *when a big tree falls the Earth shakes*. I was too young to process the lack of shock, and the force field of hate, in the new PM's words. The massacre didn't raise a single hair on the PM's body. Limited vocabulary of a pogrom, and equally bad physics: *when a big tree falls the Earth shakes*. Slowly my feet dragged me automatically to the waiting room. Only one bench was free, but I decided not to occupy that tiny space. Don't know why I stood paralysed in one corner with my luggage until I heard those seventeen-year-olds playing antakshari ... At first the loud singing and clapping annoyed me ... but listening to 'Chingari Koi Bhadke' I felt they were the only lyrics that Bombay cinema had minted which understood my inner turmoil. Kishore Kumar's melancholic, mildly inebriated voice kept running through my mind, *majhi hi jo nav duboyeh usay kaun bach- ayeh*. Then someone sang an A. R. Rahman song and my eyes became moist.

Only once have I seen my father cry. After the wedding of his younger sister. That day he wore a mint-coloured safari suit, male fashion of the seventies, and right after the sister's car took off he created a rare spectacle by sobbing uncontrollably. Only once have I cried for him. Because I thought we had lost him. Until the age of seven I slept on the same bed with my parents, in the middle, more towards my father. I loved his smell. Some- times he would mutter nonsense in his sleep. But that gibberish only increased my resolve to become someone big and significant. Like him. I wanted to dance. Like him. Sometimes he would break into a foreign dance in his uniform. In his khaki uniform he took me to Tihar

231

jail once, and showed me a 'thief', a 'murderer', an 'arsonist'. In the wing for women he showed me a prostitute. She had small hands, the smallest hands I ever encountered. To this day I remember the shape and size. I stood close to the iron bars and she threw a hand outside and quickly touched my brow. This is real life, he said. You are 'oversensitive'. Sonny boy, acquire a thick skin, he said. Other people's children are different. He was so much more articulate than me, so much more judgemental. But he knew how to listen, analyse, suspect. How to enjoy. Spin around . . . Most of my memories of Father are pale vortices, overshadowing love. And the objects he gifted me . . . Did they speak of his everlasting love? That old metallic camera of his, my first real introduction to the magic and science of photography. How excited I was to receive the gift that would help me freeze the order and disorder of time. Just before we set out on the journey to the highest mountains. Rohtang Pass. Mount Affarwat. Nanga Parbat. Back home I took the camera and the rolls to the developing shop, and that technician of a man very hesitantly delivered bad news. That I had basically shot pictures of NOTHING. Because on the left side of the camera a tiny cavity had exposed the film, damaging it irreversibly due to leakage of light, whereas the film should have been wrapped and sealed by perfect darkness. My father cares about me, but I am afraid of him.

When the two men shook hands on the dark railway platform (Father and Professor Singh), although they were strangers, they trusted each other (I assumed), and I was the object of that trust . . . *Take care of my son, he has just recovered from jaundice* . . . Two days later when Father did what he did, he betrayed the Constitution, his oath, his

232

profession; more important, he betrayed me, and I never saw it coming. For a long time I could not process the betrayal. I lacked the proper vocabulary or concepts to understand it, and there was no time, for heat transfer and mass transfer and diffusion equations and mechanics of materials and failure analysis and thermodynamics would occupy all my time . . . Then I started preparing with a certain madness for the GRE exams to escape India. But I don't know for sure. We always take the past and bend it to our current awareness.

In Delhi I checked into a hotel. I called voluptuous calves, but she had changed her number. (The Kindle is still with me. What else can I do?) I continued taking notes, but the whole project made little sense now, not until I arranged a meeting with Father. And that is exactly what my whole body resisted. I tried to imagine the father–son meeting, but the experiment was a disaster. For days I felt shocked and paralysed. As if an unknown electromagnetic field had irreversibly changed my body chemistry. Then a professor friend of mine from the PhD committee invited me to watch a film by Pasolini at the IIT campus. Reluctantly I agreed. The cabbie, a young Sikh with a baby face, dropped me in front of the boys' hostel. Glazed red-brick building named after the ancient mountain range Aravali. The room was packed, and although I arrived late the screening had not started. They had also changed the film – no longer Pasolini's *Oedipus Rex*, but a film called *A Taste of Cherry*. From where I stood it was possible to scan the profiles of all those in the audience, and I spotted my friend at the very front, sitting next to the empty chair he had saved for me.

'Pasolini has been cancelled,' he explained. A gay professor's expulsion from one of the IITs had polarised

233

the campus. The IITs have a history of unjust expulsions, he said. During Mrs Gandhi's Emergency many professors were expelled or arrested. Are you really interested in watching *Oedipus Rex*? I will have no problem borrowing the DVD, he said. I know the organisers of cultural events, SPIC-MACAY. You are also welcome to borrow Kiarostami. Sheer poetry. Who is Kiarostami? I asked. Perhaps the most important contemporary film-maker, and he lives in Iran. What I like about his cinema is that the characters re-enact their own real life stories. *A Taste of Cherry* is about an ordinary man who seeks assistance to kill himself. The film has a beautiful ending, perhaps the best in cinema.

Listen, I said, is it possible to skip the film? He agreed without much fuss. We abandoned the student hostel and walked through the campus towards the Wind Tunnel. He, too, was in a bad way, a state more fragile than mine. Dressed in a mere tracksuit. His hair messier than before. I detected he, also, had been drinking alone. Soon we passed by the faculty residences, and he admired the jacarandas. A professor of mine used to live in that house behind those trees, I told him. Professor Singh would park his white Fiat there, and once I saw him mopping the Fiat with a yellow rag, then he sprinkled the leftover water around the purple trees.

'Will you help me kill myself?'

That line didn't come as a surprise. The surprising thing was that I, too, was facing similar impulses, hard to articulate.

I spent another week in my hotel room in Hauz Khas. My black Calvin Klein socks had developed big holes. For the first time I didn't shave for a week, didn't shower. I would stand against the wall, helpless, squinting at the thick curtains. On the floor I lay sick, breathing heavily, persuading myself that it was all a redundant dream, an old tape that could be rewound. Room service delivered lunches and dinners, and I ate gluttonously to forget the simple fact that I had a parent. In Shimla in the archives when I was going through the files I could not share my discovery (Father = Mass Murderer) with the staff members. To do so would be to betray Nelly. But at the same time I could not resist borrowing from the files a newspaper cutting and a photo of the pogrom widows. Perhaps 'borrowed' is the wrong word. 'Stealing' is the right one. Over and over the stolen photo stared at me. Over and over in the hotel room I read the yellow cutting. Then I took to walking. Random aimless walking. Day and night I walked in the unwalkable city, the air heavy with petrol and diesel exhaust and other nefarious molecules, and I judged harshly the city and its part imperial, part box architecture, and ugly roads and countless humans trapped within countless million miseries. All the existential anxieties of my teenage years returned as I zigzagged towards the ring road and the outer ring road. During my teenage years I didn't find history interesting, and now the only sites that beguiled me were connected to the past.

Only the poor walk in Delhi. And they kept walking with me – the dead. Holding my fingers, unable to cross the streets by themselves. I took refuge in the zoo, gazing at the eyes of the animals, gazing at the specular eyes of captive elephants, tigers, panthers, snow leopards. I begged and begged again the dead to liberate me. In return I was prepared to do anything, even murder the caretakers of the zoological conc. camp, and obliterate my tormented selves by puting a noose around my neck. I walked in circles and spirals and straight Cartesian lines. But the dead continued to walk with me. After the fourth day my shoes looked visibly damaged, and no shoeshine boy grasped my leg. My left knee started hurting. Hurting, I felt a sudden need to see Nelly again. She called that evening. And left a voice message. She was going to take the bus to Delhi.

After listening to my messages I checked the papers. There was a huge ad in the local paper – a high-school reunion. Not my school, but I decided to attend. Professor Singh once talked about this old school of his fondly, without a hint of revulsion. In '84 the school (next to the Chilean Embassy) was vandalised and looted before it was reduced to ashes. The classrooms, the laboratories, everything.

Now a new structure, a new generation.

The principal told me that Nelly was expected any time after the assembly; he took me to the assembly and introduced me to the students. Before ardas I spoke a little about Professor Singh, Helium-3 and moon missions. The students heard but didn't listen. The principal, a Sikh gentleman, did not know Mohan personally, but he knew the details. I hung out with Mohan's 'class fellows'. And that is where, once again, I found her an hour later. Nelly had come for two days from Shimla, a survivor mingling with other survivors.

Now that I think about it she was happy to see me. Obviously she had overcome some of her fear of Delhi. I was about to tell Nelly about something new I had read in the papers – the US court and the summons it sent to the Congress Party – when her cellphone beeped, and soon afterwards a very intense man, who would have been about her son's age, with big eyes and a neatly trimmed beard, introduced himself. 'We would like to do a piece on you.' Now, that annoyed her a little. I witnessed her face, filled with anger and anguish; it was clear she was not in a mood to be interviewed. But soon she changed her mind. The journalist's own story was very interesting. He became quite animated while sharing it. Several years ago he moved to Chicago and decided to study engineering. Then, in the middle of his PhD, he dumped school and travelled the entire continent, Yukon to Yucatan, on a motorcycle, and afterwards switched over to journalism, and decided to return 'home'. A chill went through me when he told us his name.

Arjun.

He was both shy and confident, and now and then tilted his head, which accentuated the beauty of his big eyes. I checked with Nelly if she wanted me there. She held my hand. We walked through the science block. Maroon pebble-dash walls. Several times I peeked in the laboratories, the walls crammed with colourful displays. Lateral Section of a Flower. Life Cycle of an Angiosperm. Chandrayan. Not far from the school bell there were three fire extinguishers. Walking through the corridor we also watched young boys and girls play volleyball. Such noise!

'To this day I don't know the rules of volleyball,' said Arjun. 'I wish someone had taught me at the right age.'

'Do you feel bad?' asked Nelly.

'No,' he said. 'This was just a passing thought.'

237

We walked to the huge banyan tree close to the swings. For a fleeting moment, it seemed, we managed to escape the past. Briefly the three of us sat on the swings, red and yellow. One or two repressed memories made an attempt to surface, but I refused permission. Boldly I dismissed them. My gaze fell on the blackened school wall. A few red bricks and the rest black like a child's hair. On the other side of the wall – a DTC bus depot. On our side, piles and piles of abandoned furniture. Chairs, desks, antiquated computers, Godrej almirahs. By the swings Arjun told us something that has continued to haunt my hours.

'Right after the pogroms the names of the guilty were published by PUDR and PUCL,' said Arjun. 'A senior Congress leader called Maken, who was also the son-in-law of the Indian Vice President, appeared prominently on the list. But the criminal Criminal Bureau of Investigation or the legal system did nothing. In the new government several of the accused were made cabinet ministers by Prime Minister Rajiv Gandhi and subsequent Congress governments. Yet this is not the image transmitted to eloquent books of history. The Congress Party today is no longer the same. But it is the same. The party gave India its first Sikh prime minister. But he has done nothing ... Not a single politician, cabinet minister, bureaucrat, diplomat, judge or a high-ranking police officer has been brought to justice. Manmohan Singh, after enormous pressure from human rights groups and the opposition, did issue an absurd apology, or semi-apology, whatever it was, without acknowledging the crimes of those at the very top, and no sense of justice. But look at the current government. The Minister for Trade, Kamal Nath, accused by tons of victims, human rights reports and eye-witness accounts. (How will he, I have often asked myself, be remembered by history?) He visits foreign lands (resort towns like Davos) on big business missions. Sonia and Rahul Gandhi often shake hands and do photo ops with the foot-soldiers of November 1984. The Harvard-trained Home Minister calls another genocide-denier (who until recently was the Minister for Overseas Affairs) 'my friend'. However, Maken's case is different.

'In '85 he was murdered at his house. Maken's daughter was six years old then, she didn't know that in November '84, on her father's orders, hundreds of innocent people were burned to death in the most brutal fashion.

'Maken was gunned down by three militants, one of them a young man who had heard about the pogroms; his own father (a highly respected agricultural scientist and a professor at the university) was in the same neighbourhood where the Congress Party leaders, operating as merchants of death, are reported to have set up their killing machine.

'He was nabbed many years later in the US by Interpol, where he was kept in a high-security prison. He confessed his crime and requested a trial in India. He was extradited in 2000. At the trial he confessed that he had nothing personal against the Maken family. Why didn't the Indian state bring the Congress leaders and top police officers to justice?

'In 2008 the case took a strange twist when Maken's daughter decided to meet the man in the prison.'

Nelly was staring at Arjun.

'You have a huge book there,' I said.

'I am writing it as a tiny article for the paper,' said the journalist. 'These days I don't have much time. I got married last year and now I perform the role of a new father. To write books one needs time, and time is the only thing I lack.

'Anyway, the daughter had grown up hating the prisoner,' he continued. 'Who would not? But she decided to meet him. He had confessed his crime, and he enrolled in

239

the distance education programme to continue his studies, a Master's degree in agricultural sciences. She told him she had grown up hating him. He had snatched away her precious childhood. The prisoner exploded, 'Your father snatched it away from thousands of children. Look, Indira Gandhi's assassins were hanged, but those who ordered the pogroms and those who actually killed innocent people have still not been brought to justice. So many years have passed by, so much ruined time. Twenty years, twenty-five years. Soon all those who witnessed will die and the victims will die and thousands of widows will die and then all we'll be left with is a big void. One day people in India will write plays about that Event. But justice is more important than plays and poetry, he emphasised.'

'After the meeting the daughter told the media that she had forgiven the murderer. She also started lobbying for clemency.'

Arjun fell silent.

I decided to leave, he was waiting for me to leave in order to begin interviewing Nelly. We shook hands. Then I made it to the school gates. Outside I saw a rickshaw over-loaded with freshly varnished furniture. Dressing table, dining table and a bed, all on one rickshaw, and I realised I hadn't asked the most important question, so I turned back, literally running, noticing the labs and classes in progress. I made it to the reunion room breathless. They were still there. My reappearance made the journalist emit a piercing smile. Nelly was half expecting me.

'Did you ever?' I asked Arjun's namesake. 'Did you ever meet the man?'

'Yes, I did. As a matter of fact I did. And the first question I asked was: Why did you kill Maken's wife? She was innocent. She had no role to play in the pogroms. I didn't want to kill her, he said, I waited for several hours and acted when the man was alone, but in a split second she appeared from nowhere running and embraced her husband in an attempt to save him.'

On the way to the hotel the auto-rickshaw driver turned on FM radio. Radio Mirchi, 98.3 FM. Neither the driver nor the rest of the city listening to the songs on Radio Mirchi had the faintest idea about the stuff going through my mind.

Because I didn't charge my cellphone for a couple of days my voicemail filled with messages. Messages from IIT, and from Nelly. She left four or five messages. While checking the messages I dealt with one of my worst fears. What if unable to connect with me she decided to visit my 'home'? What if she visited Amrita Sher-Gil Marg and Father received her at 'home'?

When I returned her call she was already on the train. Part of me was relieved, but I raised the worst-case scenario.

'Did you go to Amrita Sher-Gil Marg?'

'What for?'

Nelly was travelling, and that is precisely the reason I postponed revealing the truth about my father. Yet again.

Arjun's interview appeared a week later. Nelly's photo spread over two pages. And that is how I found out. Halfway into the interview she spoke about the trip to Italy, the fascist railway station. She and her boy returned after they ran out of money and spent a couple of days in a relief camp in Delhi. A few men at the camp were making plans to kill the pogrom instigators. Volunteers? She thought Arjun was too young, and that is why she didn't warn him. When she woke up in the morning the

241

boy was gone ... There was another immensely moving piece in the same magazine, the story of a Chicago immigrant, an engineer like me. The engineer, Raj Singh, his real name, made me cry (and laugh) and I felt my six-foot cylinder of a body burning. The piece hit me like a concrete block. My doppelgänger was apparently tortured by my good father or one of his colleagues. How does one really forgive the unforgivable? The engineer's story convinced me that a so-called apology amounts to nothing. Reconciliation is impossible without justice. Raj Singh writes:

How little I know about my childhood. And yet I remember the sheer astonishment I experienced on finding out at school that it takes around eight minutes for the light of the sun to arrive on Planet Earth. Or the puzzlingly constant speed of light. Another thing that never fails to astonish me is the origin of life – chances are if the big bang happens again no life would form. Life is the biggest coincidence we know of on Planet Earth. I have no idea why I ended up choosing metallurgical engineering. Why I focused on microstructures of steel. Why I spent ten years of my life researching corrosion and vibration. Metallurgy was not even my first choice. Meteorites. I really wanted to study cosmic accidents; objects older than our earth. In November '84 we were in Delhi. We were spared. Our neighbours gave us refuge ... Our neighbours hid us in a dark room only after we agreed to cut our hair. (But once inside their storeroom we refused to cut our hair.) These neighbours were slightly better than those neighbours and a woman who sided with the mob. (I would like to believe she has become human again.) In some other city this is where the madness would have stopped ... Soon afterwards we got a notice from our landlord to vacate the house – we had signed the lease for an entire year, but he asked us to leave ... I would often eat at the landlord's place and play cricket with his children completely oblivious to what was going on ... My father was summoned by the court. At first he kept me in the dark. I found out and accompanied him to the hearing. Over there they abused him verbally, 'sardar-ji aa gaya, sala sardar-ji aa gaya,' then the judge scolded the lawyer representing us, 'Are you out of your mind?' The landlord wanted us out because he was afraid some 'lumpen' might set his property on fire. The court ruled in his favour; we were served an eviction notice. Three or four men came and dismantled our house; so many of our objects resisted being moved, but on two lorries the men took our objects away. We went by train to Punjab to stay with our relatives. On the way, close to Panipat, the train made an unexpected stop, cops in khaki (and black leather belts) barged in and demanded IDs and arrested me arbitrarily. They took me to a prison inside an old fort, where they tied my hands behind my back with my turban, and then tied them to a rope, which was attached to a rod on the ceiling and a pulley. I was suspended in the air by the pulley while the police beat me with lathis on the soles of my feet and knees. Later a heavy wooden roller moved up and down my thighs until I lost consciousness. Cold water was thrown on my face, and then the cycle recurred as if an experiment. I don't remember wearing my clothes, perhaps I had my under-wear on. I try not to dwell on that image. All I want to say is that I learned a lot about the strength of materials in that crumbling fort, and a lot about physics and chemis-try and biology and the human body. Later I acquired

243

words like 'fibrosis', 'dislocation', and phrases like 'tenderness of thigh muscles'. I still don't know the proper Hindi or Punjabi word for torture.

These days I am reading a book titled *Reduced to Ashes* by a Vienna-based human rights expert. Within its pages I found something I did not know, and it made me feel lucky, because my father was able to generate ten lakh rupees for the Inspector General of Police to secure my release. Thousands of innocent people 'disappeared' then and the police killed thousands in custody and carried out secret cremations. Vienna-based Ram Narayan Kumar spent the last two decades of his life uncovering the truth about the secret crematoriums. The police, he writes, also created a climate of moral revulsion, sometimes they would themselves engineer heinous crimes – just like the terrorist – killing innocent people.

Sometimes a feeling grows within me to stop everything and scream like the magic-realist dwarf narrator in that German novel called *The Tin Drum*. Scream and shatter all things made of brittle glass. The body that they tortured is still within me. Sometimes it dissolves completely and it feels as if the process of dissolution is irreversible, but then it swells again, becomes bigger than me. I don't want to stay like this for the rest of my nights. I want the swelling to shrink, to metamorphose into an invisible dot, I want the weight within me to become weightless, I want to experience weightlessness.

Not a single year goes by when I don't encounter a person from the diaspora who claims that 'you Sikhs deserved what you got'. 'Achha hua.' Huge violence in those two words. Often such characters are highly educated professionals. When I narrate the short version of my story their eyes pop out – but we never meet again.

244

What hurts me more than anything else is that my father never painted after we moved to Chicago; he grew his beard long, but never recovered from the shock. He drove a cab and that is how he raised me. He gave up what he loved the most, he had rebelled against his family members to study the visual arts, and he gave it up to drive a cab. No more Picasso, Matisse, *Lady in Moonlight*, Jamini Roy, Karkhana paintings. He purged art from his everyday life. Even the cab stopped after thirteen or fourteen years, he aged before his time, he would stammer, and lost the use of both hands, he was unable to apply torque with his fingers, unable to unbutton his shirts, unable to put socks on by himself and tie shoelaces. I feel like writing my own book and dedicating it to him. The narrator would completely repress his painful memories; he speaks the language of silence. But silence is not a real language. My father was like that, and I don't want to become him.

Next day, after a lot of unnecessary resistance, I took a taxi to Trilokpuri slum. The clean-shaven, dishevelled cab driver was around sixty years old and carrying more wrinkles than he deserved. An entire era was visible within the confines of that rugged face. He was a bit puzzled when I mentioned the destination. We passed by a big DLF mall and an ice factory, and just before the zebra crossing he accelerated. I don't recall how our conversation turned to 1984. Bodies on fire. Generating ash and grit. The carcasses . . . He told me stuff that in essence resembled the account in the disintegrating paper cutting, the one I stole from the archives. Sitting in the cab, I thought back to my days in Shimla and the abrupt return to Delhi. The previous night in the hotel sauna I'd had a similar conversation with a rich old man. The temperature set at eighty-two degrees Celsius. Only the facts matter, the 65-year-old had said in a calm and collected manner, his towel as white as mine. His loose, flabby skin absorbed the same fragrant eucalyptus oil vapour, and the heat of the rocks. The more 'facts' he narrated, the more agitated he grew, his language more vulgar. We were the only two in the sauna. He checked if I understood Hindi. *Chaurasi*, he said. Tattey kaat deney chahiye thhey sab saalon kay? We should have chopped their balls off then? . . . Only then I understood. Did you see it from up close? I asked. He paused. Were you part of the mob? Did you burn a Sikh? He was sweating, but not because of what I asked. Slowly he turned his neck in my direction. Young man, all I can say is that the motherfuckers didn't get enough.

The cabbie was driving at near Mach speed. I asked him to turn back just before the bridge over Yamuna River

and make towards an alternative destination. 'Home'. No longer my home. Amrita Sher-Gil Marg was no longer my marg. Red tiles, and thriving aeroelastic palm trees. A thought flashed inside my liquidating brain. What if? What if? The man dropped me, and within an instant, seeing large numbers of police guards by the gates, fled without payment. There I spent a few minutes with the well-tended plants in my father's garden. The creeper on the brick wall had no roots just like old times; it derived nourishment from the particles of soil trapped inside the cracks. Our old gardener saluted me and carried on watering the patch of yellow hibiscus. I borrowed a cigarette and smoked. One never forgets no matter how long the gap of time. Then I walked into my father's study, and scanned the books he surrounded himself with, the study where he translated my myths, or ignored them; this is where Father kept his diaries, the daily orders he received and the actions he took. Inspired by the legendary officer DGP Rustomji my father had started keeping thick diaries, and they were meticulously labelled. All the diaries were there. Only 1984 was missing. Why in his retired life was it missing?

On his desk, a Rubik's cube and letters. One of them from Clara. It was open and I was tempted, but I know all the polite meaningless words Clara mails him in that old-fashioned way now and then. She maintains a correspondence with him; my estranged wife and my father have formed a mutual admiration club and exchange polite meaningless words every couple of months. She believes my problems with him are 'normal' and 'usual' problems 'normal people' have with normal parents or the older generation. She has no idea that being the son of a mass murderer is a dreadful condition. She has no idea.

Now that I think about it I decided to meet Father purely for the sake of maintaking my sanity. It was impossible to move forward without a brief encounter. If someone were to ask me: How did it go?, the first thing my body would do in response to that question is to shake mildly, not violently; the mildness would tell my interlocutor the intense hatred I feel, revealing also the truth hard to admit. That I must have loved him in a different season.

He was not home. My quick-witted aunt, who cooked for him and controlled his drinks (and she was still a little in love with him, and I could not understand how anyone could harbour such feelings) told me that Father had gone to the Doordarshan TV Channel to participate in a panel. Is the show today? It is on the security of the international athletes expected to attend the Commonwealth Games. I don't know when they will air it. I turned on the TV. A panel was discussing censorship and art – the ninety-year-old painter (the Picasso of India) had been forced out of the country by men who belonged to the Hindu Party. Men in sinister khaki shorts, religious extremists, had slashed and destroyed two more canvases of his. The Picasso of India had 'offended' their so-called sentiment by undressing the gods and goddesses. The Picasso of India was unable to find an inch of space to hide himself in the whole of India. The TV camera focused on an overdressed liberal who was verbally attacking a right-winger. My aunt checked if I was going to join them for dinner. Don't wait for me, I said. I got the car keys from her. Then I drove towards the Doordarshan TV building. Normally I don't drive when in Delhi but that day the fear of the Indian roads disappeared. I drove carefully and carelessly (establishing my own rules), and that is the proper way to drive in the city of cows, jams

249

and Bentleys. Delhi makes one a child again. Even the toll highways are bumper-car rides. The pedestrians? An afterthought for urban planners. In twenty-five minutes I made it to the Doordarshan parking lot. Full. I paid extra money to get in. From where I planted myself I could see Father's car; the driver waved at me, and walked up close. Sa'ab is inside. 'Yes, I know.' Now I have to make a request: 'when Papa comes out don't tell him I am here, just go on driving wherever he is headed and don't mention me.' He gave me an odd look. Do as I say. Twenty or thirty minutes later Father walked out of the building, stick in his hand, but he really didn't need it, he uses the stick like a bandmaster. He was not alone. Father was accompanied by a serving police officer; the two men entered the car chattering cheerfully. I followed. Behind the car was a security jeep. The car was headed to the airport. Before the exit to the terminals the car took a detour and made it towards Gurgaon. Then the service road to the statue. It didn't take me long to understand.

The car stopped in front of the eighty-foot-high statue of Shiva. The monument of excess. Thermodynamics of new materials and materialism. A strong, reinforced god, looking authentically metallic with a little help from car paint.

From the parking area the two men followed the concrete path to the base of the statue. My father in civilian clothes, stick in hand. His companion, ten or fifteen years younger, in IPS ceremonial dress (khaki tunic, tie, belt, hat). I observed them from a distance.

They sat, the two dwarfs, next to concrete Shiva and watched the planes land just across the highway. The new terminal at the Indira Gandhi International Airport was ready. This is where Commonwealth athletes from seventy-one countries (ex-colonies) were going to land in the near future.

From the parking lot I marvelled at drive-by religion, and I marvelled at the tourists, picnickers, stalled motor-cycle-wallahs and other devotees. They stood little chance of gaining proximity to the god; the ones closest were the birds. On Shiva's hand, arm, snake, drum, trishul and fluted hair. Rose-ringed parakeets, pigeons, sparrows.

Twenty minutes later I stepped out of the car and walked slowly on sharp pebbles. The guard came after me. 'Sa'ab, you forgot to lock.' I used the remote control to lock the vehicle and resumed my walk to the giant foot of Shiva. Behind the statue the sun shone brightly. I looked up and up. God. There was a strange glint in those dark blue eyes. Two starlings circled and swooped around Shiva's head before vanishing in his copper-sulphatish tresses. Father was a bit surprised. He didn't hug (he rarely hugged me in public), and of course we did not have a model father–son relationship.

He introduced me to the IPS officer. 'My son'.

'Exactly like you.'

'How is Father?'

'Son, we just did a panel for the Doordarshan TV. How happy I am to be alive to witness this moment, this airport. This new terminal is nearly ready and, you see, our subway system is the best in the world . . . The panel was on the security of approximately seven thousand athletes . . . Our new Commissioner of Delhi Police –' he patted the IPS officer on his back – 'was there! He is a lucky fellow, he will provide *holistic* security. No such opportunity presented itself when I was active in service.'

But you did get the opportunity, Father, and you were a disaster. I wanted to press charges. It was not the right moment. Father and I for a long time were not able to have any meaningful conversation because he would not listen to me and slowly I stopped listening to him.

'Sir, I will make a move,' said the new police commissioner. He saluted the old man and extended his hand towards me, and although I had nothing against the new chief I felt I was shaking hands with the Devil.

Father used his cellphone and asked the driver to drop the new hero at his bungalow.

Suddenly he looked frail and weak. No longer 'significant'. But he has always looked terribly significant, even in old photos.

'How is your health, Father?'

'Nothing wrong with me, son. I am more worried about you. Do you remember? It was your mother's anniversary last week. I called several times, left three or four messages. You didn't even bother to return my calls. Are you still upset? Why didn't I inform you about my surgery? Why didn't I write to you before the operation was over? But, son, you would not have come anyway, you didn't even come home for your own mother's cremation.'

I felt like crying.

'Keep Mother out of this.'

Father was tactful.

'Is IIT keeping you busy?'

'If you don't need me here, then—'

'Son, let's have Scotch tonight. I do need your assistance. There is a girl.'

'A girl?'

'She is around thirty-two years old. A journalist. She has been after my blood regarding my alleged role.'

252

'Your role in what?'

'Remember '84? In the month of December, gas leaked in Bhopal. The Union Carbide, it turns out, got the license to set up a pesticide plant with flawed and obsolete design, unfit for Virginia, during Indra Gandhi's Emergency years. A few journalists are tracking everyone down who played any role, any small role, in facilitating the release of the CEO of Union Carbide. Warren Anderson. That man has blood on his hands. Bhopal was our country's tragedy, bigger than 9/11, and we allowed Warren Anderson to flee. He lives in a big mansion in Long Island somewhere. All I did was follow the PM's and the CM's orders.'

'And there are reports, Father, about your involvement in the anti-Sikh massacres?'

'Oh, the Sikhs we can handle, but the Carbide case is bigger. I want you to help me. Last time you asked me if I wanted to emigrate to the US; I declined. What would I do there? But I have changed my mind. When are you headed back? I have a tourist visa anyway. We can leave at the same time.'

'Father, will give me time to think?'

'What do you mean? If you need money, we can sell the house. Son, it's yours anyway. It is, as you well know, worth a lot of money.'

There was a long pause.

'Raj, I'll help you raise your daughters. It is time you went back to your family. Clara is a kind-hearted, beautiful woman. It is time you stopped living recklessly.'

'Reckless? That is the wrong word, Father. I would like to drive with you. I want to show you something really shitty and reckless. Please sit with me in the car, and we will drive around the city. That's all. Lunch is on me (and I promise we will drink Scotch in the evening). In fact you

253

will need a lot of Scotch. But first we will go across the river. Not far from the new stadium under construction for the Commonwealth Games. Tell your driver we don't need him any more.'

'I am glad you have started driving.'

'It had to begin some day.'

And I drove him to the other side of Yamuna. The river looked tense, the volume of plastic and toxins more than water. My father knows most of the roads of Delhi and on the way he kept reciting their names, even the one named after the most intolerant Mughal Emperor, Aurangzeb. Father feels rooted only in Delhi, and spouts a lot of trivia. He pointed out an unusual tree, one with red buds. They are ready, he said, ready to open and astonish with the beauty of their blossoms. More roundabouts reeled behind us. 'Son, Delhi is inclement weather for trees and despite that they continue their business.' My father, my navigator. We zipped past Type III flats, and then the road was empty. It felt strange. In Delhi the roads are never empty. 'Son, there are powers in this world who don't want India to become a superpower, they don't want to see us becoming a permanent member of the United Nations Security Council. In the larger scheme of things all of these small issues from the past are raised to dismiss, diminish and disempower us.'

'When I was a child, remember, you helped me prepare for the school UN exams?'

The memory surged out of me without proper processing.

'Yes, you had to learn by heart all the data, when the UN was formed, and the names of the secretary generals.'

'Do you recall my performance?'

'How can I forget! You stood second in the exam.'

'I was very worried I had not stood first, and I delayed returning home. I intentionally missed the school bus. The peon, by mistake, locked me in the classroom. You came to the school to collect me. I was still crying because I had come second, I had made a serious error. I hugged you outside the classroom and cried more. I had misspelled him. Kurt . . . Kurt Waldheim of Austria.'

'Yes, he later on became the President of Austria.'

'Well, turned out that Kurt Waldheim was a Nazi, Papa.'

'I never heard.'

'Of course. But it matters to me.'

'Did I say it didn't matter?'

'If they gave you a UN position would you accept it, Papa?'

'Well, there is an Indian who almost became the Secretary General in lieu of Ban Ki-moon. The Government of India is well aware that I understand the mechanisms of this new world better. I will not say no if I am offered that important role. Where are you going?'

'We are going to look at your deeds, Papa, not direct deeds, because your hands didn't strike a match, your hands don't know what it means to use a metal rod or a rubber tyre. You didn't rape the women yourself, no, you didn't mutilate their genitals. You were not the "mob", but you made the mob. We are going to look at all that you enabled in '84. It was your job to protect the people who lived here, and you failed them, you were a disaster.'

I stopped the car next to a handpump.

'Block 32, Papa. Trilokpuri. Remember? This is the site where the worst massacres took place. The so-called streets and the houses in this resettlement colony, in this slum,

255

have outlasted those who lived here, and they will outlast you. Even if you bulldoze them. Even if you help eliminate the new occupants and build a new sports complex. You see that handpump over there? That handpump knows the details of every single crime you enabled. The water flowing out of the pump is cleaner than your morally pulverised soul. That bicycle there (on top of its faint shadow). It knows each one of your compromises. Do you see the jute cot? Are you listening?'

I made my father read a newspaper article by a witness (Rahul Bedi, *Indian Express*). He, my unreformed father, refused to read. Look at the aching spectacle you created. I displayed a black-and-white photo. Three Women.

Uneasy silence filled the car.

Most who died in '84 lived in slums, the wretched of the earth, twice or thrice dispossessed. People with nothing, pushed further to the limits of nothingness. They wove jute cots or worked as carpenters. It won't surprise me if I hear that the sons of those dead fathers have grown up to become drug addicts and gang members. Substance abuse. Life goes on. Criminals. Delhi, the city of criminals. Delhi, the city of miles and miles of haze and guiltless criminals. What is sad and infuriatingly tragic is that the instigators and inciters and facilitators of the pogrom and their loyal protectors walk the streets of the criminal city or get driven around (and they get level-Z security from the police) . . . They run our country. My father was shaking and angry. A kind of convulsive shaking. (If they ever make a film, they will make him stare at his hands shaking convulsively, an orgy of shaking.) It was strange. In the past I was the one who would shake in his presence, and now he was, uncontrollably. 'Have you no shame?' my father said. He ordered me to drive home. It was then I told him that he was a true 'scholar' who needed a bit of extra reading. Of late you have become careless, Papa. Carelessness, you well know, corrodes morals. The library in your study is not up to date. I see you have stopped reading crime stories. Please allow me to give you a bag of essential books. Crime thrillers. The problem with 1984 is definitely not the lack of books: *When a Tree Shook Delhi* by Manoj Mitta and H. S. Phoolka, *The Other Side of Silence* by Urvashi Butalia, *Who are the Guilty?* by People's Union for Democratic Rights and People's Union for Civil Liberties, *November 84* by Ajit Caur, *I Accuse* by Jarnail Singh, *Scorched White Lilies of '84* by Reema Anand, *Gujarat* by Siddharth Varadarajan . . . And the film: *Amu* (uncensored version), and the documentary: *The Widow Colony*.

Watch them, read them, Papa. You are a real hero. Let
these macabre books act like an axe to break the ice within
you. And if you feel like it, translate. Even if you wreck the
text, at least you will have read the crimes you co-authored.
And if you feel like it, go ahead, use a black marker. Because
no matter how hard you try you cannot erase. Strike a
match, and the paper won't ignite. The proof exists in libraries all over the world. In a few years little boys and girls will
read about your deeds on Kindle. You have become literature, Papa, a monster. You have become a grand crime story.

Did I call you a hero? Fuck, no. Nothing extraordinary
about you, Papa. You are not diabolical. You are not Evil.
You are so ordinary. And that is what makes this a bigger
crime story.

At home he walked into his study. 'Bloody fool,' he said
and slammed the door behind him. After a couple of hours
he stepped out, unusually quiet and sweaty, and several
times climbed up and down the stairs, defying doctor's

orders. Then he strolled in the garden for a long time.

During dinner he didn't defend himself, sitting in the tall chair with tribal tapestry, he didn't ask me the dreaded question: What would you have done? I broke the uneasy silence with my ideas of justice and violence and my ideas of India. New India.

'Father, we all need a little private madness and a little lie in order to live. I shall be the first one to acknowledge this. Normally the little madness and the little lie don't harm others. The problem is that your madness and your lie harmed so many. Do you understand? Are you listening?'

'I had no choice.'

'Some chose differently.'

'I think it is you who is refusing to listen,' said Father. 'What happened THEN cannot be understood from what is happening NOW.'

'But, Papa, what happened THEN was also illegal THEN.'

Again silence.

'Answer me, Papa.'

I asked him again, and then I asked him: 'Now what should I tell the press?'

My father laughed. I have yet to watch a human being laugh like that. In 1984 he would have laughed too, exactly like that. One often forgets that 1984 was also a year of excessive laughter.

I walked to my hotel via Khan Market. The place gleamed like a phosphorescent jewel at night. *How could you forget?* I heard an echo of my aunt's anguished voice. Just for a minute we were face to face and she had implored me.

He is after all your father.

259

On the pavement, not far from Khan Chacha's kebabs, a magazine-wallah sold me three weeklies. All of them covered news about mass graves found in Hondh-Chillar, fifty kilometres from Gurgaon. Bones of an entire village in what is now the Millennium City . . . Dark spherical objects, some stained by indigo . . . Massacre in Pataudi.

How could you forget?

A court in the United States of America had summoned the astonishing Congress Party. Three separate articles informed me about the Alien Tort Claims Act. Finally some hope.

There is a molecule called alloxan. Primo Levi writes about it in *The Periodic Table*. In the next few days I reread the chapter on nitrogen, and was particularly struck by alloxan.

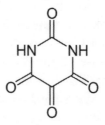

It is a pretty structure, isn't it? (asks Levi). It makes you think of something solid, stable, well-linked. In fact it happens also in chemistry as in architecture, he writes, that 'beautiful' edifices, that is, symmetrical and simple, are also the most sturdy: in short, the same thing happens with molecules as with the cupolas of cathedrals or the arches of bridges.

Levi's alloxan for some strange reason made me think of indigo, the word, the molecule, pronounced by Nelly as if it carried a latent possibility to take her breath away. But as soon as I thought of indigo I tried to forget the painful associations.

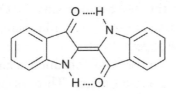

How would Nelly describe her perturbed state as a function of that grand independent variable Time without invoking the colonial history of a bird or a molecule? I have often wondered. Driving through Dilli's Ring Road these thoughts would come to me on their own.

Our next meeting took place three months later. I was admitted to the Trauma Centre of All India Institute of Medical Sciences. Because I slipped into a half-conscious state while driving, my BMW collided with a lorry on National Highway 8. When she heard the news, Nelly immediately took the Volvo bus to Delhi, and a prepaid taxi to the hospital. On the way the driver asked, 'Memsaab trauma kya hai?' The beautiful Hindi word 'sadma' was on the tip of her tongue, but at that moment no matter how hard she tried it escaped her.

She must have walked straight to the ICU. Only a few traces are lodged in my memory.

'You see my problem, Mrs Singh?' I must have detached myself from the pillows. 'I want to remain human.'

She must have sensed correctly that I had prepared my words carefully. She looked so delicate and graceful sitting close to me, a dead silkworm. I can never fully imagine what thoughts passed through her.

'You will be all right.'

'No matter what I do or don't I will never be all right.'

Stuttering, I think I spoke about molecules, and after a long awkward pause I recited aloud the names of my daughters, and then felt compelled to talk about the woman who gave birth to me. In the past every time Nelly had expressed curiosity about my mother, I managed to steer the conversation towards the physical and chemical world of objects.

Mother didn't attend the ceremony. When Father got his gallantry medal in '85, she stayed home. She didn't attend the pompous event, and I had no idea what inner calamities she was going through. She mailed me a letter saying she was unwell. She included a photo of herself submerged in the pool. I never saw it coming.

Mother didn't see it coming either. She believed in passive resistance. 'Nelly, are you listening?' I almost said. The difference between 'passive resistance' and 'passive acceptance' is like the difference between the value of 'gravity' in London and Delhi.

'Disintegrating' is the right word. Before Mrs Singh, before Nelly, lay a patient completely disintegrating. Mr Absolute Zero. I try to imagine her thoughts then. Was she thinking about my daughters? Do Raj's daughters understand even a trace of what their father is going through? But children have a way. They know. They are more resilient than we think. Children understand. They pay for the crimes of the parents. By hiding. By lying. By atoning.

'Let me tell you,' I paused. 'The truth about my father.'

She withdrew her hand.

'He is faking it.'

'What do you mean?'

'He is faking it.'

My father was faking Alzheimer's. Clearly and concisely I told her the details. She responded as if it was not the right moment to discuss something so grave.

'You will be all right,' she repeated the lie. 'Time will heal you.'

Then she was speechless. A complete conflagration of words. I am unable to forget the fading colour on her face in the midst of a phase transition. She was absolutely unprepared as my father wandered in.

No longer the man on the railway platform. Different from the man she nearly had tea with. In the past she must have wondered how she might respond if such a human ever entered the same room. What language, what gestures to use in his presence? Dull anger is not enough. Nor a lump in the throat, nor an involuntary drying of the upper mouth. I bit my lips. Nelly's body shook. Something within her was still crying.

Please don't leave, Mrs Singh. You are allowed to say anything to this criminal. He is listening. He pretends he doesn't comprehend any of this . . . Of course, it would have been best for all of us if this man had set himself on fire.

The nurse was listening. Her face beyond a shadow of doubt resembled the younger version of Shabana Azmi. Nervously, she kept moving a metallic object in her hand.

My mother, too, looked like that beautiful actress, whose films have comforted me. I have no idea how to make sense of the fact that Shabana got married in 1984. My mother, when she got married, also resembled the poet Amrita Pritam. I had no idea how to deal with all the traces my mother carried in her.

'Nelly,' I said, 'I have spent long hours of the night listing the various ways to bring an end to his life, an honour killing of sorts . . . Who would have thought this strong physiological and moral need within me to see him dead? Why so much hostility?'

The nurse, repulsed by my words, asked me to be still and ordered Nelly to leave, but I insisted on two more minutes.

'This man murdered my professor, and by doing so he killed me, and so many who are still "living". I do not use words loosely here. Several times I have thought of making his body into a work of art – tattoos, all over his body . . . Nazi swastikas . . . To make a tattoo is to write on butter with a toothpick. The pain he will have to endure is minor compared to the pain he gave so many people . . . I have thought of driving Papa again to the slums, to the Widow Colony, where he will ask forgiveness for each individual death.'

'You think that is absolution?'

I could not respond.

'The women in the colony are the ones most betrayed,' she said thoughtfully (and my father was listening). 'The women die every day, they relive the trauma over and over. Just because they survived, outlasted, they feel the weight, the guilt, they bear the burden of shame, and witness the shamelessness of the conductors of the pogrom. Layers of layers of evidence . . . But not many believe . . . November 1984 never happened. November 1984 is not an Event in our nation's history. Men don't talk about sexual violence. Men use women to humiliate "other" men. History has used these women in the worst possible way. The state would like them to live without a past.'

'Nelly, I understand your anguish, and I, too, would like to stir up the past, and shame this man . . . Perhaps this act will save me . . . As long as he is alive he can't deny . . . And I would like to shame the entire Indian justice fucking system . . .

'Father has given a new meaning to shamelessness. He paid his doctor an insane amount of money, the doctor has diagnosed Alzheimer's, which is really an insult to all those who truly develop Alzheimer's, and an insult to all the caregivers and family members of those who actually suffer from real Alzheimer's.'

She grew unusually silent. Her frozen state made me think she was questioning me: but how could you be sure? People in old age develop Alzheimer's, and the field of trauma is large and complex, both the victim and the victimiser undergo trauma.

'The doctor has made loads of money, the money that should have gone to the victims of '84. The doctor called me to his clinic and revealed the "bad news" that my father has Alzheimer's. "Dementia is invading his brain." Grey matter has declined dramatically. Aggregates of misfolded proteins are migrating to the key zones of the brain. He talks kachumber and pees in his pants. If you have failed to notice so far, you will soon. On the wall (in the clinic) there was a calendar, Nehru on a polka dot horse. The MD pointed at the calendar, and said your father has forgotten the face of Nehru. Right now he is aware that that man is a human

265

being. Soon he will even forget that. And one day it will be difficult to distinguish the horse from the man riding the horse. Then only the polka dots, and then nothing.'

The nurse reminded us that the time was up. 'Wait a minute. I am not done yet,' I protested.

The nurse gestured her to leave. In the parking lot Nelly might have encountered a stranger going through a different crisis. In those two or three seconds the two of them might have done something comforting for each other: a quiet validation.

Where did she go next? I try to imagine the taxi she took. How she released the taxi-walla. The hotel room. Perhaps I will never know if she walked to a friend's place.

Would this constant note-taking ever create the precise conditions for healing? (asks Nelly.) So far his experiment had failed, in fact writing and words, and language had stirred things up, remembering had left him more wrecked than ever. The past had come like bitter drops of helium, but he didn't know how to handle it; this helium was neither inert, nor invisible, nor light, and refused to disappear. Was there a better way to handle the incompleteness of history, a milder way to encounter the dead, because no matter how hard one tries the dead keep returning.

On recovery I returned to Ithaca. I promised myself 'never return home'. Four years kept me going with conferences on rheology. Lab work consumed me. I published thirteen papers, edited an anthology, completed the unfinished monograph on bitumen, shale and tar sands, and got a promotion. For a while I even collaborated with my colleague on carbon fibres, a hot new topic – fibres so strong, a single strand is able to stop a plane on the runway. But my mind was not in it, I kept working mechanically because I could think of doing nothing else.

Several times I tried to tell Clara about Nelly, but our divorce proceeded with such bitterness, we never got a chance to talk like humans. She got custody of our daughters.

During those days of discomfort I called Mr Gopal's daughter, Gul. So much time had passed, a huge gap of years to catch up. She told me that the old man was still around. She was in Connecticut for a year, and, like me, she too was recently single. We decided to meet midway in New York City. The concert at Lincoln Center was her idea, and I drove straight after my morning class. Despite heavy traffic I arrived a little early. After parking my car I wandered around the energetic city. The sun was about to set, and New York looked needlessly beautiful in its last light. Ten minutes before the concert I planted myself close to the ticket window and waited patiently for Gul. No call, no text message, and this got me worried. I stepped out of the hall and waited by the plaza, but she was still not there, nowhere to be seen. Inches away from me thousands of humans condensed and evaporated, and the sounds of sirens did nothing to diminish my anxiety. Waiting, panicking (outside the Alice Tully Hall), my mind went through the most rational (albeit a little absurd) algorithm. Miss the concert and continue to wait for Gul outside the hall, or leave the ticket with the clerk and go in. The first piece was 'Subito' (for violin and piano) by Lutoslawski, followed by 'Sarabande and Toccata for Harp' by Nino Rota, and the last one Rachmaninov's Cello Sonata in G Minor, Opus 19. South Korean pianist. Chilean cellist. Flawless is the only adjective that comes to my mind. (Flawless apogee of Romanticism. Grand structure. Sublime.) Followed by a standing ovation.

The cello sonata, now that I think about it, resonated with the audience deeply, and comforted me; the slow andante drifted my thoughts into a reverie, and I found myself meditating on the most independent of all variables. Time, I thought, was itself a Brownian motion (like the constant jostling of particles). Bits and pieces moving and mingling randomly, gathering mass, strange coincidences shearing past invisible blows and that includes stuff yet to come. If time is a river, then is it a river of discontinuous ice? Perfect balance between the instruments, the piano, I felt, swirled startlingly around the cello. With his big energetic hand the Chilean allowed the bow to linger longer and longer on the strings, unaware of the shadowy figure behind him, who would stand up now and then, take a few steps towards the piano and turn and turn again the page. All the advances in technology had still not made the page-turner redundant, I thought. Once in a while my gaze would fall on the pianist's ever-replicating hands in the black paint of a mirror, which reminded me of the composer Rachmaninov's huge hands and the Marfan's

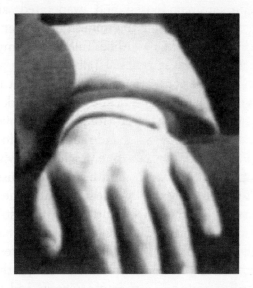

syndrome he suffered from. The duo wrestled with every single note, refusing to play the score in front of them, but struggling to create that score for the first time. There I wished the concert to go on for ever. When the two musicians (in black) walked back to the wings, I remained still for a long time, literally staring at the chair on the stage, solitary and empty, and so was the state of the chair next to me. It remained empty throughout the concert. Gul, I found out later, had lost her phone the previous day, and as a result completely forgot the concert.

Nelly, during those days, would send me an occasional email. Once in a while a longish letter with a CD. *Hi Raj. Dear Raj. Warmly, Nelly.* She would write less and less about her personal affairs, and more and more stuff about others. She would dispatch audio files and old photographs, digitised sepia, which had the eerie quality of Goya's *Los Desastres de la Guerra*. The only things missing were the appropriate captions. But really there are photos which require no captions. She had established an 'oral history' institute in Delhi, not far from the Widow Colony. She did not like the extra-polluted air of Delhi, and developed a nervous belly. Sleeping was always a problem. But the survivors poured their hearts out, and she would listen to their stories over and over. Old photos made so many open up. Certain personalities, who claimed they had nothing to tell, especially opened up after seeing the photos. She witnessed unbearable 'rage' and 'agony' (as I write these two words down, they feel like an understatement). Once she broke down physically, and had to be put on medication. She did not inform me, but, as I said before, I have my sources. She found the behaviour of 'Dilli' men towards women despicable, but knew living in that city was important. Moving back gave a sense of urgency to her work. Some of her emails sounded as if she was trying to grasp the psychosis of Delhi. Those who ruled the city were still above truth. Schools and colleges in her own country (in 'my' country) didn't teach 1984 honestly. As a result the younger generation knew nothing. The youth didn't even know what they didn't know. Only the 'official version'. Funding was always a problem. Once or twice I received photos of women in the Widow Colony sewing or stitching clothes as if they were the forgotten daughters of the night.

Then it happened. Nelly sent a collective email once to several of her acquaintances, and that is how I connected with Maribel. The moment I saw her long, earthworm-like

270

email address on the computer monitor I was compelled to contact her. She was going to heal me the way she had healed Nelly. I composed my message quickly and pressed 'Send' without giving it proper thought. That message to Maribel, I feel now, was a huge faux pas. 'I am assuming you know a few things about me via Nelly.' My email ended with a request. 'Please, if possible, keep our correspondence confidential.' *Please not a word to N.* 'But it is important I contact you. These words come to you in good faith. Hope you will not disappoint.' That last line sounded so old-fashioned and inappropriate. Obviously she didn't respond.

I sent another email a month later. My tone apologetic. At the same time I informed her about my firm intention to visit Mexico City. I was headed south of the border to participate in the Rheology Society's annual meeting and it would be 'a privilege and pleasure' to see her. Perhaps the two children as well. I sent her my exact dates and the hotel coordinates, etc. Once again she didn't respond.

Despite no response I decided to go ahead with the trip to Mexico. There I attended almost all the panels, the most exciting one was on the lava flows in the Trans-Mexican Volcanic Belt, and a Plinian eruption scenario at Volcán de Colima. A young grad student also presented findings about the monogenetic Parícutin, the one that will never erupt again. One thing we can be sure about . . . However, I found mingling with colleagues a chore. So I hung out with an older professor, a local, who turned out to be a Renaissance man. During drinks in the hotel bar he told me, among other things, about a few years spent in Italy, where he met Levi in 1984. I don't recall now how he figured out my continuing obsession, how our conversation stumbled upon Levi (the most likely trigger was the newspaper report connected to the trial of some Italian seismologists), but when I demanded the exact details, the professor scratched his grey goatee and said that he would rather jot those impressions down. I still remember every single word of that email of his, which arrived within a couple of hours.

Señor Raj, I must apologise for sharing the information in written form. I don't understand fully why I felt uncomfortable doing so in the oral form. Perhaps it has to do with my English. I did have the occasion to meet Levi briefly, and am happy to resurrect my recollections of that evening in November of 1984.

Those days I was teaching two semesters – dragging my feet on my doctoral dissertation – in Lugano. There I made acquaintances of a few fellow professors, who knew Levi. I believe there was a gathering of the old friends at a reading of a Pirandello play in Milano, and a talk as well by Primo Levi.

He had come to Milano for this occasion, though he lived in Turino. I remember the reading of Pirandello, but have no recollection of the subject of the talk by Levi (my non-existent Italian didn't help either), except for his gentle manners, soft voice and his piercing eyes.

Levi knew Marco's father (a Buchenwald survivor, and editor at *Corriere della Sera*) and Jardena's father (a classmate from Ferrara, who fought against and died at the hands of Il Duce's goons). So, the gentleman joined our dinner table briefly to chat with Marco and Jardena.

At the time, I had read Levi's Auschwitz memoir, his *Periodic Table*, and collections of his short stories. I was deeply moved by his humanity in the midst of madness . . . So, it was an honour to meet him in person, while regretful of my language barrier to converse with him. I was shocked, as were my Italian friends, to hear of his apparent suicide only a few years later. Such a man, who stood so resolutely for *life*!

On the last day of the meeting I skipped the gala and visited the Museum of Anthropology and wandered through its labyrinths to finally stand in front of the Aztec calendar, and the sun god, Huitzilopochtli. It was hard to tear myself away from the Fire Serpent. When I returned the hotel clerk handed me a yellow slip, a message. Someone had called. Is the name Maribel? I asked. No, sir.

Why don't you come over to our place? the local professor had suggested. He left his phone number as well. I took a cold shower, and before stepping out checked the Internet, and, yes, there was a message from Maribel. *Something happened that made me change my mind. Let us keep in touch via email. But I am not ready to talk to you in person. Safe travels.*

The professor's place was in San Angel, at the edge of Coyoacán, walking distance from my hotel. On the way I noticed a heavily-ribbed statue of Gandhi, and not far from the statue a bookstore called Gandhi. Walking to his place I got a sinking feeling: that I was actually walking to Maribel's place. I didn't know what she looked like. Several times I tapped the metal knocker. The maid opened the door finally ('*un momento*') and took me straight to the courtyard. She was sitting by the fountain, reading, the professor's wife. Seeing me, she stood up and smiled and took off her glasses. We shook hands. Her hairless dog sniffed me briefly. She looked much younger than Nelly. The moment I sat down a young man emerged from the house and took his leave with a single kiss on the cheek. We were not introduced. He is our son, she explained. Then the professor stepped out.

Both were extremely open with me. Our son came to persuade us to pay for his travels to Europe. We have no problem with that, she said. But he wants to take his Argentinian girlfriend along and he wants us to pay for her trip as well. The professor's wife had short hair, dyed brown, but her features resembled that famous painter, or perhaps I was desperate to see Frida Kahlo in her. Or perhaps I had imagined Maribel as Kahlo. The maid (from Oaxaca) served us hot chocolate and finger food. 'Gracias', I said. Something about the wife gave me the impression that if she accepted one as a friend then it was for life, and if she rejected one then it was for life. And she would do anything for the sake of a friend. Her nose ring gleamed like a mathematical singularity. Most likely she had acquired the stud of a jewel from an Indian shop. Her son didn't look like her; he didn't resemble her husband either, I thought. He could easily have passed as Nelly's son. Our

274

son. My mind was becoming mushy again. What if Nelly was pregnant in October '84? What if she had asked Maribel to raise our child? The professor and his wife saw my outwardly smiling face, they had no idea what was brewing inside. Later they drove me to the university campus and gave me a guided walk of UNAM, now and then pointing at the murals. Briefly they mentioned the 1968 student massacre. I didn't ask any further questions. I'd read about the massacre in a book by Paz.

There I stood unable to tear myself away from the murals.

Soon afterwards the professor showed me photos of the 2 October Tlatelolco demonstrations on his iPad. I borrowed the iPad and sent an urgent email to Maribel. She, much to my surprise, responded right away, in real time.

'What is it really that you want to ask? I don't think I will be able to betray confidences.'

'Nelly,' I wrote. 'Did she know the truth about my father? I could not tell her in the beginning. It took me so long. But did she find out on her own?'

'You sound worried.'

'Please. I wouldn't have come otherwise.'

'You are an engineer, aren't you?'

'I am sorry.'

'But don't you see? Your father's story is in the archives. It is public knowledge.'

'Nelly never once mentioned my father's involvement to me. She didn't know for sure that the man who is mentioned by his rank (and not his name) in the archives happens to be my father. No, there is something I don't know.'

'Don't you see what everyone sees?'

'I have one more question.'

'Last question.'

'How many children do you have?'

'Three.'

'Is the last one really your child?'

Maribel was mad at me, I know for sure. One can always tell such things. Finally someone was mad at me for the right reason. I had gone to Mexico prepared to extend my stay if the need arose. Now I felt the strong need to return 'home'.

Two or three months after my return from Mexico (for reasons that remain unclear) I invited her to visit me in Ithaca. After initial hesitation, a 'categorical no', and four phone calls, she came. I insisted on paying for the ticket. Those nineteen days with Nelly are perhaps the happiest in my life.

I rented a furnished place for her. A pastor and his wife were headed on an RV holiday to Utah and they left behind the duplex, a curious combination of antiques and modern amenities including a home theatre.

After her jet lag relaxed, I gave her a guided tour of Cornell's 'campus Gothic' architecture, we had lunch at the students' union, then I took her to my rheology lab, and Gergina's locked office. We spent almost half an hour in Professor Singh's old lab in the physics department. Laboratory of Atomic and Solid State Physics. Professor Osheroff did revolutionary Nobel Prize-winning work in the same lab. One afternoon, Nelly and I drove to the Cornell Ornithology Lab, where she bought a book of birdsongs and a couple of posters. From the university store she picked up a book by David Foster Wallace. Another by Carl Sagan, and almost bought a thick blue volume of Nabokov's butterflies. The long silences during our conversations made perfect sense, although at times I felt we were like two figures haunted by the same picture that needs no caption. I tried to persuade Nelly to extend her stay. Nothing would give me more joy than the sight of her at the pastor's house sitting on the sofa with a book in her lap, allowing the weight of both hands to keep it open. One afternoon we were driving around Cayuga when she told me how Professor Singh, during a lighter moment, demonstrated ice hockey to the children, Arjun and Indira. He used a golf club, a carrom board striker as a puck and Rollerblades. The demo – a prelude to his 'Coldest Experiments' – took place on the roof terrace of the IIT house one night when the sky was very dark but the stars were very bright and low. She repeated the story two or three times (within a span of twenty minutes) during the drive, with exaggerated gestures, and for some strange reason I thought about that night when from behind the bougainvillea I watched them together, dancing.

'It was in the late sixties when Mohan first moved to Cornell,' said Nelly. 'He didn't know baseball or ice hockey. Field hockey and cricket, yes, but no one around him played those sports. His Jewish room-mate taught him how to skate. On ice. I see him struggling to learn on the rink. *Single-mindedly he sheds his fear of falling. Every time he falls he becomes a child. Then rises like a physicist. Over there his body is pure force. Pushing and gliding slowly, and slowly he swirls, and swirls, and is spinning around in widening circles. Now F, now A, now G, E, D – he is fast becoming one of those of grainy rings of Saturn. I see it all and hear as well. Frozen water. Debris of ice. He is all of those cosmic rings of Saturn. Also the rings of the moon, Rhea.* Arc after metallic arc the old-fashioned skates generate an ensemble of sounds I cannot get used to.'

277

Once the two of them crossed the border, Nelly reminisced. Mohan and his room-mate drove all the way to Montréal, Canada, to watch a game of hockey. At the border all the cards they presented (read 'flashed') were mere university ID cards. Those days such things were possible.

Nelly repeated the skating story, the 'ensemble of sounds' she found difficult to get used to, as we were driving around Cayuga. How far is Montréal? she checked. Whimsically I turned the car back. Quickly we collected our passports (in Ithaca) and drove non-stop to Montréal to watch a game. It was my first time, and her first time too. I don't recall now the teams, and neither one of us knew the rules of the game, but we held hands, locked, for a couple of hours. Afterwards we drank red wine, 2004 Shiraz. Perhaps the only time I saw her consume wine after '84. We talked about Faiz and Feynman and the wine, and she told me that it was in Montréal, of all places, the two friends had also gone to attend a sitar concert. During the concert, said Nelly, a string broke (according to Mohan) and Pandit Ravi Shankar very gracefully replaced the string as if it was the most natural thing to do, and then continued with 'Rag Megh Malhar' as if no accident had ever happened. Nelly and I stayed in the restaurant until the waitress (from Haiti) informed us in French that it was past closing time. The restaurant parking lot was filled with Volkswagen Golfs. *Je me souviens* licence plates. I translated for her sake and for my sake. *Je me souviens*. How painful those words became when translated. But not to have translated would have made them calamitous, I thought. Still inebriated, I tried to persuade Nelly to write her memoirs. 'Please consider. The sayable and the unsayable.' She was mad at me. My words must have touched a raw nerve. She didn't speak to me during the drive back to the US. We patched things up just before she flew 'home'. Despite that needless waste of time towards the end my overall state was 'happy'. I could no longer say that happiness was impossible.

She died. It was a natural death. She left no objects behind for me, only courage, warmth, affection, dignity, and they glow to this day like the nest of a rare Andamanese bird. I found out while I was teaching a class on viscoelastic liquids. Her co-worker phoned with the news. I cancelled all my engagements and took the first flight to Delhi. The city was wrapped in miles and miles of dense January fog. It felt like that sincere (elegiac and celebratory) day in Mexico, the day of commemoration. After the cremation I had a meal with Maribel not far from Jantar Mantar, but the meeting was brief, she was headed home that very day. M was different from the picture I had formed in my mind, and I knew our first meeting in all probability was also our last. She told me something I didn't know. Nelly, too, had grown up afraid of trains. This was followed by a long silence, and in silence we parted. Later in my hotel room I skimmed through local papers. There was nothing on Nelly. It was already old news or no news. The media was obsessed with the Indian Premier League, and motorcycle gangs, and a couple of ghastly crimes.

A week later I stood outside the house (that was once mine).

Three or four private security personnel posted outside like attack dogs.

Under a dark overcast sky, it was raining mildly and I was carrying an umbrella. A figure appeared on the upper balcony, stick in hand, gazing at the clouds, the wind grew stronger and ruined my umbrella, and the wind lifted the old man's white kurta pyjama for a brief second. Then he spat and the wind gave his spit a strange parabolic trajectory.

I looked at the house and the dogs as if I was looking at them one last time. Then I took an overnight taxi to Shimla. As the car rolled into the night I experienced a flood of thoughts, and I knew what I had to do next. The Hague, I knew that was the road I would take next, but before The Hague a lot of work. Work, and save the truth from extinction.

In the taxi I felt as if she was with me, her voice, and her unfulfilled promise. She had agreed to write a memoir, and now it would not happen. She had even chosen the title. *Observatory Prose*. I hear, I hear her still telling me about the ylang-ylang fragrance she received as a gift from Maribel. She tells me about lukkan-mitti, hide-and-seek, in sugar-cane fields, her Hero cycle, rope swings and tube-well vacations with cousins, the way her body responded when she first saw a combine harvester.

I arrived in Shimla just before sunrise with a terrible head-ache and dehydrated and checked into a no-name hotel with macaque monkeys dancing on the roof, staring at me as if I was totally irrelevant in the grand scheme of things.

Two days later I walked to the institute.

Outside, in the shade, there was a long line-up of colourful tourists, Indians and foreigners, one or two very old in wheelchairs, a figure from the days of the Empire, an Englishman in a trilby. I bought a ticket and joined the guided tour. The guide took us very close to the glass entrance, we stood under a hundred-year-old Belgian chandelier. People marvelled at the pale crystals of light. You are allowed to peek inside, a voice said. Quiet, but very quietly. Shh! Among the tourists there was a young mother with a daughter, around three years old, and the mother said, 'Auntie ko hello karo', and the child waved at the figure on the other side of the partition. Then she pushed open the door and took fifteen little steps towards the desk. The man at the gate stirred but didn't stop her. A voice commanded the mother to fetch the girl back. 'Koi baat nahi', said the librarian. She bent low, shook hands with the startled girl, who pivoted on her tiny left foot imbibing as much as possible of that wondrous crumbling space, and at that point a recently married man standing next to me tapped his fingers on the Burma teak panels. 'This has been made by such levels of patience', he told his wife. I, too, touched the wrinkled panels (and almost whispered, 'But why don't you mention the patience of the books on the shelves and the patience of the custodians of books?'), and after the mother and daughter returned our guide led us to the Viceroy's tea room, the new seminar room, and the billiards room with its Khatumbund ceiling, partitioned round table and glass mosaics stolen from 'Burmah'. High up on the wall a Dutch pendulum clock with the exact shapes and degrees of the moon. A. V. Oostrom, 1826. The hands jerked forward. 'We wind the clock once a month'. That is when I separated from the tour and returned to the glass partition. The figure was back at her desk. I saw a pile of dusty books, her black shoes, and felt as if I knew nothing about her, or the crumbling colonial building. I stepped out, trying to regain my ground, and for a brief moment gazed at the distant snow-clad mountains. The castle was colder inside . . . and during lunch she stepped out as well and sat on the empty bench under the tulip tree, and ate her sandwich. From where I was she looked like a dwarf in front of the building and as she started eating for some unknown reason I heard my aunt's anguished voice. How could you forget?

The librarian shared the last bit of her sandwich with the birds. *For my son I will do anything.* Slowly it occurred to me that Nelly had obviously known about certain things – she never told me that she always knew about my father's involvement. And that day I left Shimla abruptly because she had known it all the way along. A real scientist might say, 'Raj himself knew about his father all along, but he was in search of another proof, and Nelly's work confirmed what he feared, what he already knew but was afraid to admit.'

When I met Maribel after the cremation, she apologised for not meeting me in person in Mexico. 'You deserved better. But I was genuinely angry at you, and not just because of that absurd question. Now I know how mushed up you are because of '84. The fact is that Nelly always knew, and she kept postponing telling you about your father's involvement, just like you kept postponing telling her. Do you understand? Do you?'

My project is done, I thought. Now I know more or less the essence of the story. And I am going to assemble it all in Shimla.

'By any chance are you the new librarian? The new archivist?'

The woman flashed a thin smile. 'Yes, I double as both.'

282

Her gaze, like her hands, delicate and patient, filled with an exuberant curiosity. What are you working on?

'I am a new fellow at the institute,' I told her, 'and I am interested in the discovery of helium.' Among the colonial papers she led me to I figured out that the question of 'discovery' was still not a settled affair. An Englishman based in the UK? Or someone based in occupied India? In one of the files I read that, in 1868, a French scientist came to Shimla; he had just observed the solar spectra in Guntur, in the south, and one bright yellow line just didn't make sense. India was the best place to observe the sun that year (a perfect twelve-minute-long solar eclipse), and he had arrived with state-of-the-art equipment, and perhaps the yellow line (he thought, on the verge of discovery) was simply the fingerprint of a previously unknown element. In Shimla, high up on Observatory Hill, he reanalysed his data, the anomalous wavelength, 587.56 nanometres, and even thought of an appropriate name for the new element: Helios. But he was filled with mist and doubt. Perhaps the bright, unexplained line, the anomaly, was simply an error. The Frenchman, like other colonial scientists, didn't know then that 23 per cent of the universe is made up of this lightest of all inert gases, and 'rare' only on Planet Earth. When an electric current passes through a sample it glows like a peach or becomes canary yellow. Helium was also responsible for the extra luminosity of Saturn. This new element would help us determine the age of our Earth, and tell us about the inner lives of stars. Superfluid helium would make CERN's Large Hadron Collider possible, the discovery of Higgs Boson-like particle, and the origin of mass. Without an element as small as hydrogen we humans, the scientists didn't know, would not see the way we see, because so much of our seeing depends on particles that

283

come to us from our sun, and what creates those photons also creates a slightly bigger element called helium. In 1868 they knew nothing about its atoms, how they stuck together, how they vibrated, their anomalous behaviour, spin or iso-spin, and as I sifted through more boxes evening descended, and the archives room grew very cold.

Acknowledgements

Alexandra Pringle, Jackie Kaiser, Gillian Stern, Alexa von Hirschberg, Kathy Belden, Dr Jaswant Guzder, Nancy Marrelli, Surinder Jodhka, Olivier Fuldauer, Uma Chakravarty, Peter Balakian, Hartosh Singh Bal, The Singh Twins, Satish Abbi, Enrique Servin Herrara, Umaraj Saberwal, Anthony Whittome, Marni Jackson, Prashant Panjiar, Raj Kumar Hans, Colin Carr, Taras Grescoe, Anne Mclean, Rui Coias, Arvinderpal Singh, Hamish McDonald, David Albahari, Michael Hulse, Aparna Sundar, Kajri Jain, Simon Dardick, T. Sher Singh, Chiki Sarkar, Andrew Steinmetz, Lida Nosrati, Anvita Abbi, Marc Parent, Gunstein Bakke, Denise Drury, Christabelle Sethna, Swaati Chattopadhyay, Jim Olver, Patricia Uberoi, Juan Vera, Grazyna Wilczek, Katherine Fry, Rahul Bedi, Shohini Ghosh, Puneetinder Kaur, Audrey Cotterell, Farhang Sajed, Kim Williams, Donald Lee, Jessica Auer, Arpana Caur, Brigid Keenan, Beatrice Monti, Edward Moulton, Bhupinderpal Singh, Theresa Rowat, Arwen Fleming, Diya Kar Hazra, Rick Stroud and Dilreen Kaur. My parents.

MacDowell Colony, Yaddo, Bloomsbury, Ledig House, Fondation Rowohlt, Canada Council for the Arts, Santa Maddalena, Banff Centre, and Natural History Museum (London).

Who are the Guilty? by Peoples' Union for Democratic

Rights and Peoples' Union for Civil Liberties. *When a Tree Shook Delhi* by Manoj Mitta and H.S. Phoolka. November 1984 films, documentaries and texts listed on page 257. *Primo Levi: A Biography* by Ian Thompson. Books by Richard Feynman, Allan Octavian Hume, Raaja Bhasin, Salim Ali and W.G. Sebald.

Grateful acknowledgement is made to Amrit and Rabindra Kaur Singh (p. 64), Dr. Jaswant Guzder (pp. 96, 176), Gauri Gill (p. 247), Ram Rahman (p. 256) and Valerie Campos (p. 280) for reproduction of images. Gauri Gill's photograph came with the caption: 'Taranjeet Kaur's grandfather Jeevan Singh was killed by a New Delhi mob on November 1, 1984.' Professor Uma Chakravarty provided complete access to her private archive connected to the pogrom; images on pp. 144, 219, 246, 258 relied on her collection.

The author and publishers express their thanks for permission to use the following material:

TEXT

p. vii   Extract from *Vertigo* by W.G. Sebald, published by Harvill Press and reproduced by kind permission of The Random House Group Limited.

pp. 65, 112 Extracts from *The Periodic Table* by Primo Levi, translated by Raymond Rosenthal, copyright © 1984 by Schocken Books, a division of Random House, Inc. Used by permission of Schocken Books, a division of Random House, Inc. Any third party use of this material, outside of this publication, is prohibited. Interested parties must apply directly to Random House, Inc. for permission.

p. 112   Extract from *Moments of Reprieve* by Primo Levi, reproduced with permission of Simon & Schuster, Inc. Translated from the Italian by Ruth Feldman. Translator copyright © 1979, 1981, 1982, 1983, 1986 by Simon & Schuster, Inc. Copyright © 1981, 1985 by Giulio Einaudi editore s.p.a copyright © 1986 by Primo Levi.

p. 113   Extract from *Exterminate All The Brutes* copyright © 1992 by Sven Lindqvist. English translation © 1996 by Joan Tate. Reproduced by kind permission of Granta Books, UK and The New Press, US, www.thenewpress.com.

p. 180   Extract from *The Collected Poems* by Primo Levi reproduced by kind permission of Faber and Faber Ltd.

IMAGES

p. 4   Creative Commons. http://en.wikipedia.org/wiki/File:Ashsem_small.jpg

p. 15   Copyright page copyright © 1984 by Schocken Books, a division of Random House, Inc., from *The Periodic Table* by Primo Levi, translated by Raymond Rosenthal. Used by permission of Schocken Books, a division of Random House, Inc. Any third party use of this material, outside of this publication, is prohibited. Interested parties must apply directly to Random House, Inc. for permission.

A NOTE ON THE AUTHOR

Born in India, Jaspreet Singh moved to Canada in 1990. He is a novelist, essayist, short story writer and a former research scientist. He received his doctorate in chemical engineering in 1998 from McGill University, Montreal, and two years later decided to focus full time on writing. *Seventeen Tomatoes*, his debut story collection, won the 2004 Quebec First Book Prize. *Chef*, his first novel, about the damaged landscapes of Kashmir, was a 2010 *Observer* Book of the Year and won the Canadian Georges Bugnet Award for Fiction. He has also been a finalist for four awards including the Commonwealth Writers' Prize for Best Book. His work was longlisted for the DSC Prize for South Asian Literature and the International IMPAC Dublin Literary Award, and has been translated into French, Spanish, Italian, Punjabi and Farsi. He lives in Toronto.

www.jaspreetsinghauthor.com